OF ELVES AND MEN

DESA FILES #4

Christian Warren Freed

Cover design by BroseDesignz
Author Photograph by Anicie Freed

Warfighter Books
Holly Springs, North Carolina 2754
0https://www.christianwfreed.com

First Edition: July 2024

Library of Congress Cataloging-in-Publication Data
Name: Freed, Christian Warren, 1973- author.
Title: Of Elves and Men/ Christian Warren Freed
Description: First Edition | Holly Springs, NC: Warfighter Books, 2024. Identifiers: LCCN 2024906193| ISBN 9781957326467 (trade paperback) | ISBN 8781957326474 (Hardcover)
Subjects: Urban Fantasy | Epic Fantasy | Fantasy

Printed in the United States of America

10 9 8 7 6 5 4 3 2 1

The Northern Crusade
Hammers in the Wind
Tides of Blood and Steel
A Whisper After Midnight
Empire of Bones
The Madness of Gods and Kings
Even Gods Must Fall

The Histories of Malweir
Armies of the Silver Mage
The Dragon Hunters
Beyond the Edge of Dawn

Forgotten Gods
Dreams of Winter
The Madman on the Rocks
Anguish Once Possessed
Through Darkness Besieged
Under Tattered Banners
A Time for Tyrants
A Good Day For Crows*

DESA Files
Where Have All the Elves Gone?
One of Our Elves is Missing
From Whence It Came
Of Elves and Men
Save the Queen!

Tomorrow's Demise: The Extinction Campaign
Tomorrow's Demise: Salvation
Coward's Truth
The Lazarus Men
Repercussions: A Lazarus Men Agenda
Daedalus Unbound: A Lazarus Men Agenda*

A Long Way From Home+

<u>Immortality Shattered</u>
Law of the Heretic
The Bitter War of Always
Land of Wicked Shadows
Storm Upon the Dawn

<u>War Priests of Andrak Saga</u>
The Children of Never

SO, You Want to Write a Book? +
SO, You Wrote a Book. Now What? +

*Forthcoming   + Nonfiction

OF ELVES AND MEN

.

ONE

Daniel Thomas heaved the last of his storage boxes into the back of his new Volkswagen SUV with a grunt and sat down on the edge of trunk. Familiar pains shot up his back from the waist, reminding him he wasn't getting any younger. He attributed his aches and pains to hard army living, sleeping on the cold, wet ground, and burning through countless pairs of boots as he marched up and down dark roads with seventy pounds of gear and body armor. Of course, jumping out of planes certainly didn't help either. Old before his time, that's what his father used to say. Huffing out a breath, Daniel closed his eyes and let his thoughts stray to the half-empty beer fridge in the back of the garage.

Any sense of peace evaporated when two overly large Bernese Mountain Dogs stormed out the front door with wagging tails and joyful barks. They slammed into his legs, jarring his back in the process. Daniel's eyes snapped open—the dogs pounced. He failed to throw up a protective arm before the female leapt into the back and flopped on him. The male popped up, bracketing him with his forelegs and barking exuberantly in his face.

"Are you done goofing off?" Sara called as she joined him.

He rolled his eyes and laughed. Daniel went in for a quick kiss only to be blocked by a hairy face determined to lick his. Shoving the dogs away, he accepted the cold bottle of beer she offered. "Do you realize we haven't had any privacy in years?"

"What's privacy?"

Between two children and two dogs, work, and their adventures in the hidden world of the elves they barely had time to think straight. He sighed. "True."

"I haven't gone to the bathroom alone in a decade."

On cue, the male Berner bounced down and slipped between her legs, his tail threatening to knock the beer from her hand. Sara reached down to scratch the thick fur around his neck before he trundled off to pee on their rose bushes.

Swallowing a mouthful of beer, Daniel gestured with the bottle. "How he hasn't killed those things is beyond me."

"It's been a decade, and they still bloom three times a year," Sara countered. "Maybe dog urine is good for roses."

"Uh huh." He grunted. "Thanks for the beer."

"It's the least I can do seeing as how you're out here moving all these heavy boxes."

They'd been through this a hundred times. Each weekend he had a show he spent the better part of an hour ensuring his boxes were packed and the displays and signage loaded. Each weekend he had a show he grumbled and complained. As much as Daniel enjoyed the resurgence in sales and popularity since turning indie, he lamented the long drives before the sun broke the horizon and the even longer drives home.

Sara professed to not knowing why he did it. Every time he came home, he was beyond exhausted. His throat hurt from giving the same sales pitch to hundreds of people and, depending on how he did, his mood fluctuated. Daniel knew he pushed himself to the limit of tolerance with each event. Perhaps more so with this one.

After three years, he still didn't understand the whole con scene. Much of what he saw didn't make sense, leastwise not to what society deemed normal. The attendees reveled in their costumes and the opportunity to meet their favorite celebrities and share their love for all things geek. He attributed much of the rising popularity in cons to the string of successful fantasy and science fiction movies over the past twenty years.

Regardless, Daniel travelled from town to town across North and South Carolina, occasionally branching into Virginia and Tennessee if the table cost was worth it. Since taking over his own publishing destiny, he found himself in a constantly evolving string of events, deciding which were profitable and which were a waste of time or money.

He glanced at the stack of plastic boxes holding his display books as well as three copies of each of his twenty plus books. Big events in Raleigh were hit or miss for authors. Most of the time attendees weren't interested in carrying heavy books around while they browsed over seven hundred vendors. Daniel didn't blame them.

Still, he did well enough to justify returning year after year to the Sword and Sorcery Con. It was one of his biggest events of the year and, despite his reservations that never seemed to disappear entirely, Daniel found himself looking forward to the four-day weekend. He'd made friends through the years and couldn't wait to catch up.

Sara didn't get why he had reservations and still insisted on attending. He didn't expect her to. She was business focused and remained disinclined to dive deeper into his fantasy worlds even with everything that had happened. Daniel suspected she was leaving out key elements to her adventure on the coast but didn't push.

Not that he blamed her. They'd both been through so much over the years, with each new adventure drawing them deeper into the elf clan schemes. Daniel loved the story fuel at least. He hadn't heard from the Department of Extra Species Affairs, D.E.S.A. for short, since returning home from upstate New York. The longer the silence went the more he grew concerned. Not that any good ever came from dealing with the government, especially agencies who officially didn't exist, but them being quiet concerned him. He couldn't help but feel there was always a set of eyes looking over his shoulder, waiting to draw him back in.

Slamming the trunk shut, he and Sara wrangled the dogs back inside, a feat neither took for granted and often lost as much as they won.

"You know, I could use a back rub later," he joked after they got inside the house. "I think my kidney stones are acting up."

"Good thing you haven't had any for two years," Sara tossed back. "I could use help preparing dinner."

He shrugged. "Hey, you can't fault a guy for trying. What's for dinner?"

"That's what I need help with,"

He hummed, looking around to make sure the kids were still upstairs finishing homework. With a grin, he sidled up behind her and wrapped his arms around her waist.

"Daniel…"

He began kissing the side of her neck. "I have an idea."

"That's not helpful," she purred.

"Depends on how you look at it."

She gave him a playful elbow to the ribs and pushed him away. "We need to feed the kids too."

"The kids are old enough to make what they want," he protested.

She glared at him. "You do remember what happened the last time we let either of them cook unsupervised, right?"

Daniel winced, following her gaze to the pasta stain on the ceiling. "It's not my fault one of his dumbass friends told him that's how you test pasta to see if it's done."

"No, but that can of paint in the garage is waiting on you to use it."

Daniel finished his beer, setting the empty bottle on the counter. "As much as I'd love to do yet another home renovation or help with dinner, I do need to get going. Set up only lasts another few hours."

"You have to do this tonight?" she fussed.

"I don't like feeling rushed in the morning. Better to set up now and forget about it," Daniel replied. "You know, it would go a lot faster if you helped. We could grab a pizza on the way back."

Daniel followed her into the kitchen and was amazed with the speed and efficiency she showed in hauling out select produce and cuts of meat. She had a knife in her hand and cutting board on the island before he knew what was going on. *Thought you didn't know what was for dinner?* She spun on him, kitchen knife waggling. "I told you, never again. That freakshow in Fayetteville was enough for me. You go have fun with your little friends, but remember, it's a school night. Be home before the lights come on."

"Yes, Mother." He kissed her forehead. She had a point. Normally events were held on Saturdays, but this one kicked off bright and early Thursday morning. "I'll be back as soon as I can. Put my food in the microwave if I'm not here on time."

Accompanied by the dogs, Daniel grabbed his keys and headed for the front door.

Sara waited for him to leave before stabbing the knife into their cutting board. A headache was forming. Nine times out of ten he was the one in the kitchen. The perks of being retired, he called it. Sara wasn't sure about that but felt a pang of jealousy if she paused long enough to think too hard about retiring. She busted her butt every day and came home to find him doing all the typical household chores.

Her friends were envious. She lost track of how many times this friend or that complained about their husbands over a cup of coffee or hasty call while Sara hurried to work. Their dissatisfaction with their lives prompted her to 'gift' Daniel with a brand new Traeger smoker a few months before Christmas. It turned out to be the gift that kept on giving. His biggest triumph to date was taking a pork belly and turning it into bacon.

Chuckling at the memory of his boasts about smoking any sort of meat under the sun, Sara pulled a pack of carrots from the fridge and started peeling. Daniel hated cooked carrots. He'd told her a hundred times and still hadn't figured out that it was on the menu every single time she was irritated at him.

"Let him enjoy that," she mumbled to the dogs, who had returned to the kitchen and were patiently waiting for her to drop a morsel. "Serves him right for taking off when I asked him to help."

Wagging tails was the only reply.

Across the street and half a block up, Norman Guilt sat in his new red Challenger and watched Daniel drive past. Morgen often chided him for taking so much time watching over Daniel's wife, but that was a queen's prerogative. Norman swore an oath, and a gargoyle was always true to his word.

Norman had no qualms against Daniel. Daniel was a good enough man but unable to keep his wife safe. The entire hidden world was aware of the human family from North Carolina. Therefore, Norman remained determined not to let anything bad come to Sara Thomas. She'd earned the respite and, in no small measure, his respect. Fully recovered from the wounds suffered from their last adventure, Norman resumed his watch. A growl in his stomach left him wondering what Sara was cooking for dinner. It had been too long since his last home cooked meal.

TWO

Summer was in full swing as Daniel hummed to his favorite tunes. The windows had started rolled down until the humidity registered—it was high enough to make him reconsider the next hour or so. He wasn't looking forward to being drenched in sweat and smelling as foul as a troll pit after the effort of making several trips from the parking garage to the show floor. Still, the work was generally worth the reward. Ten-hour days aside, his bank account and occasionally wavering self-esteem would appreciate all the effort.

Heading up 401 toward Raleigh, Daniel wove in and out of mid-afternoon traffic. The heavier traffic became, the more restless he grew. Since his last tour in Iraq, he found driving in cities to be difficult. Years may have passed but he still scanned the sides of the roads for bombs or potential ambushes. His wife no longer called him paranoid at least. *Paranoid. What did civilians know? This is called situational awareness.*

Dodging a car trying to merge, he reflected on the many reasons to enjoy living in North Carolina. The beach was a few hours away and the mountains about the same distance. It was still considered country in most places, the way of life a few paces behind the rest of the country. Daniel enjoyed the lack of urgency—it was no New York City crazy. The rudeness and air of self-importance of those places he used to visit left him with a foul feeling in the pit of his stomach. More and more northerners flocked south, polluting the state with their northern arrogance. Being from up that way himself, Daniel loathed all they brought to the state. A car horn beeping, the plates reading *New Jersey* had him rolling his eyes.

Feeling a little sticky, he turned up the AC. What he didn't care for, and never would, was the humidity. North Carolina in summer must have been close to the outer circles of Hell. He'd have flashbacks of sweating through uniforms during his time in the army and having salt stains that were impossible to remove. Being retired and choosing to become a keyboard warrior, Daniel preferred sitting inside any day. Even the dogs refused to be out in the sun longer than necessary.

Daniel wheeled into the parking garage on the corner of W South Street and exhaled a deep breath. This was the moment of every event he despised. Loading the truck was one thing but hauling everything across the street and through the impossibly large convention center … *All part of the experience*, he lamented to himself. Few people saw the behind the scenes work that goes into a con. Then again, no one wanted to know how the sausage was made, only that it tasted great.

He figured it was the same for his books. Only a handful bothered asking questions about how he came up with the names and stories. Most people were just happy to get an autographed copy and move on. The one thing irking him was how his dedicated fans expected him to churn out new stories with a rapidity he doubted anyone could manage. If they only knew how much went in to writing a good book.

Daniel snatched his dolly from the backseat and started loading boxes. Experience taught wisdom. He longer brought every copy of his books along. He instead tailored his supplies to the size of the event, not the desire to sell out. Already sweating, he adjusted his ballcap and wiped some of the sweat off his forehead.

Normally he stuck with the easy to carry handhelds one the first trip and took his time bringing in the rest, but he knew Sara would be stewing over him ducking out *after* she asked for his help and wanted to get home as soon as possible, if for no other reason than to ease her ire enough he got a good night's sleep and, hopefully, avoid having another dish laden with cooked carrots. Straining, Daniel began the long drag down to the registration table on the lower-level showroom.

Chugging the laden dolly and once again underestimating how much books weighed up the long ramp toward the front doors, Daniel was amazed to find scores of people in costume already lurking outside. He shook his head. The event didn't start until tomorrow and they were already camping out. He watched as security kept refusing non-vendors entry without an access badge. Security waved him through the glass doors and soon he was heading to the elevator.

The cool air hit just right, tempting him to stop a second to take it in but he knew the sweat would turn into chills soon enough. Daniel waved at the next level of security, nodded his head at fellow vendors he passed who were getting a jumpstart on setting up and headed for the registration table.

"Who are you with?" a pleasant young lady wearing a Sword and Sorcery Con official shirt asked without emotion.

He didn't blame her. There were over eight hundred vendors expected to attend. He was just another face in the crowd. "Daniel Thomas. I have an artist alley table."

Rifling through the surrounding boxes, she unearthed his vendor packet. "Do you need help finding your table?"

"Nah, I can manage. Thanks," he replied after she checked off his name and handed over the packet. A throat clearing behind him sent him hurrying off.

The sights and sounds soon bombarded him. Daniel enjoyed looking at each section he passed. Sara used to chide him for not buying anything he had liked because he complained about missing out later. Eventually he managed to explain that while he did complain, he went to these events to make money, not spend it on things that he might think were cool. Truthfully, Daniel didn't know what he'd do with half the things he liked if he did buy them. Better someone else bought them so they didn't get shoved into one of his closets and forgotten.

Daniel found his table and got to work.

Set-up didn't take long. It seldom did. The eight-foot table provided more than enough space for his books, an email signup sheet, and the small collection of dragon statues he had recently gotten into selling.

He saw a few looks his way after he stacked the last box he had, noting their envious expressions at how quickly he'd set up, and later they'd give him similar looks once he tore down. He adjusted the last item on the table, grabbed the dolly, and headed back to the truck for the rest. He was ready to go home to smoke a cigar and relax. "I wish I could do it as fast as you," a middle-aged man with a long beard remarked.

Daniel checked out the massive setup the man was doing, by himself, and let out a low whistle. It was all part of the gig. "It's easy when you just have a little. I wish I could compete with what you have going on!"

Chuckling, he waved and head off.

Wincing as the summer sun almost blinded him before he slipped his sunglasses on, Daniel left through a side door and headed back to the parking garage. He half expected to find Agent Blackmere or another D.E.S.A. agent lurking in the shadows, ready to whisk him away on another mission. A rue grin spread it wouldn't have been the first time an event was interfered with. A year ago he had just finished a major book signing when Agent Blackmere came for him.

No one lingered around his truck. Daniel snorted at the brief flare of disappointment he felt and tossed the dolly in the back. Snatching the last few items for his display, he made the longer trek back to the convention center floor. The building was surrounded with more doors than he could count yet only the front, and furthest away from where he needed to go, were open because, of course they were.

Soon enough he was back on the show floor and finishing his table prep. Shoving aside the feeling of being watched, he took the obligatory social media pic that he'd post later and decided to stroll through the massive space in search of familiar names and people he'd grown accustomed to seeing on the circuit.

Daniel passed an Army MRAP and chatted with the recruiters, graciously accepting a new travel coffee mug to replace the battered one Sara insisted on throwing away whenever she washed it. They spoke for a while. Daniel felt good having at least one booth he related to. No matter how man shows he did, he never felt comfortable. He nodded to those who made eye contact, made small talk with the endless wave of security personnel stationed throughout the building. He learned from his first time attending that the event organizers ran cons across the eastern half of the United States, from Ohio to Florida, and the only way to keep their cash cow rolling was through enhanced security—a security guard had said this. Daniel respected that, even when it slowed him down as he had to constantly dig for his access badge on show days. If they only knew what lurked among them, especially here in Raleigh, at the heart of the elf kingdom…

He frowned to find the sun concealed as he exited the building. The temperature had already dropped, though not enough for any sane person to be comfortable. He paused on the wide steps leading into the convention center and looked past the guardian statue of Sir Walter Raleigh and focused on the upper floors of the Wells Fargo Building a few blocks up the street. The queen of the dark elves, and the sole surviving heir to all the clans, was watching. She always watched.

Repressing a shudder, Daniel hurried to the parking garage. Any chewing out by Sara proved far preferable than falling under the queen's judgmental gaze.

A strange flavor rode the winds. Morgen shivered at the raw power buzzing over the heart of downtown Raleigh. A score of vultures lined the roof across from her building, staring at her patiently. She ignored them. Once, Morgen used the creatures as scouts in her great war against her late husband. Now they were little more than unpleasant reminders of a different age.

Her gaze was pulled across the city, to the ever-shifting North Hills skyline and the budding storm darkening the horizon. Licking the air, she cringed. Fell intentions swept over the land, though from what she failed to discern.

Frowning, she slipped through the utility door on the roof and hurried back to her inner sanctum. Daylight fading, many of those who came to the private club were already heading for their homes. Their power deals for the day were finished. Today was a rare day when no one petitioned her or forced her to make decisions.

Morgen entertained many of the members, for they were the elite of local society. She'd twisted and manipulated them for decades without any growing wiser. A silly game, one she no longer found appetizing. Her people had enough issues of their own to keep her occupied. Recent events in upstate New York threatened to bring the clans to their knees. Basil Kadis, longtime rival and former prime minister, had made his play for power. His death left a vacuum in the clans. One she failed to fill. His apparent suicide, at the insistence of the Old Guard sent to collect him, echoed the loss of her daughter and the former Champion of Light, Xander. Morgen had never felt more alone. Under other circumstances she might have reveled in the challenge—not now.

The budding storm ensured she would find no rest this night. *But why? What am I sensing?* Another frown burrowing deep creases in her brow, Morgen settled in her favorite office with a cup of fresh mint tea and pondered how much more she, and the elves, could withstand. She was tired. Old aches tingled in her bones.

THREE

The storm picked up sometime after sundown. Neon lights clicked on, lighting the city center in a kaleidoscope of greens, reds, and blues. Not that anyone noticed or appreciated the beauty right now. The wind slashed through the corridors of downtown Raleigh with a banshee's wail. Citizens pulled their shirts closer and their hats down, some struggled with umbrellas, in a desperate attempt at keeping the cold air and rain from blasting them further. Trash and debris kicked up, tripping some. As quickly as it started, the storm faded. Confused, the people of Raleigh continued about their day. If the local weathermen couldn't predict the weather with any consistent accuracy why should anyone else bother?

.

The heavy sound of guitars tuning at the amphitheater across the street from the convention center soon replaced the ill wind. A popular concert venue, the site competed in crowd attendance with the hordes of cosplayers descending on Raleigh. Police officers patrolled the streets, ensuring the peace was kept A pair of burly businessmen, brothers based on appearance, strode down the middle of the sidewalk, ignoring any civilian they passed. Their gaze was fixed on the stage being erected on West Cabarrus Street.

They had the look of paid bounty hunters, or so they've been told. In truth, one was an investment banker and the other owned and operated one of the more popular jewelry stores in the state. Their tailored Italian suits did little to conceal their bulging muscles or soften the hardness in their eyes. To the common citizen they remained anonymous. Just two more faces in the increasingly populated area. Those who knew better gave the Schneider brothers a wide berth.

A cigar tucked in a corner of his mouth, Angus scowled. "That time of year already? I had hoped the little freaks would stop coming."

"Seriously?" Fritz replied with a roll of his eyes. "You know they aren't going anywhere. If anything, their little movement continues gaining momentum. Seems being a geek is popular these days."

"I'll show them popular," Angus growled. "Beat a few to a pulp and the rest will wither away. You'll see."

"I seem to recall some law preventing us from doing such."

Angus waved; ash spilled down his shirt. "Bah! Laws. The queen has never been this weak. Mark my words, brother, she won't be long on her throne unless she changes with the times."

"We've resisted change for hundreds of years. She won't do so now unless there is good cause," Fritz replied. His eyes pinched.

"It's all that little human shit's fault," Angus muttered. "We'd be fine if that high and mighty fantasy author hadn't stumbled into our world. I'd like to break his fucking neck."

Thanks to the now infamous Daniel Thomas, their world hadn't been the same since the high king was assassinated by his own daughter. Fritz and Angus played a huge part in ensuring further damage hadn't been done that night and, accordingly, were counted as heroes of the elf clans for their deeds. That honor did little to assuage the animosity Angus held towards the human and his interference.

"I don't think the queen would approve," Fritz chided. He enjoyed pointing out the obvious to get a rise from his brother. They'd done this too often for him to be invested in it.

"Like I give a damn what Morgen thinks. The dark elves have too much power as it is. Something needs to be done to restore the balance."

Fritz sighed. "What does that have to do with Sword and Sorcery Con?"

Angus shrugged. "This, all this, is a distraction from what needs to be happening. Every year we get swarmed with thousands of these … people. I'm tired of it. Sick and fucking tired."

Fritz wisely avoided pointing out how they managed to take vacations during this one weekend a year, until now. Business matters kept them in town, forcing them to endure the four-day festival of all things fantasy. "We could make the most of it," he suggested.

Angus shook his head. "You already said the queen would be pissed for that."

Fritz smacked his brother on the back of the head. "No one said anything about killing, idiot. I was thinking more along the lines of getting into costume and seeing what all the fuss is about."

"You mean—"

"Dress like dwarves!" Fritz grinned.

"I'm losing my mind." Angus rubbed his head.

"Come on. It would—"

"You know what, fuck it. Why not? It's been a long time since I donned the old armor."

"If it still fits," Fritz teased. He stepped away before his brother retaliated. "This is going to be fun."

"There had better be mead, and lots of it. I'm not drinking any shitty craft beer."

Bickering as the warmup band launched into their set and surprised by the ease with which he convinced his brother, Fritz did his best to ignore the returning wind and the gnawing premonition in the back of his head.

Wally Rutherford pulled into the parking garage three hours later than he planned— a blown tire and the embarrassment of learning he needed all four replaced if he expected to make it to Raleigh alive had caused considerable delay. The Sword and Sorcery Con was his biggest event of the year and there was no way he was going to miss a second of it, especially considering how much it cost for him to secure a table.

"Anything for money," he muttered and began the hunt for a parking space.

With the concert already raging across the street, parking in downtown Raleigh was at a premium. He made it to the fourth deck before finding a spot as far from the elevators as possible. Grumbling about his day going from bad to worse, Wally checked his watch. He still had an hour to complete setup before the organizers closed and locked the doors for the night.

He hopped out and began loading his boxes into the wagon he and his brothers used for their events. With the con being so far from home and lasting four days, Wally found himself once again abandoned to do it alone. *This is the last time. They will come with me to help or… or else.*

Picturing him telling his brothers this when he got home, Wally closed the hatch on his car and headed for the elevator. He really hated being late. Not that the security guards bothered asking. They were used to people squeezing in at the last minute. Struggling to find his access badge they mailed out over a month ago among his things left him asking if he was doing the right thing. Sure, he had a real job, but instead of languishing behind a computer screen all day he longed to create.

Launching his own comic label was supposed to have been the beginning of a creative empire. Five years later, he continued struggling to get it off the ground. It wasn't for lack of talent. Wally had that in droves, or so he had been told. He lacked the commitment to match his drive. Thanks to a bad string of events last year, Wally considered dumping the label and going back to the real world.

Any doubts were quickly smothered the moment he stepped on the con floor. There was an energy he felt here. Wally rejoiced in letting his inner geek free where he was surrounded by like minds. His wife often found his work bordering on ridiculous, though she professed to supporting his passion. A small victory, but one he gladly accepted.

"Cutting it close, man," a security guard announced as he walked towards him.

"You know how it is."

The lights were off in half the building. Maybe a few hundred people, vendors and organizers, remained on the floor putting their last-minute touches to their display booths and tables.

After a brief stop at the registration table, where an annoyed woman huffed as she rifled through the file box to find his packet, Wally strode past booths filled with sword replicas and magic wands, toys and collectibles from every major popular franchise—he'd already been warned not to come home with anything new—and a ton of comic vendors. It all made sense. At least it did until he passed the booth with handcrafted soaps. *Why is there always a soap lady at these things? And is that cereal in the bar?* He walked faster when she tried to catch his eye. Not everything had to make sense, he supposed.

He found his table tucked in among an endless succession of rows stretching the width of the floor. He was among hundreds of independent artists, authors, craftsmen, and more looking to leave their mark on society and, if the gods were kind, take their brand to the next level. Sadly, most would abandon their dreams before success ever found them. Wally had seen plenty of friends come and go. Each one started with high hopes and near impossible dreams, but that's what it was all about. They rose through the ranks, battling for recognition among the big producers and then just stopped. Gave up. A sad truth had become evident to him over the years—far too many treated their work as a hobby instead of a business.

Wally found his table. Not the ideal placement but still close enough to the main walkways to attract potential customers. His mind focused on the task at hand, he began unpacking and settling for what he hoped to be a killer weekend. He started feeling that raw energy. The kind he got every time before a show. A smile crawled across his face. This was what he lived for.

Finished with his setup, he took a moment to look around the nearby tables to see if he recognized anyone else's work. Big Gene was two tables down—Wally brightened at the prospect of continuing their running conversation of who was the most powerful superhero. Wally roved up and down the aisles for a little in search of the one person he hadn't seen in over a year. The elf master himself, Daniel Thomas.

"Your attention please. The show floor closes in five minutes. Please finish setting up and head for the exits."

Looking around the now almost empty show floor, Wally scratched his chin and muttered, "I guess I'll see you tomorrow."

Wally yawned. It had already proven a long day and he was ready to grab a quick bite and crash on his buddy's coach. These events drained him, but he couldn't wait until morning. It was another chance for Wally Rutherford to prove his worth.

Chuckling at the thought, he made his way back to his car. The band playing across the street got his head bobbing. A connoisseur of all genres, Wally considered staying in the parking garage and listening to the show. His body begged otherwise. Giving in, Wally fumbled for his keys. There was plenty of time to enjoy the scene, later. The keys slipped from his fingers, clinking on the dirty concrete. Wally groaned and reached for them.

"Get up. Put your hands up and step away from your vehicle."

FOUR

Wally tensed. Heart hammering, he rose slowly. Everything sharpened around him. Music was blasting loud enough to vibrate the concrete structure of the parking garage. The smell of fetid trash shoved in the corners and overlooked by cleaning crews mingled with spilled beer and urine, was amplified by the trapped heat from another sweltering day. His nose wrinkled. Lights swirled and changed from the concert across the street. *Focus.*

"Hey, man, it doesn't have to be like that," he started. "I don't have what y—"

He turned and the words caught in his throat. Wally never counted himself a particularly brave person, though he had been known to stand up when the need called for it. He'd been robbed before and got away without injury. But what he saw confronting him was beyond his expectation and imagination.

"Look, I don't know what this is about, but you got the wrong guy," he started again, raising his hands shoulder high. "I'm just a dude trying to slip on home for a bite and some sleep before the show tomorrow."

Seven men and women spread out in a semi-circle around him; a white van idled nearby. Only one man was armed. Wally spied the shake in the man's arm as he kept the pistol trained on him. Eyes narrowing, Wally took in their ragged appearances. Short, no taller than five feet, each had a similar haircut reminiscent of Moe from the Three Stooges. Their thick foreheads sloped over the rest of their faces, accented by a single eyebrow dragging across their eyes.

They were heavily muscled and, unless his mind was playing tricks on him, had the sharp dagger points of fangs slipping out from under their upper lips. Stained and torn clothing clearly having seen better days curled Wally's lip. Tufts of hair jutted from behind their ears, lending them a wild appearance.

"Who are—"

"We know who you are, Mister Rutherford," the same voice from before interrupted. "Now, if you will be so good as to get in the van we can be on our way."

Wally took a step back and shook his head. "I'm not going anywhere with you. I need to get back home. Take my wallet if you want, but I'm leaving."

Murmurs spread through the group. The van's engine cranked over before dull yellow headlights nearly blinded him.

"That is not going to happen, Mister Rutherford. One way or the other, you are coming with us," the man with the weapon said. A growl accented his words.

"Nope! Not happening." Wally turned and reached for his car door—he never made it.

They leapt for him, driving him to his hands and knees with a barrage of small fists and boots.

His lower lip split. A crack tremored through his side. Stars spotted his vision. Wally collapsed to his stomach.

"This is some bullsh—"

A loud whack sounded.

Hiding in the shadows of the closest pylon, the figure watched as the pack of goblins kidnapped the human. Not a fan of humanity with its noise and pollution, he found the deed unpleasant and unprofessional. Worse, it signified a shift in longstanding peace treaties. The elf clans already balanced on a dangerous edge, threatening to plunge both sides into unending chaos. Should word of this blatant disregard for the treaty reach the queen it would tear their world apart.

Scratching an itch on the corner of his mouth, he frowned. He needed to move quickly to prevent Morgen from getting involved. There was one in the city capable of helping—if he could be convinced. Too bad for him, that meant exposing himself to the creatures he most despised. Stuffing his hands in his pockets, the man turned back to the concert, lost in thought.

Pain. Excruciating pain threatened to tear his head apart. Consciousness slowly returned to Wally's instant regret. Wetness spread through his hair, trickling down his neck. He groaned and opened his eyes, seeing nothing but darkness. That's when he noticed the scruff of fabric against his skin. Each inhaled breath dragged the cloth into his nostrils and scratched his eyelids.

What the fuck? I've been kidnapped?

Wally groaned again as he jerked to the side. He was still in a vehicle, probably the white van.

Bad things didn't happen to him. In fact, not much of anything exciting did. He went to work, spent his free time working on the family farm with his wife, and developing his comic label. Hell, he hadn't gotten a speeding ticket in the last seven years. Perhaps it was due to living in the country or maybe the positive influence his wife had on him. Perhaps it was because his cousin was one of the county deputies.

Country living suited him, though his wife often argued for moving closer to Wilmington, citing the thirty-minute drive to the grocery store repeatedly. Wally always shifted the conversation. The land had been in his family for three generations and he was the only son with any interest in keeping it. Wally didn't mind. He enjoyed getting his hands dirty while living up to his family's expectations. What did that say about him as a man if just gave it up without cause?

"He's waking up!" a female whispered shouted near him. The words drove into his skull like iron spikes. Wally tried lifting his arms only to find his hands were flex cuffed. His already bad day continued worsening. He felt the vehicle speed up, each bounce and rumble eliciting fresh waves of nausea.

"Quick! Hit him again!"

"Yes, knock him out."

"Too soon! Too soon!"

Wally caught three different voices begging to administer another round of thumps. He curled up into a fetal position to prevent more damage.

Minutes passed.

The clamor of calls to knock him unconscious faded. He got the impression his kidnappers were losing interest. Oddly enough, Wally found it insulting. *Damn, did they already stop caring? I'm not even putting up a fight.*

When it became evident no rain of fists awaited, Wally cleared his throat. His voice, when he tried to speak, was hoarse. "Hey."

"He speaks!"

"Keep him from speaking!"

"A curse he will put on us!"

"Water," he croaked.

"No water for you. Not until we get home," a voice shouted over the inane babbling. "Much work to do. Yes. Much work. You get water when we get home."

"How much longer?"

Chuckles burst into laughter from a dozen voices at his question.

Wally felt his confidence dissolve. One or two he might have been able to handle, but the voices swarmed him from every direction. Yet … *How many people did they fit inside the van? Was I kidnapped by circus clowns?*

He snorted a laugh, regretting it instantly.

"Funny man. Funny man, what's so funny?"

"Tell us, funny man!"

"Tell us!"

A boot clipped his hip when he stayed silent, reminding him of the direness of his predicament.

Out of moves, not that he had many to begin with, Wally worked on controlling his breathing in the hopes of washing away the pain. Years of forced couples' yoga, a small compromise for dragging his wife to far too many shows for her liking, put him in tune with his mind and body. Unwilling to admit it aloud, Wally had come to enjoy quiet moments of meditation. A sense of calm was his only hope of retaining sanity while the van sped down the road.

Away from his life.

Away from his home.

Away from everything.

Panic would end his chances for escape just as quickly as doubt. Leastwise that's what he learned from watching endless hours of television. *Stay calm. Do your breathing and see if we can get one of these people on our side. Yeah, that's it. Turn the tables on them! Man, if I could only get that gun I'd be in business.*

The van rumbled on in silence far longer than Wally found comfortable. The repetitive click-click-click of tires hitting cracks and small reflectors in the road told him they were now on one of the major roads. I-40 cut through Raleigh while 440 and 540 did concentric loops around the capital. None were in great repair despite the endless amount of construction hampering traffic over the better part of a decade.

Wally had no idea what direction they traveled or where they were headed. Images of his wife flashed in his head, causing his thoughts to spiral. How was he ever going to explain why he didn't, perhaps never, come home again?

Tears welled. The prospect of death bothered him, but it was the idea of being killed and tossed in an abandoned place of the world where they'd never find his body. A life left unfulfilled. The dreams of turning his hobby into a successful business erased. He briefly wondered if his titles would take off after his death.

That's it. Game over. I'm gonna have my face on a milk carton. Who are these jokers? What could they possibly want with me? He feared any answers wouldn't be forthcoming.

His thoughts turned to his captors. They looked like normal people, but something felt off. Unable to narrow it down, Wally searched his memories for obvious abnormalities. The fact they were all approximately the same height and shared an obviously defective gene with those heavy foreheads and single eyebrows aroused his suspicions. Not normally a paranoid man, Wally began to question *what* they were more than *who*.

He didn't believe in any of that mumbo jumbo of aliens, monsters, and other mythical creatures. Sure, the child in him wanted them all to be real but how many times had a special presentation drawn him in only for there to be no actionable evidence at the end? The last straw was a show on yetis. The hosts tried turning the 1959 incident of the Dyatlov Pass in the Ural Mountains where nine Soviet college students died mysteriously into a full-blown Yeti attack. In fact, the one host brought up the subject and said there was only one thing in the world capable of killing those kids, a Russian killer bigfoot.

That's when Wally turned the TV off in disgust and vowed to never watch another similar show again. Of course, that vow lasted only until the next alluring hint at the Bermuda Triangle sparked his interest. Could he be part of one of those shows now? The thought made him shake his head. Ridiculous.

He grunted when the van rolled over a deep pothole. The pain in his side felt less than before, prompting him to think his rib might not be broken after all. If that was the case, Wally's chances of fighting back at the first opportunity rose. Not that he was much of a fighter. He'd lasted the ten free karate classes bought through Groupon and never went back.

The van slowed, then he shifted, they were likely going around a long turn that meant nothing to him. He wasn't familiar enough with Raleigh to know where he was going without checking gps. If only he wasn't blindfolded. He might not have a way of contacting his wife, or the police, but he would at least have a general direction of where to go if he escaped. A road sign, mile marker, anything. He could figure it out, maybe.

FIVE

Daniel lay in the dark, staring at the clock. He could count on one hand the number of times the alarm went off instead of him already being awake. He has had endless nights of tossing and turning, glancing at the angry red letters, in anticipation of the following morning. Giving up, he would rise feeling drained then drag his way into the new day more tired than when he went to bed.

A glance at the clock had him shifting his hand over to the clock as the final minute hit before the alarm went off. Yawning, he dropped his head back on the pillow and closed his eyes. Beside him Sara made a noise. Daniel wasn't one for the snooze button like she was. His years in the army conditioned him better than that. Nor did he proscribe to Sara's theory of setting the clock ten minutes ahead. How did that make sense? Tired, Daniel slipped from the sheets and headed to the bathroom.

Washed up and dressed, Daniel snuck back into the bedroom to give Sara a kiss on her forehead, drawing back when she shifted. The last thing he wanted was to wake her before the sun rose. A point she continually chided him over. He lost track of how many times the first thing he heard coming through the door was 'why didn't you wake me?' instead of the obligatory welcome home.

Shoes in hand, he crept downstairs. A pair of wagging tails and excited looks from the dogs as they scrambled to their feet threatened to undo all his careful efforts upstairs. Their joy proved contagious. How could anyone be in a bad mood after being bombarded by unconditional love first thing in the morning? He pointed a finger at Otto when he spied the dog preparing to throw his head back and howl. Daniel rushed them to the back door and hurried them outside.

Retreating to the stove, he turned on the burner with the glass percolator coffee pot sitting on it, some called it a relic, but he found the taste of fresh brewed coffee better than any Keurig or Nespresso. Some things just tasted better. Daniel grabbed his favorite mug and waited. He'd been raised not to waste time. A fact inspired by his late grandfather's favorite saying—let's go, we're burning daylight hours, before the sun rose. He missed those simple times when all that mattered was ensuring all the poles and tackle gear, with a few snacks, were loaded before they headed out to a nearby river or mountain stream for the day.

The coffee finished percolating at the same time the dogs bounded back up to the deck and begged to come inside. Daniel clicked the stove off and opened the door. They swarmed him as he grabbed their bowls and headed into the garage for their breakfast. *Mission accomplished: Dogs taken care and wife and kids still asleep.*

Noting the time, Daniel filled his travel mug, grabbed a few croissants, and headed off to the first day of Sword and Sorcery Con.

After paying the ridiculous parking fees, a sore spot for any large event he attended, Daniel closed his eyes and tapped his forehead against the steering wheel. This was his ritual of preparation before any event where he was attempting to manifest success. Focused and prepared as only a former army paratrooper could be, he grabbed the much needed coffee and headed for the building.

Crowds lined the street. An array of costumes blocked his path to the doors. Pushing towards the front of the makeshift lines, he flashed his lanyard with the vendor badge and slipped through the anxious crowds. Behind him people crowded close.

Daniel let out a low whistle, taking it all in. Dozens of hired security worked to keep the crowds at bay. He watched as each time a guest or vendor headed to the escalators the awaiting crowd surged a little closer, eager to get their first glimpse of this year's layout. Daniel put on his best scowl in the hopes of keeping too many from stopping him; the less talking the better. He knew his throat would be sore by the end of the day.

The escalator ride down was his last chance at finding focus. He closed his eyes for a moment, listening to the mechanical hum and the murmuring crowd. The air was electric. He couldn't help but be excited even as nervous energy filled the floor. Vendors were busy conducting their pre-show rituals. Daniel reached his table and removed the black sheet he used to cover his display. He spent the next few minutes adjusting his table displays, ensuring all was where he wanted it.

The five-minute warning came over the distorted loudspeakers.

"Game time," he told himself.

Daniel just made it back to his table with a refill of coffee when the flood gates opened, and the crowds poured in.

"Thanks for stopping by. I hope you enjoy," Daniel said with a forced smile as he finished signing the book he just sold.

Smiles in return, the two women took their books and blended back into the stream of people. Daniel watched them go, still trying to figure out their costumes before he broke out his ledger. The first day always proved slow and he never had fun until making back his table cost. From what he counted; he had taken a fair chunk out of the hefty cost. The weekend proved promising if this continued.

A pair of shadows fell over him. Without looking up, Daniel said, "I'll be with you in just a moment. Feel free to look through the books and let me know if anything catches your eye."

"You couldn't pay me to read this bullshit."

The gruff tone raised the hairs on the back of Daniel's neck. Raising his gaze, he found himself staring up at a pair of familiar, and hostile, faces—Fritz and Angus Schneider. Burly and out of their element, yet fitting in among the costumes, the dwarf brothers loomed over him. Daniel spied the clenched fists on the brother on the right, Angus if he remembered right.

"No one's asking you to," Daniel replied with as much pleasantry as he could, which wasn't much considering their one and only meeting.

They once fought alongside each other in a string of running gunfights from downtown Raleigh to halfway across the state. Daniel learned more about dwarves than anything his imagination might conjure, and they had left him rattled. He thought he'd been around true warriors in his time. He was wrong. The Schneider brothers were among the roughest men he'd ever encountered and, until now, he had been glad to have them on the same side. Looks like they didn't hold any admirable feelings towards him.

Angus folded his thick arms across his chest. Veins popped. "I thought you would have learned your lesson after that fiasco with the king. Looks like you hummies just aren't too bright."

Heads turned their way. Curious faces. Daniel knew what they saw—another character come to live. Making him the bad guy. Crap.

"Smart enough not to bring up sensitive subjects around people I don't know," Daniel fired back, ignoring the look of disdain he received. "Look, fellas, I'm busy here. It's been a long day and I have plenty of customers to meet and greet. Grab a book if you want and I'll sign it for you. Just don't hog my table time."

One thing he learned was how fast people were to bypass a busy table.

Fritz elbowed his brother. "What my brother meant to say is it's good to see you again, Daniel."

"Uh huh."

Fritz fixed his brother with a baleful glare when Angus grunted. "Isn't that right, Angus?"

Glowering, Angus gave a clipped nod. "Sure, what he said."

"There, see? He can be civil!" Fritz beamed and Daniel rolled his eyes. "Daniel, how have you been?"

"Well enough I suppose." Daniel kept his gaze on Angus. "Work has been taking up a lot of my time lately."

"Explains why there hasn't been a new book," Angus retorted.

"Among other things."

Fritz lowered his voice and leaned conspiratorially close. "Word around town is you were involved in something big up north a while back."

"I wouldn't know anything about that," Daniel balked.

Fritz hummed. "So, you haven't heard about Xander and the Princess getting killed in a shootout in upstate New York?"

Shit, how do they know? I hope they don't bring up Sara's encounter with the werewolves. Daniel nodded at a pair of kids passing by. "Nope. I try to stay in my lane."

"Look, buddy, we're old friends, right? You can tell Angus and me…"

"Fritz, I like you. At least I think I did," Daniel started. He wasn't sure what they were getting at or why they were talking to him now, but he wasn't interested. "But you have the wrong guy. I don't have anything to do with your world or DESA anymore."

"Oh, for fuck's sake!" Angus burst out. "You sit there and look at me with a straight face while you lie through your teeth."

He snatched Daniel's newest book off the wire rack and brandished it like a weapon; Daniel tested ready to dodge. "What's this? Just another tall tale to wow your audience? This has DESA's taint all over it, army boy."

"Okay, fine." Daniel finally rose. He held out both hands to calm the dwarves before they did something all three would regret. "I was there. Blackmere grabbed me. Said it was a top-secret op and I needed to be there. Xander got sprung from some secret prison—"

"The Grinder," Fritz supplied.

"—by the prime minister and was sent to assassinate a handful of power players. I led a team that stopped him. That's it. You'll have to ask Blackmere for the rest."

"Book doesn't say anything about Xander buying it." Angus sneered, crumbling the book almost in half and tossed the ruined copy back on the table.

Daniel frowned. *There goes fifteen bucks.* "Wait, you really think I detail every little encounter or strange happenstance?"

"Convince me otherwise."

Shrugging, Daniel said, "Well, I haven't included an asshole dwarf for a character yet."

Fritz's laughter prevented Angus from launching a right hook that he had started to pull back.

Daniel tensed. A glance from the corner of his eye spied several potential customers approaching his table. One wore an excited look. He forced himself to relax and go back to work mode. "Look, fellas, it's been great catching up, but I am trying to run a business. Feel free to swing back around at the end of the day and we can talk all about it over a beer. My treat."

"Whisky and a cigar," Angus grumped.

"Sure, sure," Daniel agreed, already turning to face a man that had stepped forward. "Hey there. See anything you like?"

The man ran an index finger over the cover of the nearest book without looking at him. He licked his lower lip and whistled low. "You're the author?"

"I am, all twenty of them." Daniel beamed. "Which one caught your eye?"

"Oh, I'm not much of a reader." The man shook his head. Long strands of greasy black hair dragged across his neck; Daniel caught the reek of armpits and forced down a gag. "Name's Damon Pender."

"Maybe I can change your mind." Daniel felt a familiar warning in the pit of his stomach. "Nothing wrong with a good book, Damon."

Anger flashed in his eyes, his skin darkening a sickly shade of grey. "I said I don't read. Are you deaf?"

"If you don't read you don't need to waste either of our time," Daniel replied, trying to remain calm. He glanced at the Schneider brothers who had moved to stand at the other side of his table. "There's plenty to see here. Have a good day."

"I did not come here for books. I came for you, Daniel Thomas."

The dwarves reached for weapons they didn't have. Angus snarled and spat, stepping back as his brother fell into a fighting stance.

"Stay away from him, Daniel," Fritz warned. "Don't let him touch you."

"What?"

Angus snatched a doll with a small animal's skull from the next table over and readied to attack. "Move Daniel."

SIX

Daniel recoiled, ensuring he was out of reach.

The dwarves rushed in. Their bulk only surpassed by their proclivity for violence. A small crowd formed at the end of the isle, eager to see what happened next as the dwarves, suddenly in full dwarven regalia, prepared to battle. Daniel sensed danger wafting from the stranger and moved back to let the dwarves work. He scanned the growing crowd for security.

Damon offered a thin smile resembling a predatory leer and raised his empty hands. "I didn't come here looking for a fight."

"You shouldn't have come at all." Angus jabbed a thick finger at him. "I thought we killed you."

"What can I say? The dead don't always die," Damon replied. "Please, Schneiders, I come in peace and with an important message for this one."

Daniel sighed. "Not me? I don't want any part of this."

"Your friend is in grave danger."

Daniel tensed. *Friend?* "What friend?"

"The comic book man. Rutherford. He has been taken." Damon's voice carried a lisping song akin to a wet lizard crawling across stone. "Gone from here."

"Wally? Are you sure? He normally plays it close on these things. I'm sure he's at his table," Daniel insisted. He tried looking for his friend earlier but ran out of time.

Damon's eyes lit and electric orange hue. "Yesss. Wally Rutherford. The comic man. He has been taken captive by goblins."

"Bullshit," Angus growled.

Fritz gasped. "They wouldn't dare break the treaty!"

"Wait, goblins?" Daniela asked. "You're kidding, right? This is all a prank he's pulling on me for that incident in Greenville."

Damon's head cocked. "What is a prank?"

"There haven't been any goblins in this part of the state since the end of the war," Angus interrupted. "I was there when we beat them back and forced them to submit."

"Which war?" Daniel asked.

"Civil," Fritz supplied. "The goblin hordes were defeated in 1864 outside of Charlotte. They have not been allowed within five hundred miles of the king or queen since. Damon, are you certain it was goblins?"

Murmurs rippled through the crowd. Several were filming. A few took pics of Daniel's table. Others whispered about *having* to buy his books.

Damon regarded him. "Many goblins. They took him from the parking garage last night."

"How do you know it was him?" Daniel insisted. "You could be mistaken."

Another shrug. "Go to his table and see if your friend has arrived."

"I can't just leave my table like that." Daniel tried to ignore the doubt eating at him again. Maybe it wasn't a prank. Though Wally was as jovial as they came and staging his own kidnapping wasn't beneath him.

Angus snorted. "Go ahead. Doesn't look like too many people are dying to buy your rags, hummie."

Seeing no battle forthcoming, the crowds dispersed. There was too much to see to stay holed up in one section for too long.

"Easy, brother," Fritz cautioned. "We're in enemy territory here."

"Ah, the infamous Schneiders continue their internal bickering," Damon cooed. "Give me an hour and you will not be so…lively."

"You say one more veiled threat and I'll take your fucking head here and now, treaties be damned," Angus fumed. "I should have made sure you were dead."

"Oh, but I am," Damon cackled. He straightened, rising to his near full seven-foot height. A shadow and a pall fell over the isle that had the crowd oo'ing and aah'ing.

"Go Daniel Thomas, see I do not lie. When you believe me, and you shall." He turned away. "Come and find me in the capital building. I am not hard to find. Just whisper my name in the dark. But I warn you, time runs short. Goblins are known to … devour their prey."

Damon Pender slithered away.

Tense moments passed without a word. The crowd surrounding them dispersed, any notion of a cosplay battle ending in frustration.

Daniel shook himself back to reality and noticed the vendors on each side of him staring with open mouths and flushed cheeks. He didn't know where to begin to clean this one up. *The one time you need a professional D.E.S.A. agent around.*

"We do this sort of thing all the time." He felt lame saying it aloud and, judging from their looks, the other vendors weren't buying it. "Spices up the quiet days, you know?" Daniel shifted his focus from the people he most likely would never see again back to the dwarf brothers. Angus' chest heaved. Fritz stood looking as if having seen a ghost. Neither moved. Daniel saw a break in the crowd and motioned for the dwarves to join him.

The dwarves followed him to the convention center's back wall; they wedged between opposing bathrooms and trash cans. "Somebody care to explain who that was?"

"A bloody lich." Anger simmered in Angus' eyes. "One of the last."

"But we killed him." Fritz shook his head. "This is impossible."

Daniel frowned, searching his already crowded memory for anything describing this lich. He had nothing. "You mean like a soulless bloodsucker from Dungeons and Dragons?"

Angus glared. "Idiot. Do you have any idea what happens if that thing touches you?"

Fritz clapped his hands. "Instant dead. You've become one of his minions. A plague forever damned to wander the planet until the breaking of the world."

Daniel's mouth fell open. "You mean a zombie?"

Angus drew back. "Sure, hummie. Whatever you want to think. He shouldn't be here, and neither should those damned goblins."

"If what he said is true," Daniel countered.

"I don't see why Damon would lie," Fritz said. "It's not like you're important enough to get the lich king's attention."

"That's just a rumor and you know it," Angus mumbled. "We don't have time for this. We need to warn the Old Guard. Let Morgen deal with him before he can rebuild his cult."

"Fellas!" Daniel's voice rose with exasperation. "What about Wally?"

Angus blinked. "Who?"

"My friend!"

"Oh yeah, another one of your fuckhead friends making a life off my people. Go see for yourself."

Fists clenching, Daniel ground his teeth to keep from snapping. He decided to ignore the angrier brother. "He does space and alien stuff. Fritz, can you two watch my table for me until I get back?"

"Do I get to sign the books?" he asked, a wicked gleam in his jewel-like eyes.

"No, and don't let your brother destroy my product. I'll be right back."

Daniel hurried off, slipping through the throngs of costumes in search of his friend and praying this was all a misunderstanding.

They decided they would look as imposing as possible, practically blocking the table from passersby because they weren't sure how to answer the questions they had been asked so far. Impressive in their mass and stature, the dwarves conjured imagination in young and old alike—or at least they thought so after hearing some comments. Their leather armor, faded and dull with time, fit snugger than either remembered. Their vambraces and gauntlets lacked the luster with which they were first forged. Neither had worn traditional dwarven combat gear in so long they almost forgot how.

It had been too long since they last wore their gear. Being able to do so now, among the throngs of costumed characters and unsuspecting bystanders, proved confusing on multiple levels. Trained warriors, nothing in their experience prepared them for all that surrounding them today. Being in public, no longer hiding, the dwarf brothers felt like they were breaking the law.

Life among the humans trapped them behind power suits and gaudy ties. Today at least provided an opportunity to untie their hair, braid their beards and clank mugs of mead in toast to each other. The only thing missing was their battle axes. Weapons were banned, for good reason. Not that either minded. Both had grown fond of the standard light machine gun over the past few decades. Then they ran into the lich king and all their plans evaporated.

Angus popped a cigar in his mouth and fumbled in his pockets for his lighter. He took a few delicious puffs, blowing smoke rings toward the ceiling and sighed. This was the life. If only they had a few dark elf skulls to crack. "You can't do that in here."

Angus opened his eyes, searching for the perpetrator. A pair of Star Wars characters walked by, earning a well-deserved sneer that had them walking faster, and then a handful of teenage girls dressed far too inappropriately for any good parent to be comfortable with giggled.

"Cool costume, man," one claimed.

"Yeah, hi, you can't smoke in here," the redhead repeated, waving at Angus from the table across the aisle. "It's no smoking."

Angus took a deep puff and blew the smoke her way. "Is that right?"

He took a step forward before his brother gripped his upper arm.

"We're trying not to stand out," Fritz warned. "Pummeling her isn't a good PR move, Angus."

"I wasn't going to hurt them," he replied with an innocent look. "Just shove this cigar so far down their throats they fart smoke for a week."

"Been working on that line long?"

Angus shrugged. "Long enough."

"I can't leave you two alone for a moment, can I?"

Angus dropped the cigar. Ash and spark dancing across the trodden floor. He stiffened, as if reprimanded for pulling a school prank. Turning, with a nudge to his brother, they bowed to the slender woman confronting them.

"Angus and Fritz Schneider. I thought as much when I inhaled the stench of that foul thing," Morgen announced as she glided closer.

Her black dress, complete with raven hair swept back in a tail and power heels conveying every ounce of royalty, fit just loose enough for her to act if need be. Danger clung to the corners of her eyes like cobwebs in an old house. Despite her age, Morgen's skin remained flawless with just the right hint of golden tan.

She terrified them.

"Are you the cause of my dire warnings?" she asked. "Perhaps riding the storm as you dwarves did in the old days?"

"No, your majesty," Fritz said, regaining his composure first. "The storm hasn't been called in centuries. We just decided to blow off some steam and stop hiding for a bit. No harm in it, we figured."

"No harm indeed." She swept her gaze over the isles, admiring yet abhorring the endless stream of pretend elves, wizards, and more. Her gaze fell on the array of books behind them. "It must be coincidence I find you here."

They remained silent; hands clasped behind their backs in a display of subservience: Morgen remained a power neither dared cross. *Good.* She studied them, seeking signs of deception. Not a fan of dwarves and their often-filthy ways, the queen looked down on them with thinly veiled contempt. The Schneiders, she knew from her spies, were instrumental in the action the night her estranged husband was murdered by Xander and Gwen. It was only through a plea deal from the government that both continued living. Morgen ran a manicured nail over a row of books, impressed with Daniel's resume.

"Tell me, dwarves, where is Daniel Thomas? I would very much like to speak with him," she commanded.

"I'm right here, lady."

She turned, smooth and graceful, to watch him walk up from behind. While he appeared defiant, she noticed a hint of dejection. *A defeat, perhaps?* Morgen let her carefully manicured smile slip into place. "I am a queen. Remember your place, mortal."

"Not my queen," Daniel snapped. Folding his arms across his chest, he met her gaze with fire. "We have problems."

"Indeed, we do, but this is neither the place nor the time to discuss them."

SEVEN

"I really appreciate you doing this, man," Daniel said for the third time as his long-time friend and sometimes show companion settled into the chair. "You got everything you need?"

Telly gave the table the once over, again. "Yeah, dude. I'm all good. Go take care of whatever you need to. I'll handle this easy enough. Besides, Thursday and Friday are the slow days. It'll be fun."

You have no idea. "You're a lifesaver. I owe you."

Daniel hefted his old army assault pack, transformed to carrying snacks and promotional items instead of ammunition and MREs, and paused. He felt guilty for throwing his event on Telly with no warning.

"Get out of here before I change my mind," Telly chided. "You know my kids want me to bring them here. I can't afford that."

Lips pressed together, Daniel gave a clipped nod and hurried off.

With the end of day one approaching and a slew of nocturnal activities planned, the real party was set to begin. Daniel never stayed for any of that. This was work, not fun. He seldom enjoyed himself at cons. Dressed in his standard Grunt Style t-shirt and army themed ball cap, he was a far cry from the pirates, creatures, and scantily clad damsels perusing the isles.

The Schneider brothers waited at the base of the stairs. Impatient scowls darkened their faces enough for other attendees to give them a wide berth. Though as he was heading toward them, he saw Fritz agreeing to a photo op. Another group tried for pictures next but after a few colorful phrases from Angus, accomplishing more than blushed cheeks and huffed attitudes, they got the hint. A handful of empty plastic beer mugs lay scattered about them on the nearest counter; Daniel's attention was drawn to the drip of golden liquid from an overturned mug. *That's not a bad idea. I could use a drink.*

"Are you ready?"

"What took you so long? We saw that slinky hummie head down twenty minutes ago," Angus said after a loud belch. "The queen don't like to be kept waiting. Especially not by one of your kind."

"Yeah well, I don't work for her," Daniel gripped. He shifted the weight of his pack to the opposite shoulder. The only reason he agreed to go was to get to the bottom of the Wally mystery. "Are we walking or not?"

Angus squinted, menace in his gaze, then stalked off. Daniel saw he was opting for the lower-level side door rather than swimming through the crowds heading down from the front.

They were soon outside and marching toward the Wells Fargo Building where Morgen, queen of the dark elves, built her lair. All those times he and Sara were members of the City Club they never imagined it held such a deep secret.

Daniel saw the dwarves' tense at the attention they were getting, as if both were prepared to lash out at any fool enough to get too close. He didn't doubt they would either. Though Fritz projected calm and common sense, he too was a viper coiled beneath that old armor. Memories of that fateful night he was introduced to their world resurfaced. Together, the dwarf brothers were unstoppable, slaughtering dark elves by the score. Ash and dark dust had littered the Raleigh streets, and halfway across the state, thanks to their unleashed fury.

They arrived at the building and hopped in the elevator to the top floor, jarring him back to reality. Daniel had no idea how he was going to explain two medieval dressed dwarves to the receptionist.

The chime announced their arrival to the twenty-eighth floor. Daniel took a deep breath, politely gesturing the Schneiders out first. Angus led the way without pause. Much to Daniel's surprise, the young woman dressed smartly in a black skirt and executive jacket beamed when she saw them.

"Ah, Mr. Schneider. I trust you and your brother had a good time at the event," she greeted with a smile leaving Daniel in shock.

Angus returned the smile. "That we did, lass. That we did. Nothing says let your hair down like mixing it up with the locals. This town needs more of it."

"He's been drinking," Fritz explained when she laughed and shoved his brother forward before the man made a fool of himself. "Thank you, Emily."

Daniel followed, unsure what he was seeing as Frit winked at her.

When they were alone in one of the side corridors, he asked, "Is she an elf?"

"Emily? Oh no. She's only been here for a year or so. Just got her degree from State and is trying to figure out which direction in which to take her life," Fritz explained. "She's a good kid. She has to be to put up with his nonsense."

"Stow it, brother. It's been a long time since I gave you a good beating," the bigger dwarf warned without looking over his shoulder.

Fritz rolled his eyes and nudged Daniel in the ribs. "He only says that because he doesn't remember the thumping I gave him. Some men only think with their muscles, eh Daniel?"

"Uh, right." Daniel began to question everything he thought he knew about life.

They found Morgen in a small room overlooking the North Hills area. Ever graceful, if Daniel didn't know better, he might have taken her for a wealthy heiress instead of the cold-blooded killer he knew her to be.

"I am not in the habit of being kept waiting," she said without turning.

"Told you," Fritz mumbled.

Daniel spied her glare in the reflection on the window and swallowed. "I wasn't under the impression you needed me. The Schneiders convinced me otherwise."

Morgen stiffened, barely. "They did not lay hands on you I trust."

"Not a finger, your Majesty," Fritz hastily confirmed. "Not a one."

The smell of fresh roses filled the room, throwing Daniel off his game. He struggled with the sudden urge to go home. *Sara! Shit.* He reached for his phone before remembering where he was.

Morgen turned and gestured for them to sit. Fingers of red and orange streaked across the sky behind her, promising to bring the darkness behind. She made a show of studying them, pausing to look deep into each of their gazes before moving on. Daniel frowned but held his tongue. It was a tactic he'd seen far too many senior leaders in the army pull.

"Why am I being drawn to this pettiness?" she began, pausing to enunciate each syllable with applicable force. "The clans are in turmoil, and I must now waste my precious time, of which there is never enough, on you three."

"Pender is back," Fritz said a moment after.

Morgen placed her hands over her lap and smoothed the wrinkles from her skirt. "I see. Is there anything else?"

"Your Majesty? The lich king has returned," Angus emphasized with a frown. "He must be dealt with before he begins another cult."

"He shall be. I will deploy the Old Guard to ensure there will not be another plague," Morgen mused.

Daniel cocked his head. How could she remain so calm?

"Perhaps I did not make myself clear. What else are you hiding? I have known you both for far too long to be fooled by witless deception. Answer me—"

"My friend was kidnapped by goblins," Daniel interrupted.

The dwarves fixed him with opposing glares. Daniel realized he was weary of playing their games. Tired of walking on eggshells around Angus, who he almost considered a friend during their previous encounter, and, most importantly, fed up with being dragged from the comforts of his life by the elves on their terms.

"Goblins have not been seen in this state for decades," Morgen hissed. "They know the consequences of violating the treaties. Entire villages were wiped out in retribution the last time. Did you see these goblins? How many? Where?"

Daniel's cheeks reddened. "Actually, no. None of us did. Damon Pender told us."

"Tell me everything and make sure to leave nothing out. All our fates may depend on it," she commanded.

He considered leaving now and phoning Blackmere. Let the government handle this, but it was his friend. He owed Wally at least an effort. Like a good soldier, Daniel obeyed.

Finished, Daniel leaned back in the chair and let out the anxious breath choking him. Until now, he hadn't realized the stress he'd been under. Wally was a good friend and didn't deserve whatever foul fate the goblins had in store for him. The sooner they got him back, the sooner Daniel could focus on Sara who was going to have his hide for getting involved once more with the elves and, if he was lucky, get back to the convention.

"While I find the lich most distasteful, there may be some merit to his offer. Go to him, the three of you. Find out what he knows and bring me intel on his lair. A lich never gives from the heart. Damon is most assuredly playing an angle and I need to know what," Morgen instructed. "Upon your return I will have you fitted with whatever arsenal you need to move forward should it be necessary."

"What if Pender gets handsy?" Angus asked.

"He is not to be harmed, leastwise not by any of you. Leave Damon Pender to me. I will ensure he does not spread his filth again." Morgen's tone left no room for discussion. "Now go."

They rose all, awkward and appreciative. Daniel didn't know whether to bow or not. His brief interactions with the queen had yet to produce a moment where it came up. A bump from Angus convinced him not to when he started to bend at the waist. He tugged his shirt to cover the motion and was almost at the door when Morgen called out to him.

"Mr. Thomas, I trust you will want your darling wife to have a measure of protection."

"That would be appreciated, yes. Thank you," he replied.

"I'm sure she will be glad to see Norman Guilt again. They have grown to become close friends since the werewolf incident," Morgen admitted. An odd mirth was in her words. "Oh, and boys, change out of those ridiculous costumes. It's bad enough you're dwarves. You mustn't look foolish being such."

Halfway to the elevators, Daniel pulled out his phone and started texting.

EIGHT

First occupied in 1840, the North Carolina State Capital Building was all but a shell of its former self. Having closed earlier in the year for much needed renovations, all offices but one were displaced to different venues spread across the city. Nestled in the heart of downtown on what was once the plantation of Joel Lane, the building represented the heart of the state. Surrounded by majestic oak trees towering over the sidewalks, benches, and statues and monuments, the building was within walking distance of the museums and a block away from Fayetteville Street.

It was a five-minute walk from the Wells Fargo Building and Daniel hoped the start of finding his friend and getting back to his event. Daniel tried to focus on his job. Nothing in his previous experience with the elves suggested this would prove easy, however.

Crossing the street, they stood looking up at the sturdy building, more imposing in the night. A handful of pedestrians walked through the designed park. Others sat on the benches making out. Daniel spied a handful of youths talking quietly in a circle off to the shadows. A patrol officer walked down the sidewalk along South Salisbury Street, watching from the corner of his eye.

Daniel caught the echoing thunder of drums and guitars from the stage outside of the convention center signaling the shift from the vendor floor to the party atmosphere. Part of him wanted to go back, to take the opportunity to finally see what happened during the infamous after hours after years of fighting it. The other part of him reminded he hadn't called home yet.

Daniel fumbled in his pocket, pulling out his phone just as it started ringing. He winced upon seeing Sara's face pop up on the screen. *Well, shit.* "Hey babe. Did you get my text?"

"You know damned well I did," Sara fumed. "Why didn't you call me?"

"About what?"

"About what?! How about the fact you're working with that freaking witch instead of shutting down your table?"

"Sara, I—"

"Don't even try. Norman called."

Fucking gargoyle! He hadn't even made it out of the city yet and Norman Guilt already had him pegged. "It's not like I want to be here. I was dragged into it. One of my friends has been kidnapped and I'm on the way to see about getting him back. Don't worry, I'm not alone. The Schneider brothers are with me, remember them?"

A pause and the click of her tongue on the roof of her mouth. "Angus and Fritz? I thought you said you didn't want anything to do with them again?"

Grumbling from one, perhaps both gave him pause. He winced, failing to consider they could hear through the phone. "Sara, I must do this. I'm the only one who can."

"You better not get hurt. If you do, I will be there with Norman and the others so fast you won't know what happened," she replied angrily before hanging up.

Others? What others? I should have paid more attention to what she told me happened in Wilmington. Slipping his phone back in the pocket, Daniel turned to see the undisguised disdain on their dwarves' faces. "Sorry, the wife and all." He offered a light laugh. "Where do you suppose Damon is hiding?"

"My guess is as close to the sewer as possible." Angus picked at a piece of meat jammed between his teeth and flicked it at the ground in front of Daniel.

Fritz passed Daniel a pistol. "Listen, Daniel, this is no joke. Lich are dangerous creatures wrought from twisted magic. Damon Pender is one of the worst. He's a carrier. A creature capable of spreading the blight—he's done it before. You must be careful."

"Do as we say and you should be fine," Angus added.

"I will be," Daniel affirmed, wondering what history the dwarves had with Damon and how it might affect what came next. "Have either of you ever been in here?"

"Once," Fritz said. "Long, long ago. Angus is correct. Damon will be as far underground as he can get."

"How did you all wind up in North Carolina?" Daniel surprised himself, and them based on their expressions, in asking. "There are so many better places in the world to be."

"Wasn't always North Carolina, fool," Angus muttered then barreled past him. Instead of his machine gun, which Daniel expected, the dwarf produced a pair of foot and a half blades. "Are we going to stand around talking about the past all night or can we go in and find this fiend?"

Envious of the blades, thinking they made the dwarf look like a Roman legionnaire, Daniel fell in line behind him. They scampered up the short flight of steps, ducked around the side of the building containing the security office, and to the plastic covered chain link fence. Angus wasted no time in slicing through the locking chain. Fritz swept in, a soldier clearing the immediate surroundings with his short barrel rifle.

The dwarves were impressive to watch. Trained and experienced beyond measure, Daniel felt like a raw recruit as they swept the interior perimeter before collapsing on the side access door. Feeling inadequate with naught but a twelve round 9mm, he longed for better weapons with greater power. He never had quality weapons on these adventures, unlike his counterparts.

Angus laid a gnarled hand on the doorknob and looked back at them. "We go on three. Heads on a swivel. Damon may have invited us in, but he is not to be trusted. There's a good bet he's already turned others and they are waiting for us."

"Why would he spring a trap?" Daniel was confused.

"Because he's as close to the fucking devil as this state has ever seen," Angus replied. "Any more stupid questions?"

Screw this. Daniel squared on the dwarf. "When this is finished, you and me are going to have words. I don't know what your attitude with me is, but it needs to end. Now. My friend is in danger, and your bullshit game of who's got the bigger dick is getting in the way of finding him."

Angus stared him down before finally grunting. "Stay between us, hummie. This is going to get nasty if we're right."

He popped the door and slipped inside, armed and ready for war. Daniel followed Fritz, bringing up the rear. The hallway was empty and dark. Dwarves, if he remembered correctly, were infamous for their night vision, leaving Daniel moving to be between them. He despised relying on others, especially when his life was on the line, but there were some instances where discretion truly was the better part of valor. Still lacking complete understanding on what lich were or how Damon turned others into zombie-like slaves, Daniel was in no hurry to find misstep and get caught.

Fritz shifted to take the lead, moving fast and sure. His steps light, betraying almost no sound of movement. Daniel figured each dwarf outweighed him by fifty pounds, making their stealth all the more remarkable.

"Show off," he mumbled.

Angus chuckled from behind.

Clinging to one wall, they hurried past closed doors until coming to the central rotunda. A miniature scale of the national building in Washington, complete with a small statue of George Washington, the heart of the building inspired and awed visitors for years. Or would again once it reopened. It was one of those places they talked about visiting for years and never got around to.

This was Daniel's first time inside. Impressive as the statue and general ambience might be, he felt a lurking presence of decay and sickness permeating the air. *Has to be the lich.* The smell strengthened the closer they got to the stairwell until his stomach threatened to rebel. Daniel glanced at the brothers to see if they suffered similarly. If they did, he couldn't tell.

Heartbeat thundering in his skull, palms slick with sweat, Daniel flashed back to his first building clearance in the northern Iraqi city of Tal Afar. He thought that was as hairy as it could get. They were supposed to clear the city of enemy fighters and wound up surrounded by thousands of people determined to kill them. Daniel thought that was as bad as things could get.

Until he confronted what nasty entity Jenny tangled with in the Fainting Goat Island Inn on his last mission for D.E.S.A. This felt like neither. The air felt … off. Daniel struggled with the sudden urge to flee. A prod from behind as he froze in mid-stride helped him refocus.

"Thanks," he whispered as quietly as possible.

Angus' soft grunt was the reply.

They kept moving down. Fritz led them unerringly, as if he knew precisely where Damon Pender lurked.

Daniel steeled his nerves as they moved down another flight of stairs. Though he may have retired from the army years ago, he always felt at home in situations like this. Time to act like it. Calling on his training and conditioning, Daniel let the past in, becoming a soldier once more. An adrenalin surge emboldened him, begged him to move to the point, with Fritz's rifle, and see the job done.

Fritz splashed through a puddle on the lowest floor and paused. Daniel spied a thin trail of wet footprints leading deeper into the darkness—a beacon unable to be ignored. A sense of dread. If Damon was here, how long had the lich had made this place his home? Shapes stirred in the darkness. Daniel frowned unsure if his mind was playing tricks on him.

"Why is it wet?" he asked.

"Pender," Fritz replied and took three steps forward before kneeling, rifle raised. "He is close."

"Daniel, take rear," Angus instructed. "Anyone comes down here you plug them. No questions. We're not in friendly territory."

"Where are you going?"

Running his blades together like a giant pair of shears, Angus grinned. "To draw that little bastard out. I don't like playing games—PENDER!"

The name echoed, slapping off the walls. Almost immediately alight at the far end of the hall flickered to life. Dull and faded, the pale light shined directly on a lone figure that stood very still.

Daniel's chest tightened. Not wanting to be foolish looking, he took a kneeling position behind Fritz and shifted his attention back and forth from the front to the rear. He didn't know what liches were, but for one to have spooked the brothers so much…

"Pender! No more games. We're here," Angus challenged.

The illuminated figure hissed a laugh and scuffed a step closer. "Games. Yes, dwarf. Ever have we played games. Tonight, this time is different, I think. No?"

Daniel heard it first. A distinct moaning. A wail that soon was carried on the funneled air pumping from the vents.

It changed into a song that was luring him with rich temptation, promising to relieve him of all worry. He licked his lips. The air tasted sweet. The stench of decay lessened, became almost pleasant. He shook his head, willing the illusions away lest he succumb and lose himself. *Not like this. I am not one of you.* He caught Damon's gaze and felt his resolve tremble. Strange shapes moved in the shadows behind him.

"Ah, yes. You hear it, don't you? The sweat song of salvation," Damon cooed. "Ever has it brought men like you to the righteous path. Come, taste in the goodness. You will find eternity."

The crack of a rifle thundered throughout the lower level. Daniel threw a hand up as the flames from the end of the barrel robbed what little night vision he had. Stunned back to reality, he stared open mouthed at the monster looming in the hallway. He froze.

"You aren't taking anyone," Fritz warned. "He's under the queen's protection."

"A shame," Damon said, cocking his head. "I would have liked to taste his flesh."

It took every effort for Daniel not to throw up.

"Enough," Angus warned. "We came here for information. Give it."

Silence.

Daniel saw his lone opportunity of learning what happened to Wally slowly slipping from his grasp as Angus took a step forward, blades ready.

NINE

Daniel's fingertip danced on the trigger. He felt the nerves
tingle. The veins throb. Every instinct screamed to open
fire and kill the creature, he no longer looked at Damon
like a man. Yet the dwarves remained steadfast. Daniel
felt shamed by his personal thoughts, especially with how
tempting it was to flee. Heat lingered in the air, turning
the hallway fetid with rancor. Stomach roiling, Daniel
reached an arm out to the wall for support and focused on
the lich.

Dancing between reality and the immaterial, Damon
Pender struggled to prevent his true form from showing.
It had been decades and he longed to reveal himself to the
world once more. The lich tasted fear on the air. Hunger
roused, he fought with base desires as the dwarves stood
ready to destroy him. His wariness for their trickery
resurfaced, a firm barrier to any foolish move. It had been
a long time since he last tasted dwarf flesh. Best to let the
arrogant take control.
"Tell us what we want to know, Damon, and we'll let you
walk free," Fritz called.
Damon scoffed. All but the human knew he could kill
them without much effort. But that was not why they were
here. He offered information. He never said it didn't come
at a cost. "Send me the human. My words are for his ears
only."
"No deal, asshole," Angus replied. "Talk now or I finish
the job I started a long time ago. How long did it take you
to recover from that, by the way?"
"Not helpful, Angus," Daniel shot.

"This is a score that's been building for over a century," the dwarf tightened his grip on his rifle. "Me and him go way back."

Daniel groaned. Were all dwarves eager to start a fight when other, usually better, solutions were available? He swallowed the lump growing in his throat and rose. "I'm here, Damon. Where did the goblins take Wally?"

"Not until the dwarf lowers his weapon," Damon hissed. "I am no fool. Dwarves are as wicked as they are cruel."

"You know me too well," Angus sneered. His swords lowered, barely.

Daniel repeated, "Where is he, Damon? Where have they taken him?"

"Oh yes, danger," Damon cooed. "Goblins have a penchant for human flesh. He seemed scrawny for my tastes, but with the proper seasoning…"

Bile rising, Daniel shoved the image out of his head. "Where, Damon?"

"They are from the Ok'tal'med Nest. Far, far from here."

"Impossible!" Fritz shouted. "We eliminated them three hundred years ago."

"Ever arrogant. It is a wonder the queen has lasted this long." Damon shook his head. "I told you what you required. Now a price must be paid."

"Price? No one said anything about a price," Daniel said. His grip on the pistol tightened, finger slipping back into the trigger well.

"Everything comes with a price, Daniel Thomas."

The finality in the tone raised the hairs on the back of his neck. Shadows deepened. Figures writhed within. Daniel heard the song again. Soft. Beckoning. His legs moved on their own accord. His eyelids grew heavy. A warm hum filled his body, drowning out emotions and thought.

BANG.

The spell broke—Daniel threw his hands up over his ears as Fritz unleashed a full mag into the lich. He caught glimpses of the decrepit body twisting and being shredded with each impact.

The click of an empty mag dominated the hall for a split second. Then the laughter started. Hissing and spiteful.

Daniel's eyes widened when the shadows broke apart and advance. Figures, multiple, were heading their way. Fritz's assault accomplished nothing but angering the lich. Shadows thickened around the undead creature, manifesting putrid vapors and covering the walls with rot.

"Run!" Fritz shouted.

Daniel hurried back down the hall, desperate to gain the stairs. The metallic schraak of swords being drawn told him Angus stayed behind. *Dwarves!* Sounds of flesh slicing dogged his footsteps. The lich's influence intensified as he fled. Bile rose. He vomited on the run, unwilling to let whatever nightmares conjured by the shadows catch him. The staircase loomed. The faintest sliver of golden light shining down from the main floor. Heart thundering, Daniel laid a hand on the iron railing.

"Daniel, wait! Angus is still back there."

Fritz's call dragged him to a halt. Regaining his wits, Daniel checked his pistol and turned to see Fritz was breathing heavily, his attention focused on what moved in the dark nearby. The dwarf dropped an empty mag and slapped a fresh one in. Breathing hard as he struggled to regain his senses, Daniel checked his surroundings. They were wedged at the base of the stairs, a dead end behind them, giving Pender one way to come at them.

"Can he win?"

Fritz shook his head. "We did not have time to prepare properly. He will hold Damon, for a time, but the end is inevitable."

Daniel frowned. "Let's go back and get him."

A tremor took the building, complaints from deep within the earth. Dust streamed from the ceiling. Daniel clutched the railing tight to avoid pitching forward. While quakes weren't common in the state, they did occur. This felt … wrong. "Angus! Hurry your ass up!"
A bellow echoed down the hallway.

Dwarf and lich exchanged blows. One drove the other back. Shadows, turned humans resembling Damon's true appearance, rushed forward in an unstoppable wave. The flesh melted from their faces, leaving only the awareness of pain in their eyes. Limbs were hacked away. Ropes of ichor and filth splashed the walls. Steam rose from the floor, hissing with each plodding bootstep Angus made. There was no give. He fought to avenge past failures and prevent Pender's filth from spreading like a plague once more.

"Duck!" Fritz shouted.

Angus bowed his head an instant before a stream of red tracer rounds sliced through the space he just occupied and caught the lich in the face. Damon pitched backward, melting into the shadow with arms and legs flailing. Minions wailed. Seeing a chance, Angus retreated as fast as possible, gaining the stairs.

"There are more of them than I thought," he coughed. Blood and saliva struck the floor at his feet.

"Morgen warned us not to engage," Fritz replied, his gaze on the floor.

Grunting, Angus slapped his brother on the back. "We need to move. Your little burst won't stop him long. He'll regroup and be on us. We need to get back into the open air. Damon won't risk an assault in the open."

"What about those people?" Daniel asked. "They are still alive under all … that."

"Nothing for it," Angus replied.

"Are you—"

Fritz intervened. "Daniel, Angus is right. Once a lich begins the transformation process there is no going back. Nothing in any of elf history has found a cure. Those people are as good as dead. So will we be if we don't hurry."

They reached the ground floor and hurried toward the exit. Hissing came from behind them. Damon and his army of minions were closing. Their boots slapped across the marble floor. The sound of water rushing taunted him. Daniel felt the walls closing in, the exit door a mile away. Angus snatched the handle and twisted. The door did not budge. He rattled it, trying to force his way out. The door remained closed.

"Locked!"

"The security guard must have found it open," Daniel muttered. *When did security ever do its job on night shift?* He remembered coming home to his condo complex in Fayetteville after long nights at the bar to find the gate guard racked out in his chair. *I guess the city can afford better personnel.* "What do we do?"

Breaking into a grin, Fritz handed him the rifle. "What dwarves do best."

"Complain?"

"Step back," Angus said, ignoring his answer. "And use that thing already. They are getting closer."

Daniel turned and knelt, picking his targets with deliberate intent. Bodies dropped. Each one delivered from an eternity of torment and shame. Daniel felt no emotion. He couldn't. The victims were just that. This was war and good soldiers did what was necessary to survive.

"They're still coming," he shouted. "I can't hold them back much longer."

An ancient war cry answered him. He turned to see the Schneider brothers crashing into the reinforced security door—the door buckled, giving way, and slammed open. Fritz shouted from the ground, "Come on!"

Daniel finished the mag, noting with a small measure of satisfaction the dissolving bodies scattered throughout the hallway, and ran outside only to trip over Fritz who was getting to his feet. Rolling, catching metal edges and dwarf elbows, Daniel got to his feet and took a deep breath of fresh air.

"Hey! What are you three doing? No one is supposed to be in there!"

The trio froze, Daniel staring incredulously at the aged security guard ambling their way. Complete with cap, his dark blue uniform blended in with the night. The man was weaponless save for a handheld radio.

"Get back! It isn't safe here," he called, holding up a hand to dissuade the guard.

The guard kept approaching.

Fritz and Angus, having regained their feet, were reaching for the swinging door. Daniel saw a trickle of water coming out and tensed.

"I'm going to need you three to step aside and don't move," the guard instructed. "You boys have a lot of explaining to do if you don't want to be hauled downtown in handcuffs."

"Mister, I don't know what you think is happening, but that door needs to be closed and sealed. Now," Angus warned.

Daniel saw the shapes gathering in the shadows. "Uh…"

Nonplussed at their attitudes, the guard produced a set of keys and stepped to the door.

"That's just what I'm doing. Now don't you mo—" He squawked as wet hands stretched for, latching onto his arms, and dragged him inside. The door slammed shut to his frantic screams.

"NO!" Daniel shouted and leapt toward the door.

Angus slapped and arm across his chest, stopping him in midstride. "We have to help him. Let me go," he protested.

Angus shook his head.

The screams faded.

Fritz sighed. "It was already too late. The poison entered his veins the moment they touched him."

Daniel felt his knees weaken. Feeling powerless ground on his psyche. There must be something he could do to save the man's life. Flashes of men he lost in combat threatened to unravel him.

"So will we if we don't get the hell out of here," Angus added. "And it's a haul to the Ok'tal'med Nest."

Daniel kept his gaze averted. "How far?"

"About four hours. Goblins made their home in old Charleston."

"We need to report back to the queen," Fritz noted.

Daniel made eye contact with a homeless man who was gaping at them from where he sat underneath an oak tree. Meeting Daniel's gaze, the man tucked his jacket a little closer around his neck and hurried away.

Numb, he followed the Schneiders headed back to the Wells Fargo Building. How was he going to explain any of this to Sara? Should he?

TEN

Bone after bone jarring bump accompanied the rumble of wheels. Wally ground his teeth, each bump reminding his bladder he should have stopped at the bathroom before leaving the convention center. His hands and feet were numb, circulation cut from the flexicuffs. The sack over his head was beginning to inspire mild claustrophobia.

"Hey," he called. "I need to go to the bathroom."

Snickers met his plea. Nothing he said or did made a whim of difference. Resolute, the kidnappers all but ignored him.

"I really have to—" Wally huffed as an object struck his chest. "What the…?"

"Silly man can't hold his bladder!"

"Tiny bladder!"

Wally tossed his head back and was rewarded with the thump of striking the floorboard. He cursed and laughter ensued.

"Just untie my hands and let me handle my business in the bushes," Wally groaned. "I gotta go!"

He didn't think they would listen, bracing for more mockery. But he felt the minivan slow before jerking to a complete stop. Rough hands snatched him to the tune of a door sliding open. Sack still over his head, Wally was pulled and shuffled down a steep bank before he had time to react. Aches from being tied up and the bruising he took in the parking garage rippled deep in his body.

Wally jerked as hands unbuckled his belt and snatched his pants and underwear down. "Hey, whoa! That's not necessary, fellas."

"The human is crazy to think we will untie him," a voice called from behind.

"Crazy," a voice to his left agreed.

Wally swallowed. *This is not what happens to superheroes, man. No one is ever going to hear this story.*

"Little man wants to go to the bathroom. Go."

"How? My hands are tied," he protested.

Wally caught the sound of a zipper being undone then the smell of urine taunted him. *Maybe this is just a bad dream ...* Small hands pushed and prodded his back. *Not a dream. This was a nightmare.*

The chants returned. "Go. Go. Go."

"It doesn't work like that," he grumbled. "I need my privacy."

"No time. No, no time! Go!"

Whether from fear or his bladder was too tired to hold on, Wally felt it rush out. His knees threatened to buckle from sheer embarrassment. Despite that, he almost tipped his head back as relief washed through him. When finished, his captors redressed him and shoved him back into the minivan.

Wally struggled with his emotions as the jostling of the wheels over bumps returned. Never in his life had he been subjected to such abject cruelty. The indignity of it rankled him but he was already feeling too beaten down to react the way his imagination demanded. It took little to envision punching and slashing his way to freedom, vowing to make his captors pay for their audacity. Just like Captain Doom against the invading Scrows.

He didn't know how much time passed before he woke up, if such could be called sleep. Head aching and mouth dry, Wally felt the first pangs of a migraine sparking. A growling stomach brought him fully awake. He knew better than to squirm or move though. Blinking the crud from the corner of his eyes, Wally made out spots of bright colored lights through the sack. Shapes took form, vague and distorted by the fabric. *Is that a sombrero?*

"Where are we?" Thus far, his captors had shown no inclination toward hurting him. Wally didn't know if this was by chance or design but decided to let it ride. A closer look at the sombrero nestled atop a rickety tower told him precisely where he was. "Are we in South Carolina?"

"He speaks!"

Soft footsteps scurried next to him. The vehicle stopped. Wally felt the cool breeze kiss the back of his hands and smelled fried food. Stomach rumbling, he subconsciously licked his lips. Hands snatched him by the shoulders, dragging him forward then sitting him up before yanking the sack away. Wally caught his first glimpse of the nausea inspired object and frowned at seeing it was an ordinary pillowcase. *There goes the last of my dignity.*

"Wally Rutherford, listen to me carefully, my name is Crispus Goldfarb. I am Nest Father to my people, and I will not hesitate to harm you if you try to escape. Am I clear?"

Wally stared at the bland features of the man walking toward him. An almond odor drifted from Crispus. Wide, flat skin a shade paler than healthy dominated by a wide nose and pinched eyes that stared back with villainous intent.

"Your people?"

Crispus stopped walking and shifted his weight to the opposite foot, displaying ragged fingernails coated in grime as he clenched his fists. "I asked you a question, Mr. Rutherford. Not answering will be most unpleasant."

Any sense of security among his kidnappers evaporated by the thinly veiled threat. "Fine. I won't try to escape."

Crispus broke into a grin. "Good. Very good! I told them you could be reasonable. A good quality for a man of your talents."

So, you're just playing tough? My talents? "Who are your people?" Wally pressed.

Crispus sat straighter, chest puffing out. "We are the Ok'tal'med goblins! The dread of the new world!"

"Goblins? Like from the Lord of the Rings?" Wally blurted. At the angry hissing that followed his words, he closed his eyes, half expecting a blow to his head. "You have to be pulling my leg."

"We only pull legs off when we plan on eating you," Crispus answered with a frown. "And if you mention those poor souls in those movies one more time, I promise we will eat you. One delicious mouthful at a time."

Wally swallowed, believing every word. "You got it. Okay, so you're goblins. Why have you kidnapped me? And why are we at South of the Border?"

Crispus perked up. "You know this place? It is a favorite of the nest. Many good times to be had here."

"Yeah, I know the place. Who doesn't?" Billboards ran north and south of the former roadside attraction for a hundred miles in both directions.

Doubting Crispus and his goblins had any notion of what constituted fun, Wally frowned as memories of his sole time visiting the roadside attraction resurfaced.

Nothing about South of the Border remotely suggested stopping for anything other than gas. It was said to be a major destination before President Eisenhower had the interstate project started. Today, South of the Border was one of those places travelers used to mark the border between the Carolinas. Boxed in by fireworks stores to the south and open farmland north, the attraction struggled to stay afloat. Weeds and grass grew throughout the parking lots. Like most places, the past threatened to swallow it whole.

Wally changed his questioning. "Where are we going?"

"Home. We have been away from the nest for too long this time," Crispus replied.

A dozen or more goblins rounded the corner of a broken-down carousel bearing armloads of junk food. Wally spied chips, Slim Jims, those nasty little stale donuts undeserving of the name generally sold only in gas stations, and cases of soda. Hungry as he was, his stomach turned at the thought of what the array of food would do late at night.

"Not going to tell me where home is?"

Crispus gave him a cautious look before retreating to the driver's side door. He ordered the others to leave Wally alone and allowed the prisoner to get back in the van on his own accord; the goblins were more interested in their bounty than him.

They were on the move in no time.

Wally looked out the window as they crossed the mile long bridge over Lake Marion. Home now hours away, Wally worried no one would ever hear from him again. It wasn't until they got off I-95 and headed east on I-26 he began to suspect their destination. If he was correct, it was a place he swore never to visit again.

Wally closed his eyes and tried to get some sleep.

His sense of peace did not last. Soon the goblins began singing what sounded like crude drinking songs. Elbows jostled him as their sugar drunk merriment spread through the minivan. Wally lost track of how many empty soda cans plinked him. He counted almost two dozen goblins crowded in on top of each other and, to an extent, on him. Wally considered looking into a van for himself if he made it out of this alive. There was something to be said for cabin space. *Maybe I can convince her to let me get one of these?*

The long ordeal came to an end an hour later as they cruised into Charleston, navigating both old and new streets as they wound their way to the old downtown historic district. Famed for oak filled parks, pirates, and Rainbow Row, the old city harbored dark secrets. It was here that the slave trade was most prevalent back in the 1600s. The first shots of the American Civil War were fired on the preserved Fort Sumter in the middle of the bay. Some say the ghosts of villains long past haunted the streets.

Wally didn't know what to believe, nor did he particularly care. The descendant of slaves, he vowed to never set foot in the city after learning the truth. The only time he'd ever been here was on his honeymoon and then only because his wife insisted. The attraction of plantations and old southern charm did little for him. He liked to say he never left anything in Charleston whenever a friend mentioned going back. Yet here he was.

They crawled past the cruise ship dock and then the aquarium. Goblins cheered as they continued down East Bay Street to the old market or when the spires of the St. Matthews Lutheran Church came into view. This late at night the streets were mostly empty. The last handfuls of partiers he saw staggered into Ubers or stumbled their way back down the streets in a daze. No one was coherent enough for Wally to call for help.

The minivan rolled into a small parking lot on a side street in the heart of the historic and tourist district and cut the engine.

"We're home! Take all your belongings and escort Mr. Rutherford to his new chambers," Crispus called over the din. "Hurry, before the sun rises."

Goblins burst into action.

ELEVEN

Daniel struggled with the urge to smash the half empty crystal decanter on the table at his side into the nearest wall and bellow his frustrations. Not that he expected much relief from that. Then there would be Morgen's admonishment, for one. Disdain from whoever had to clean the mess up, another. He didn't want to think about the Schneiders' reactions.

"Goblins from Charleston. How in the hell are we supposed to combat that?" Daniel fumed. "I can't just pick up and head down there. I have a family."

Morgen's eyebrow, impossibly manicured to a thin and menacing line with a hint of grace, arched. "Please put that back. I had it imported from upper Mongolia when the Mayflower landed on these shores."

Daniel saw the golden liquid within sloshing closer to the lip. He suddenly felt foolish, knowing he controlled his anger better than this. Daniel set the decanter back, ensuring it wouldn't fall, and tossed his hands up. "We need DESA."

"Not on your life," Angus barked.

"We could—" Fritz's words were cutoff by a simple hand gesture from the queen.

The air in the office felt confined. Daniel ran a finger between his neck and collar as he worked through the day's events. He had a destination but little else. Goblins, if they were anything like the characters in his books, were vile creatures with a disdain for light. Prone to rash actions and contemptable.

"I cannot condone your inclusion of the government," Morgen said. "Like it or not, you are this Mr. Rutherford's best chance of rescue. With a little help, naturally."

"Naturally," Daniel droned. He glanced at the decanter, wishing for a drink of whatever was within. "All I know is the goblins came from Charleston. That doesn't mean they're heading back that way or even where in the city they made their lair. The only certainty is they have a full day's head start on us."

Fritz nodded. "They could be anywhere by now."

"You and I both know goblins stay in their holes unless they have a good reason to come out, Fritz," Angus countered. "They'll head back to Charleston and force us to dig them out. That means hundreds of the buggers *with* magic enforced wards keeping them hidden."

"Angus is correct, but there is one way to find their nest and counter their protective wards," Morgen suggested.

"Absolutely not." Angus folded his arms across his chest. The strain of stitching scratched like nails on a chalkboard.

Daniel shivered as a chill ran through his body. He already didn't like what was being offered.

Morgen tsked. "The Tinker is your best chance of getting into the nest undetected and you know it, Angus Schneider. Go to him and get the tools you need."

Listening to the exchange was a lot like being lost in a fog during a battle, Daniel squeezed his eyes shut and pinched the bridge of his nose. No matter how often he dealt with the clans or what scenario he found himself mired in, Daniel felt like a fish struggling for air after being torn from the water. Goblins. Tinker. Sara. *Shit. Sara is never going to forgive me.*

"Where is this Tinker?" he interrupted.

Fritz shook his head. "You don't want any part of this, Daniel. Your Majesty, please. Isn't there another way?"

An unreadable twinkle filled Morgen's eyes. "At last, one of you has a shred of common sense. But first, the Tinker, do not ask me his name. Should he choose to let you know, he will." She waited for him to nod before continuing. "He is currently about and an hour southwest of here at a place I believe you are familiar with if your wife's story is to be believed, the Devil's Tramping Ground."

Daniel blushed, noting a conversation he needed to have with Sara when he returned home. *When did she talk to Sara about that?* "I have been there, once. Can't say I need to go back."

"This is my command: gather what weapons and devices you require and head to the Tinker. He will provide you with the rest. I will ensure your table is run for however long it takes to accomplish this task. Go now and with the good will of all elves."

"Why do you care so much?" Daniel asked.

Morgen glided closer, ensnaring his gaze without flinching. "Consider it a personal favor repaid. Your wife did me a great service last year."

She slipped him a small handheld device. "When your hour is most dire, press the button on this and help with find you. Trust no one the closer you get to Charleston. There is a greater danger lurking unseen, though what I cannot say. I feel it in my heart. Go and save your friend, Daniel Thomas."

She turned to the dwarves. "See he does not come to harm. I expect all three of you to return to my office by the end of the weekend, with the human alive and unharmed."

"What are the rules of engagement, your majesty?" Fritz asked. A different fight filled him. Not that he expected Morgen to relent on the Tinker.

"The usual," Morgen replied. "Kill those goblins as you see necessary but do not expose yourselves to unnecessary human interaction. Retrieve the human."

Fritz bowed.

Angus grumbled. "What of the lich? Damon has become powerful again."

"Andros is dealing with Damon Pender as we speak. He will not trouble us again, Angus Schneider," Morgen soothed. "I will have need of your services soon enough."

The trio filed out, leaving the queen alone with her thoughts. Without a mage or wizard at her beck and call, a premonition to help her prepare was out of the question. A shiver traced down her spine; an ill omen rising from the night. She wished she had more stalwart allies at her beck and call, but much of her authority diminished thanks to the betrayal of the Prime Minister and the bid for power by the lycans.

Morgen strode down the hall to her office and clicked the intercom, "Aislinn, bring me a cup of tea. Make it as hot as you can."

Morgen's gaze fell on the aged decanter and her thoughts returned to the lone human who had become an integral player in the direction her beloved elves traveled down since her estranged husband's murder. Briefly, she contemplated reaching out to the local D.E.S.A. office but decided against it. Cecile Barnabas proved herself worthy against the lycans but she was still a government agent and not to be trusted. There were enough developing complications with government interference.

Aislinn arrived shortly with a steam cup of Morgen's favorite tea and a handful of finger length shortbread cookies on the side. Morgen smiled. Not everything was doom and gloom. She contemplated reaching out to Constantin Andros for a status update.

Daniel stared at the massive figure looming across from him with mild interest. Standing between six and seven feet and weighing well over four hundred pounds of solid muscle, Goran the weaponsmith, who he had met once before, stretched the already thin tie dye shirt to the limits. A pair of circular rose-colored sunglasses made his wide face appear squished. Beaded necklaces hung from his neck, impossibly thick and out of place in any society. Board shorts and flip flops completed the outfit, accented by Goran's thick, sausage-like toes capped with golden rings. Soft music played in the background.

"Daniel Thomas, world renowned author and general troublemaker," Goran mused. "I didn't expect to see you again."

Daniel shrugged, an act he found himself doing far too often. "What can I say, I tend to latch onto things when they pique my interest."

"Hmmm." Goran stroked the thin beard running down his chest. "I suppose, but then again, I never understood humans. Good music though. What can I do for you?"

Questioning if anyone under fifty even knew the Grateful Dead, Daniel explained their situation. The giant glanced at the dwarves lurking behind Daniel, but so far hadn't spoken to them. Daniel figured it was bad blood, not that it surprised him. He had mixed emotions about the Schneiders as well.

"Sounds like a good time. What sort of weapons do you need?" Goran asked without skipping a beat. "Oh, I got a new toy I've been working on." He rummaged through a crowded workbench before selecting a spherical, palm-sized object that he tossed to Daniel.

"What is it?"

"Doesn't have a name. Why do humans want to name everything? Anyway, it works like a hand grenade. Depress the button on the top and throw it for your life. Should give off the heat of the sun for a five second burst—don't look at."

"What do you mean should? You haven't tested it yet?" Daniel asked. He suddenly felt uncomfortable holding the weapon.

"Come on man, look around. How much time do you think I have?" Goran replied. "It will work. I stake my name and reputation on it and that, little human, is better than gold."

Angus folded his arms with a grunt. "We're wasting time, Goran. Just fill a bag so we can get moving."

Frowning at the dwarf, Goran chose to confront him. "What else do you need from me? Yes, I'm talking to you damned dwarves. You and your weapons. It's a wonder you haven't destroyed the world yet."

Angus leered, showing impossibly white teeth. "Give it time."

"Lightweight combat rifles. Most rounds punch through goblins with little effort," Fritz chimed in.

Rubbing his temples, Daniel ignored the banter, set the weapon down as careful as possible, and began perusing the expansive racks of weapons. There'd be plenty of time with the dwarves later. He needed to clear his mind and focus. He watched the giant go to work, filling packs with magazines, knives, and what looked like handheld mines. Daniel had no idea what they were going to need landmines for, but he knew better than to question. Goran, for his part, continued piling weapon after weapon on the work bench, muttering explanations as he returned to rummaging.

Worried they were taking more than they could carry, Daniel finally interrupted. "Hey, Goran, I think this is enough. There's only three of us."

The giant halted, the light machine gun halfway off the weapon's rack. "Just three? Against a full nest? Oh, Daniel, you don't have nowhere near enough."

Chuckling, Goran grabbed the machine gun and resumed gathering weapons.

"Daniel, don't you need to make a few calls? We're leaving as soon as the big guy loads us up?"

Jarred from his train of thought at Fritz's question, Daniel nodded. "Yeah, thanks." He stalked off to a corner decorated by little more than empty charred barrels and cobwebs dancing on the heatwaves from the forge in the back. The only decoration was a blue and yellow lava lamp that suggested a vibe he wasn't feeling.

Ignoring the dwarves watching him from the opposite corner, Daniel took care of his table for the rest of the weekend first. He didn't trust Morgen as far as he could spit. Telly seemed more than happy to take the reins. Daniel suspected his friend secretly thought he could do a better job and be the first one to sell out Daniel's inventory.

"This had better be good," Sara said, her tone dark.

Daniel swallowed and decided to rip the band aid off. "I have to leave town for a bit. The queen has me and the Schneiders heading to Charleston to rescue Wally." He winced at the sound of her drawing a deep breath. "Look, before you say anything I didn't plan on any of this. Matters just sort of rolled out of control."

Silence made him wince. "Sara—"

"Daniel Thomas, what have I told you about messing with strange elves?"

"Uh, what?" Daniel asked, confused.

Sara laughed. "Relax, hero. Norman already told me you were going to be doing some work for Morgen. I can't say I approve but I also understand. Go and get your friend and get back to me and the kids in one piece. Maybe you should reach out to Thaddeus, or Cecile."

"Morgen said no DESA. Looks like we are on our own," he admitted.

The idea sat ill with him, but what choice did he have?
"That's it!" Goran boomed.
"Babe, I have to go. I love you and I'll call you as soon as I can." Daniel hung up and hurried to join the dwarves who were busy picking over the mounds of weapons.

TWELVE

Daniel had to admit it felt good being back in gear. The body armor, compact and light, yet strong enough to stop a high caliber round, fit snug and unobtrusively. Advanced night vision showed a world of unparalleled clarity the top heads at the Pentagon would be envious of. Goran's weapons were top quality, far above most international arms makers. He felt safe, as much as one could be going against angry goblins and in the company of a pair of trigger-happy dwarves.

The Schneiders slipped into battle mode. Daniel knew he was in good hands, though found himself longing to be back with the D.E.S.A. team in New York. The mixed bag of dark elves, dwarves, and gnomes gelled under his command, simplifying that aspect of the mission. With the Schneiders, Daniel didn't stand a chance of having his voice heard.

Daniel couldn't help but question whether he was making the right decision by not involving the secret government overwatch agency even if he knew better than to trust a federal government agency at face value. Like former President Ronald Reagan once said, *"the nine most terrifying words are I'm from the government and I'm here to help."*

Working with various agencies, from the FBI and CIA to agencies who officially did not exist, during his time in Iraq and Afghanistan gave him no reason to doubt there were plenty of nefarious actors hiding behind a suite and tie. Not that he thought all government employees were bad.

Agent Thaddeus Blackmere for instance was a good guy. A fellow veteran with vastly different experiences and skillsets, Blackmere had been there since the beginning.

By the end of the New York mission Daniel started feeling respect for the older man. But could he break the queen's trust and do what he thought was right? The window of opportunity was certainly closing.

"I don't suppose we can roll out in the morning?" Daniel asked, adjusting the weight of his pack so it stopped digging a burning rut in his shoulder.

Fritz slapped him on the back with a rumbling laugh. "Ah Daniel, always a sense of humor! Good, you're going to need it. The Tinker is an acquired taste for the best of us."

"Do I want to know?"

Angus popped an unlit cigar in his mouth, knowing better than to light it in Goran's workshop. "Doesn't matter if you do or not. We've got orders to track him down and that means you get to experience the miserable bugger for the first time. Lucky you."

"He's a nasty man, Daniel. Watch your back," Goran added.

Thanking Goran for his help, Daniel followed the dwarves through the winding underground passages littering Raleigh and, he imagined, most of the older city centers.

They emerged a few minutes later in a parking garage filled with nondescript armored vehicles of every make and model. He was not surprised at their collection, given the longevity of the elves and their proclivity for burrowing into positions of power. Angus popped the doors on a jet-black Suburban with asking for input and they loaded their kits in the back. The dwarves made him ride in the back.

"Do you know where Morgen is sending us?" Fritz asked.

Daniel said, "I've been there, once, but don't ask me how to get there from here."

"What the name of this place?" Angus' index finger hovered over the keys on the GPS.

"The Devil's Tramping Ground," Daniel supplied.

Daniel watched Angus struggle against the small keyboard, deleting and starting over too many times. He was just about to offer to type it in when Angus cursed then looked skeptically at the map. "It's in the middle of nowhere. Why would the Tinker be there?"

"Rumor says some freaky things go down there," Fritz said, giving Daniel a thoughtful glance.

Unwilling to relive his singular, embarrassing experience there, Daniel said, "Folks think Satan haunts those woods."

"In the middle of nowhere? Why the fuck would he do that?" Angus asked.

"Beat me," was all Daniel offered.

Fritz hummed, snatching the handle above the window as Angus peeled out of the parking spot and began the winding journey back to the surface. He shot his brother a look before speaking. "He's got a point, Daniel. Why would the devil, if he even exists, choose to haunt an empty field far from every major population center? Seems to me he'd view it more like a quiet vacation than an opportunity to increase his kingdom."

"Do you guys even believe in god and the devil?" Daniel asked, surprised the thought hadn't occurred to him before now.

The subject of theology never came up, other than selectively applied cursing the dwarves turned into an art. Daniel had envisioned multiple gods and goddesses in the pantheon of *his* elves' religion but not once did he consider if the actual elves adhered to modern human religious beliefs or had their own.

"We believe what we have to," Fritz answered after holding up a silencing finger at his brother who coughed. "Sure, we started out with our own sets of gods and monsters. What society hasn't? Like you humans, our

Of Elves and Men

beliefs evolved, eventually narrowing down to a small handful of gods. From what I learned, plenty of our kind converted to your God. Wonder of wonders. Can you imagine Angus or me as a priest?"

Daniel's imagination sparked as Fritz chuckled. Dwarves garbed in traditional vestments. An elf standing on the street corner with a sign proclaiming the end of the world was nigh. He laughed. Thoughts threatening to run away, it took little imagination to see his brother begging for alms on the street.

"No, not really," Daniel shook his head.

If elves and dwarves converted to Christianity or any of the plethora of organized human religions, why couldn't humans do the same? The prospect of druids and sun worshippers inspired by the old ways might prove a fascinating study and new angle for his next book provided he found life returning to normal after this. But where to start?

The Suburban took the curve to get on the interstate and headed west, deeper into the night and the mystery that was the Tinker. Daniel settled back into his seat and prepared for the short ride. He did his best not to think about what came next.

Raleigh to Siler City was a fast enough trip. They merged soon onto 64 west, driving down quiet roads that sparked a flood of memories of Daniel's first adventure with the elves. They passed the alpaca farm and the church where Norman Guilt brought down the helicopter trying to kill them.

"Seems like yesterday we were on this same road," he mused.

Well before Ashboro, they took route 902 south through an impossibly dark countryside filled with farms and forests. He provided little additional information. His only other time here had been in the middle of the night as well, leaving him with no real sense of where they were.

The closer they got to where the Tinker was supposed to be, the more Daniel drifted back to what he viewed a complete debacle. Sara insisted on going. She and her friend had talked about going there since seeing one of those spooky shows on the Travel Channel depicting the famed Devil's Tramping Ground, right in their backyard. *Daniel had driven. They arrived almost exactly at midnight; he took that as an ominous sign. Tensions already high in the car, they parked and took the well-worn path into the woods. Soon they found themselves in the heart of the unnatural clearing. Sure, it was spooky and a little eerie, but as much as Daniel wanted to believe in monsters and aliens, he found himself growing more skeptical the older he got. He wrote about the supernatural but that was about it.*

They took turns wandering around the clearing, tromping through the woods in a half-assed exploration before all together heading back to the car. What felt like a disappointing ten minutes had been closer to a disorienting hour. Others in the group claimed to have seen or felt something, but not Daniel. The only harrowing moment for him came when a trio of dogs stormed the car as he reversed the car. His buddy proclaimed them hellhounds. Daniel didn't agree as he doubted one of Satan's pets would have a dirty pink collar but didn't say so. After a disappointing trip and finding out he was out of beer once home, Daniel did later find a lovely tick bite right between his butt cheeks. Twenty years in the army and he got bit on a whim because he offered to take them out for a good scare.

The car jostling brought Daniel back to the present. He feared round two with the Devil's Tramping Ground was going to be just like his first experience. Though the first time had been for fun and out of idle curiosity on a random Wednesday night. This time it was to save his friend and, possibly, defeat an uprising by a nest of goblins long thought to have been subdued.

If it wasn't for his run ins at the Fainting Goat Island Inn and Craig-E-Claire, he could pretend mild indifference to the supernatural.

Sara was the one attuned to the supernatural. She claimed she had seen ghosts more than once, some even in their home when he was beside her. For his part, he had never seen a ghost, nor did he particularly want to. Sure, there was a time or two he felt impossibly cold for no reason, as if the wrath of the artic blew down on him alone, but he had no proof other than the time he swore he heard a woman's voice speaking in his ear in his own kitchen a few years ago.

He had no idea what had been said, too soft for him to decipher, but the sensation was enough to raise the hairs on the back of his neck. Even the dog tensed and growled. Daniel hated the thought of being watched in his own home and had Sara sage the house so much it smelled like Thanksgiving prep for a week. Some lines weren't meant to be crossed and, thankfully, he never had another experience.

Reluctance aside, Daniel once again found himself thrust into a supernatural confrontation he hoped to avoid. If all he came away with was a tick bite and directions to where to find his friend, the mission could be considered a success. If the devil really did exist … The best way to invite darkness stemmed from thinking it. He had his hands full enough with the clans. Best to let sleeping devils lie.

"You're kidding me. This is it?" Angus fumed, having already turned around three times thanks to the inaccurate

GPS coordinates and no signs other than the ominous Devil's Tramping Ground road sign they all missed the first time.

Daniel studied the pull off. Innocent looking enough on the surface and showing no sign of being one of the major supernatural epicenters in the state. He scanned the surrounding night for signs of wild dogs as they bumped down the road and parked on the side of the road.

"Looks like it. The clearing is a few yards into the woods," he replied.

Angus killed the engine and reached for his rifle. "Right. Let's get this over with."

"Daniel, listen to me. This is important. The Tinker is not one for small talk or mistakes. If he senses weakness, he will exploit it to his advantage and twist you until you don't know which direction you were going," Fritz warned, reaching for a rifle as well.

Daniel stuck close to the car. "Will he give us the answers we need?"

"That depends on what kind of mood he's in. Come on. We're wasting time." Angus closed the driver's door and began stalking his way into the woods.

Swallowing hard, Daniel grabbed his rifle and followed.

THIRTEEN

Every legend has a beginning. Most superstitions are born from fear, that inability to rationalize bad times. Few remember the origins, even historians lose the meaning as new volumes continued being written. Special places around the world enjoyed fame through word of mouth passed down through generations until earning a following on the internet. Sensing profit to be made as the internet expanded, locals propagated the stories into legend.

The Devil's Tramping Ground legend grew until it almost reached the point of obscurity. None alive knew the origins of the forty foot wide clearing in the middle of farm country. Some insisted it dated back almost three hundred years to a time when the western world was yet wild. Local settlers swore the devil himself came here to plot stealing souls, claiming nothing grew because of his cloven hooves.

Others said the local indigenous tribe came to celebrate victories in battle and to feast there, grass and vegetation dying because of the repetitive march of their moccasins. One far-fetched tale suggested the indigenous chief Croatan was killed and buried on the spot, his grave forever marked.

Ask a hundred people and get a hundred answers.

The one thing that was certain was nothing grew within the circle surrounded by trees. Scientists and paranormal researchers came to investigate, each presenting both sides to an unsolvable argument. Privately owned, the circle soon drew the attention of satanists and would be cultists. Reports of sacrificed animals and satanic symbols carved into trees soon spread. Those who spent the night swore an array of supernatural events occurred.

For Daniel it all seemed mundane and, almost, a waste of time. Yet now, stepping back into the trees for the first time since that night with Sara, he realized he had missed the point. While there may have been no physical evidence of demons or the occult, it was the idea that such could exist that began festering in his mind.

The first thing he noticed upon reaching the edge of the clearing was the chill. Gooseflesh prickled beneath his armor. Icy claws reaching for his neck. Screwing his eyes shut, he forced out the dark thoughts, knowing giving in meant accepting the surreal. Daniel centered his breathing and looked to see if his dwarf companions suffered similarly. They remained stalwart and resolute … *Because of course they did, can't act like a hummie.*

Mist clung to the ground, surrounding the circle without encroaching. He recalled a similar fog the night he was here. That time too it did not enter the circle. It took little imagination to return to envisioning creatures watching from the darkness, hungry for him to make a mistake so they might feed. *No more wild dogs, please.* Daniel's mouth went dry when a faint odor, strong and familiar registered.

"Why are you here? I did no request assistance in my research." The thin voice rasped from the trail leading away on the opposite side of the circle.

Daniel's rifle rose by reflex, but he saw no target. Only trees, bushes, and the emptiness of the circle. The dwarves froze in midstride; Angus took cover behind the nearest tree while Fritz dropped to a firing position on his knees. Daniel followed their example.

The night was cold. No substantial heat signatures reflected. *Impossible. I know I heard a voice. So did they.* He began tapping his finger on the magazine well, the tiny metallic echo singing like a night bird. *Come on. Show yourself. I'm already nervous enough. The last thing I need is to plug the wrong person because of a twitchy finger.*

Wind howled through the clearing, burrowing between his clothing and flesh. Daniel shuddered. Voices whispered his name, carried by the ill wind. It took every ounce of courage not to bolt back to the truck. *Why can't it just be a tick?*

That's when he saw it. Twin red dots sparking to life deep in the woods and coming closer. *The devil is real!?* Resisting the urge to swear, Daniel slipped his finger onto the rifle trigger and clicked the safety off. He had no intention of going to hell, not without a fight.

"Dwarf and human. Together. An ominous portent if the winds are to be read correctly."

Daniel hesitated, certain that wasn't something the devil would say before devouring them. He pulled off the night vision glasses to stare at the approaching figure with the naked eye. Tall, slender, and bald as an egg, the man stepped out of the forest and into the clearing with empty hands held for all to witness.

"If you are going to shoot, I suggest you do so now. I am in no mood for foolish creatures this night."

"Morgen sent us, Tinker," Fritz called. "We need your assistance."

The man cocked his head, curled ends of his moustaches dropping below his jawline. His gaze fell on each of them in turn. Daniel felt that questing hunger penetrate his armor, nestling into his soul. Then he noticed the patchwork jacket the Tinker wore. Dozens of colors, vibrant, suggesting unique stories scattered across the history of the elves, twinkled unnaturally in the darkness. He spied worlds birthed, live, and die in each panel. *Stay calm, stupid. Don't do anything brash.*

"That you Fritz Schneider? I recognize your voice. I thought I told you I didn't want to see you for a hundred years?" the Tinker replied. An annoyed flare to his words.

"It's been two hundred and thirteen," Fritz replied. "We are on a time sensitive mission. Morgen said you would help."

"Did she?" he mused. "Where is that rat of a husband of hers? Shouldn't he be giving the orders?"

"Dead. Killed by his own daughter a few years back," Angus barked. "We don't have time for this, Tinker."

"Ah, of course you are here as well. Neither of you ever managed to stop sucking on your mother's teats long enough to learn how to be a functioning adult separately," the Tinker provoked. "Who is this human fouling my presence? You know how I feel about them."

"His name is Daniel," Fritz answered. "He's the reason we are here."

"That and a nest of goblins breaking the treaties," Angus added.

The Tinker visibly stiffened. His eyes clouded. Elongated fingers clasped together, fumbling over one another in a well-rehearsed orchestra. Daniel swore the man's moustaches grew longer in the pale-yellow haze surrounding him. *Did his coat change colors?* As if sensing the internal scrutiny, the Tinker looked directly at him.

"Daniel who?"

"Thomas." It was only after he replied he noticed the dwarves frowning. He shivered, asking in his mind. *Are you in my head?*

The Tinker cocked his head to the left. *Not as weak as most of your pathetic species. Impressive. I did not think a human could hear me. Why are you here causing problems?*

Not my intent. I didn't ask to stumble into your world. Daniel's head throbbed from waves of mounting pressure. *Get out of my head and talk to me like a man.*

A shame. Not as strong as I assumed. Very well, human. The Tinker cleared his throat. "Why have you been sent to find me, of all people? I have nothing to do with elves anymore."

"I've never heard of you until recently." Daniel rubbed his temples. "My friend has been kidnapped by a nest of goblins and Morgen says you're the guy with the tools to help me get him back. These two are here for the goblins. I only want my friend."

"Assuming he has not yet been eaten. Goblins are fond of human flesh," the Tinker replied. "I wonder how far you are willing to go before the cost becomes too great."

Daniel decided he didn't like the man. Meeting his gaze, Daniel lowered his voice. "As far as I have to. They can vouch for that."

"He was a soldier and helped us with hunting down Xander when he killed the king," Fritz offered, though he didn't look happy about speaking. "Tinker, Morgen says you have a device that will get us into their nest undetected."

"I do. Made it centuries ago right after the sack of Constantinople. Dreadful time, that. In between random slaughters and the reduction of religion, in the name of religion I should add, I had too much downtime. One thing led to the next and there you have it. Thankfully I was able to test it when the king sent me on a mission to root out the nest in the Turkish mountains soon after. Worked like a charm."

"May we have it? The queen can't risk another goblin uprising after all the recent changes."

Daniel noticed that while Fritz was speaking, the Tinker was only staring at him. The throbbing in his head lessened but didn't go away entirely.

"Changes, yes. The king dead. Is Constantin Andros still in command of the Old Guard?"

"He is," Angus said. His rifle still pointed at the Tinker, contemplating firing off a few rounds on general principle.

The Tinker nodded. "That's one mean bastard I don't want to cross swords with again. Nearly took my head once. Tell your queen to send her Old Guard. They'll make quick work of those goblins. There's no need to get me involved. I have my hands full with my research here."

"If Morgen wanted the Old Guard involved, she wouldn't have sent us to you," Fritz pleaded. "Tinker, we need you."

"I told you, I'm not leaving my research." His tone darkened.

To Daniel, it appeared the Tinker, whatever creature he might be, stood several feet taller and more domineering now. His instincts screamed to act. Doubting a 5.56mm capable of inflicting much damage on the man, his best option was to retreat to the vehicle and hightail it back to civilization. The dwarves, however, still looked ready for a fight.

Fritz held up a hand. "You misunderstand. All we request is the device and a quick block of instructions on how to use it. Morgen doesn't want you to leave your business. In fact, she insisted."

The ground trembled. Trees swayed, leaves, pinecones, and dead branches crashed to the ground. Footsteps came from all directions in the night.

The Tinker stroked his moustache. "Did she now. Interesting. What games does our beloved queen weave around us I wonder? Very well. I shall help this one time. Do not expect further assistance. My work is too important for delays your kind perpetually cause."

Returning to his normal size, Daniel knew he had grown earlier, the Tinker strode across the clearing to a large sack that hadn't been there when they entered.

Daniel and the dwarves swore, all having missed it before.

Rummaging through his belongings, the Tinker produced a rectangular box with a foldable antenna attached to the back. He handed it to Fritz with obvious trepidation. Daniel looked on, only now clicking the safety on and lowering his weapon.

"There is a button on the side, here. Press it when you are within a league of the suspected nest and raise the antenna. The frequencies emitted will disorient the goblins and prevent any human interference long enough for you to rescue the bones of the one you seek," he explained, looking a tad smug. "Do not press this button until you are absolutely certain."

"Okay so then what—"

The series of howls, deep and filled with the promise of violence, echoed from every direction, cutting off Fritz's next question.

Daniel's stomach fell. It looked like they were hellhounds after all. "We need to displace," he shouted. "Now!"

"No!" The Tinker shouted, louder. "It is too late to run. We are trapped. Prepare yourselves. This is a foe unlike any other you have encountered. We may not live to see the dawn."

FOURTEEN

"Form a circle, backs to each other," Angus barked.

Sweat trickled down Daniel's face. Spasms tremored through his hands and fingers, the onset of arthritis from spending too much time behind a keyboard instead of a rifle. His eyes swept his immediate front but found nothing. Yet. Another bout of howling had him shifting backward.

"Do not let them get behind you," the Tinker warned them. "Their bite is poisonous, especially to humans. I do not have the cure to save you."

"Just bring these beasties on," Angus boasted. "We have better things to take care of this night."

Daniel didn't see how they were going to defeat a pack of ravenous hellhounds, he had no better term for them, and make it to Charleston before sunrise. It was a five-hour trip from their current location and already well past midnight. If they survived.

He flinched at the first sign of movement. The hounds circled, tightening their grip while never staying in one spot long enough for him to draw a bead. He swore he caught the faintest hint of hissing laughter coming from the night. Satan?

"Don't shoot yet," Angus warned. "Wait until they come closer and open with everything you have. No quarter."

"My night vision just went out."

"Then drop the damned things and use your eyes," Angus snapped.

At least he's behind me. Daniel dropped the glasses and focused on the forest.

The footsteps stopped. So did the laughter. A thin whistle rose, picked up by a gust of wind winding through the maze of trees and brush. Now he saw them. Red eyes shined in the night. Dozens of them in a wide circle. The stench of dirty animals made him gag. If Daniel had any question if the dwarves faced such foes before his answer came in Fritz emptying his stomach on the dirt to his left. The laughter started up again. Loud and taunting. It mocked them, almost scolding them for trespassing on this unholy site.

The Tinker scoffed. Daniel saw he stared with dispassionate eyes at the creatures before them. There was obvious animosity between him and the hounds. The slender blade in his hand, close to four feet long, stayed motionless. "Prepare yourselves. They ready to strike."

Before Daniel could ask how he knew, the hellhounds burst from the forest.

Angus roared, followed closely by his brother and the night erupted in gunfire. Hounds yelped. Some fell dead to the murderous barrage.

Daniel abandoned trying to pick out his targets. The hounds proved plentiful enough he couldn't miss. Cycling through his thirty-round magazine in no time, he shouted to let the others know he was black on ammo and changing mags. If they heard, they gave no indications. Angus continued hammering away with his machine gun, dark eyes sparkling with madness.

The Tinker flowed with unparalleled grace to his right. His blade hove through flesh and bone effortlessly. The hounds took notice and slunk away, redirecting their efforts against the perceived weaker among the group— Daniel. *Because of course they are. I can't catch a break.* Firing a burst into the nearest hound, Daniel winced from sudden pain in his right side. He looked down to see claw marks ripping his body armor. There was no blood, he just felt like he'd been punched hard enough to knock the wind from him. Daniel coughed. Bright spots floated in his vision. He barely could make out the pair of hounds that stalked him. He couldn't draw a bead; couldn't catch his breath.

They leapt— A figure danced in front of him. Fur and ropes of blood flew as the unnatural beasts yelped then died. The wet crunch of steel penetrating flesh echoed in Daniel's ears. His stomach churned.

"Fall back. Make your way to the vehicle," the Tinker ordered. He ripped his blade free. Dark blue-black blood sizzled and dripped from the steel.

A reprieve came as the remaining hounds slunk back into the obscurity of night at the call of a shrill whistle.

Chests heaving, the dwarves spat, cursed, and reloaded their weapons. Smoke rose from Angus' barrel. Daniel knew, from experience, a superheated barrel could melt. The dwarf needed to slow his rate of fire before they lost their largest weapon.

"Time to go!" Angus barked.

They collapsed into a tight triangle, Fritz on point, and began the trek back through the circle and toward the perceived safety of the vehicle. They gained the edge of the clearing before a blood-curdling howl broke the peace. It was easy to lose track of how close to the road the clearing was at night.

"Run!"

Daniel sprinted and prayed with equal intensity.

Bodies crashed through the undergrowth. Gunshots sang across the clearing. He kept running. The truck had to be close. They were only meters from the main road, yet Daniel found himself going deeper into the woods. Soon the sounds of battle faded, leaving him alone in the mist. Trapped. The cloistering effect choked him. Near total darkness turned the mist a hazy shade of grey and blue and reduced visibility to mere meters. The sliver of moon did little. Daniel found the same sight staring back from every direction. Nothing but night and scrub pines. He hated to admit it, but he was lost. He flexed his fingers, comforted by the familiar sound of leather stretching.

Calling out for help would be the worst decision he could make. With a grunt, Daniel flipped on the night vision in the hopes of at least catching a glimpse of the others. Even the hellhounds would serve to point him back the right way.

Nothing. He found nothing.

He clutched his rifle tighter. *What now?* No viable solution presented itself. He was alone in the night, hunted by demonic creatures even the dwarves were afraid of. He needed to reconnect with the others. He needed to find the truck. He briefly wondered if the others suffered similarly or if they even noticed he was missing. The chaotic events in the clearing undermanned them, turning a cohesive formation into a struggle for individual survival. Their triangle formation had been a last-ditch effort to maintain control. He knew he was running out of time. An owl hooted from a nearby tree, and he jumped. He'd been in one place for too long. Taking a chance, Daniel raised his rifle, doublechecked his ammo, and tried going back the direction he had fled.

His steps were deliberate, carefully placing each boot to avoid dry leaves or fallen branches. Night vision continued showing nothing. He sniffed the air for telltale signs of the hounds, only breathing deeper when he discovered none. *How far had I gone? Am I even still in the mortal world or had I been transported to a hellscape like Dante? ... Yeah, no thanks.*

Daniel forced the thoughts aside and focused on the task. He needed to find something—the truck would be ideal. Rifle tracking from side to side the way he had been taught on patrols in basic training, he was once again that young man fueled by adrenalin. The mist swirled around his ankles in whispered hushes. That eerie feeling returned as he found himself standing in the center of the Devil's Tramping Ground.

He was no longer alone.

In the center of the circle, ten feet tall and encircled by flame and fumes, stood a massive creature beyond his imagination. Curved horns jutted a meter high from his crowned head. Cloven hooves capped off fur covered legs. Heavily muscles and broad of chest, the figure inspired nightmares and despair in equal measure.

Daniel froze, his foot breaking a branch.

The massive head turned, staring him down with fire filled eyes.

His mouth went dry. His muscles tightened. Daniel suspected there was nothing capable of stopping this creature. Stiffening, he refused to close his eyes as the creature clasped both hands behind his back and continued regarding Daniel with unsettling intent.

"Shhh," the creature rumbled. "You do not belong here. One day soon we shall meet, but not this night."

The creature snapped his fingers and Daniel suddenly found himself in the middle of a battle with the hounds: Angus and Fritz dealt a punishing toll. The Tinker stood surrounded by the heaped corpses of his foes, his blade swinging. Those who fell melted back into the wounded earth. The battle finished before Daniel regained his senses. He doubled over, hands on his knees, and vomited.

The mist faded. The surviving hounds slipping away.

Ragged and breathless, the dwarves slumped against the nearest tree to catch their breath.

The Tinker walked through the battlefield, ensuring each of the hounds was in fact dead by plunging the tip of his sword into each. He returned to them with a satisfied look before sheathing his weapon. "That was exhilarating."

Angus squinted as he popped a fresh cigar into his mouth. "That's one way to put it, old man. I think we've overstayed our welcome."

"You were never welcome to begin with, Angus Schneider," the Tinker replied. "Do you still carry the device, Daniel Thomas?"

He fumbled through his pockets, fingers touching the hard edge. He nodded.

The Tinker beamed. "Go and rescue your friend. Prevent the next war and I shall forget I ever met you."

"What about the device?" Daniel asked. "Do you want it back after?"

The Tinker gave a flippant wave and stalked back into the night.

"Told you he was a dick," Angus exhaled a mouthful of smoke. "Come on. We've already wasted enough time here."

"I'm hungry," Fritz added as he shouldered his rifle. "Do you suppose anything is still open this late?"

Daniel followed their conversation, doing his best to forget that last experience while wondering why no one asked where he disappeared to. Come to think of it, he was hungry too. "There's an all-night diner back up in Siler City."

"What, no Waffle House?" Fritz replied.

The dwarves laugh shook the nearest trees. Daniel shook his head but didn't laugh. His mind threatened to unravel as he processed all that just happened.

They made the short trek back through the clearing to their waiting truck. After placing their weapons in the back with the rest of the kit, Fritz hopped in, leaving Daniel and Angus alone.

The burly dwarf took another puff on his cigar and placed a hand on Daniel's shoulder to stop him from getting in the backseat. His gaze would have wilted a normal man.

"You did good back there. Real good. One question: where did you disappear to?"

Daniel swallowed, the fear threatening to return. "I don't know. We broke our formation and I thought I was running back to the truck. Guess I got turned around in the woods."

"Huh. This place will do it to you. We've been watched since we got out the truck. Best we leave now and forget all about it. It' a five-hour trip to Charleston thanks to this little diversion and we're all running on fumes."

"Are we eating first?" Daniel to change the subject.

Angus barked another laugh and jumped into the driver's seat.

FIFTEEN

Endless miles rolled by, bracketed by tall pines and vast stretches of fields and pastures. Daniel never failed to be amazed at the ruralness of the state despite having financial and technology meccas in Charlotte and Raleigh. Most places remained as they had for decades.

Old men sat on their porches waving at traffic. Cars waited behind ponderous tractors and cattle carriers. Half of the towns had yet to welcome box chains or corporations. Most places were filled with fading mom and pop shops, dollar stores, and the occasional fast food chain. Graveyards and car washes mingled with western wear stores and gun shops. Tobacco and cotton fields decorated the landscape much as they had for the last two hundred years. Life in rural North Carolina proved relatively peaceful, free from the divisive politics and vitriol the media spun for ratings. All people cared about was taking care of their own, and leaving a legacy their children could be proud of.

Daniel paid little attention. He'd seen it all before, through his trips to different events across the state or numerous visits to the state zoo before that fateful night. Perhaps he took the simplicity for granted, having witnessed it time and again. Perhaps his mind remained locked on his good friend trapped and alone in the clutches of a creature he had yet to encounter, though he doubted goblins were any worse than the lich and whatever it was back ... he refused to accept what his mind tried rationalizing about the Devil's Tramping Ground.

Elves. Goblins. Satan? Wally.

Daniel tipped his head back and did his best to ignore the angry heavy metal blaring through the speakers. His stomach full of eggs, bacon, and pancakes, he found himself drifting off to sleep despite his best of intentions. *Elves. Goblins. Satan? Wally.*

He sensed, more than knew, a deeper plot was in the works, concealed behind the reclusive woman who now ruled all the elf clans. *Damn Morgen and her schemes.* Unable to escape the natural intrigue of the elves, Daniel struggled with where he fit in. Worse, he couldn't figure out how to keep Sara and the rest of his family free from it all. Thankfully, neither of their kids knew the truth, but how long could that last? Sooner or later one of them was going to trip up and then he would really be in trouble. Nothing proved as daunting as the ingrained tenacity of a teenager.

Unable to hold off the pressure any longer, the walls of sleep closed in. Thank God he stopped in the restroom to check for ticks. Once was more than enough.

"He's asleep," Fritz said, returning his eyes to the endless miles of yellow striped road.

Angus grunted. "About time. Now we can talk."

"Do you really believe Morgen cares about this human we're supposed to rescue?"

"Not for an instant. She may have softened since Alvin's death, but that doesn't mean she still isn't the cold-heart bitch we've warred against for centuries," Angus replied. "She always has an angle."

"Might be bigger than we presumed," Fritz said, idly scratching a patch of his full stomach. "The king is dead. The Prime Minister too. Brother, there's a void at the top of the food chain."

Fitz watched him picking at a resisting piece of meat stuck between his teeth with his free hand before he spoke again. "What are we supposed to do about it? We're just soldiers, Fritz. All that hero shit belongs to people like sleeping beauty back there."

"Like it or not, we're stuck right in the middle."

Angus grunted. He flashed his high beams at a rude driver roaring toward them, doing it again until the other driver got the message and dimmed his. "So what? We're supposed to second guess the queen now? Play politics and take a seat at the table?"

"No, we'd be chewed apart in no time." Fritz shook his head. "We do need to watch our backs, especially with this goblin nest. She might be trying to get rid of us."

"Morgen has always looked down on our people, treated us like fodder. The way I see it, it's about time she got what was coming to her."

"Where would that leave us? Think. I'd rather face the monster we know than the unknown." Fritz rubbed his eyes. "Regardless, we're heading into trouble. I can feel it."

"Trouble is what we do best, brother of mine." Angus grinned as the piece of meat popped free. "Worse than popcorn. So, what do you want to do? We can't just abandon the mission. We gave our word."

"And dwarves never go back on our word," Fritz finished. "We keep going but get a little reinforcement along the way."

Angus' mouth dropped open. "You're not talking about—"

"Can you think of anyone else better suited to rooting out a goblin nest?"

"No, but that doesn't mean he wants to see either of us." Angus shifted uncomfortably. "You remember the last time."

"And the time before that. And that. We're running out of options, Angus." Frustration in his voice, Fritz struggled with maintaining a positive attitude.

"There has to be another way," Angus fumed. "Anything but him."

"I'm listening if you have an idea. Those goblins never would have traveled that far from the nest unless they had strength," Fritz explained. "Combine that with the clans' weakened state and we could be facing a brand new war none of us expected."

"Goblins don't operate on their own like that. Someone must be pulling their strings."

"But who?" Fritz asked.

"That's the million dollar question," Angus said and stepped on the gas. "Looks like we're going to pick up another passenger. I hope you know what you're doing, Fritz."

"So do I." Fritz stared at his reflection in the windshield and felt his heart begin to beat faster. Desperate times called for desperate decisions. "We'll figure it out. Hopefully before it's too late."

The dwarves were prone to violence and as stalwart as the changing of the seasons, but they were never fools. He and his brother had built their reputations on their tenacity and courage, only to find it faltering now. Unable to go back and trapped into moving forward, they would have to settle their nerves and accept what fate had in store, knowing neither was going to like the result.

"Excuse me, your Majesty, Mistress Cal is here."

Morgen didn't turn, remaining a statue, hands locked behind her back staring out across the Raleigh skyline. Her black dress ran to her ankles, one of her favorites, hugging her figure with authority. Authority she felt slipping through her fingers no matter what she did to prevent it. Dark times approached. She feared the fall of the clans and, should that happen, an endless period of bloodshed and war. Countless lives would be forever lost, and for what?

Morgen released a measure of tension in her shoulders and turned around. This was not the time to show the weakness consuming her within. "Send her in, Aislinn and ensure we are not disturbed."

"Yes, ma'am."

The slender dark elf whisked away and was soon replaced by another. Viviana Cal was as rugged as Morgen was graceful. Rough around the edges and bred for a harsher lifestyle, the dark elf had a dangerous gleam in her eyes, smoldering like embers waiting to ignite. For centuries she did the hard jobs no one else could, including herself. "You wished to see me?" she asked with as much deference as possible without bordering on disrespect. A measure of bad blood existed between them, despite their eternal bonds.

"Viviana, I trust your last assignment went well?" Morgen asked, offering her the empty chair on the opposite side of the desk.

Viviana sat, her gaze never leaving Morgen. "Well enough. We managed to clean out the swamps but found no sign of the necromancer. I lost a full platoon destroying his creations."

"Such losses," Morgen murmured. Once, before the death of her husband, she would not have shied away from extreme casualties to accomplish her goals. Now, with their ranks depleted and a fresh wave of uncertainty gripping them, she feared she needed every soldier she could get. "Where did the necromancer flee to?"

"Unknown, though my sources suggest he fled the country." Viviana's no-nonsense delivery prevented further pointless questioning.

Morgen's eyebrow arched. An unspoken comment lingered on Viviana's tongue. "Is there something you want to get off your chest, Viviana? This is your one opportunity to speak to me as equals. No repercussions. Come, tell me what is on your mind."

Blowing out the breath and slapping her palms on her thighs, Vivianna nodded "Very well. The affair in New York continues plaguing my conscience."

"What precisely wears on you? She was my daughter, after all," Morgen countered.

"It should not have happened like that," Viviana replied. "Gwen deserved better. So did Xander."

Morgen drummed her impeccably manicured nails on the desk, swallowing her prideful anger so she could respond. "What more would you have had me do? They were responsible for killing my husband, or perhaps you forget?"

"No, ma'am, how could any of us forget that black day? I believe they atoned for their crimes that night fighting the Prime Minister's forces. I would not be here were it not for their actions."

Morgen noted she failed to mention the intervention of Daniel Thomas and his D.E.S.A. team. "Perhaps, but it no longer matters," she countered, a hint of suspicion lingering. No one confirmed the deaths, regardless of Viviana's report and the consolation of Agent Blackmere. She found the convenience of it too coincidental. "My daughter and her lover are dead. As is Basil Kadis. We must look beyond the past if we are to survive tomorrow."

"Survive? The necromancer is but one man, forced to rely on magic in a world where it dies daily," Viviana replied. "He is no threat to the clans."

"He is a problem. We will continue hunting him down," Morgen said then paused. "I speak of another issue I had not accounted for."

Decorum slipping back into place, Viviana smoothed the front of her shirt. "I am listening."

The queen explained the goblin situation, carefully picking snippets of information Viviana needed to hear while leaving out those she did not. Being queen for over a millennia raised safeguards responsible for keeping her alive where others fell. Her trust in Viviana had wavered thanks to her decisions in New York, prompting her to keep vital information private until the proper moment revealed itself.

When she finished, Morgen watched her right hand's reactions. The dark elf scowled at the mention of Daniel and almost interrupted when the Schneiders were brought up.

Rather than protesting or causing further division, Viviana asked, "What is it you wish me to do?"

"Travel to Charleston and do so quickly. I want you in place before those miserable dwarves arrive, but do not make contact. Watch, report their actions, and if needs be, intervene to save their lives. I fear I will have need of you by my side before long. There is something unnatural about the events, Viviana. I fear our enemies gather around us. Until I can discover exactly what, I expect you to remain on your toes, as the humans say."

"It will be done." Viviana rose, offered a clipped nod, and flowed out of the office without another word. A weapon doing what she'd been trained for.

In that, Morgen took some measure of solace.

SIXTEEN

He felt numbness running down his left arm. It was an old condition born in the aftermath of his largest dog nearly breaking his shoulder years ago. Daniel rolled his shoulder, flexing his fingers to relieve the worst of it, and yawned. His body ached, from his teeth to the arch of his foot. Being cramped in the truck induced some, though he suspected most stemmed from the battle with the hounds. He wiped the crude from the corners of his eyes and blinked away the fog.

The first hints of dawn crept across the eastern horizon. A tingling of light breaking through the veil of darkness. There had been a time where he saw every sunrise and often worked until well after sunset. His army days consumed the clock enough that when he retired, he refused to own an alarm clock, Lord knows he didn't need it with as bad as he slept, at least until his kids started going to school and then he found himself getting up just as early.

"Where are we?" he asked after a few miles passed without him recognizing any features.

"About to cross into South Carolina, but we're taking a little detour," Angus answered.

A protest formed in his thoughts until a hard stare met him in the rearview mirror.

"Good morning, sleepy head," Fritz greeted. "Feel all rested and ready to go?"

The truck clipped a pothole, jarring him enough to remember he needed to go to the bathroom. "Sure. What detour?"

"Wally's really his name? I thought you were making it up," Angus balked, avoiding the question. "Terrible. Just terrible."

Confusion washed through him. Daniel attributed it to poor sleep. "His name's not important. What matters is why we aren't there already."

"Look, Daniel, why doesn't anyone call you Danny? Or Dan?" Fritz sighed. "Anyway, most goblin nests have around a thousand goblins. Me and Angus are good for a few hundred but even we aren't enough to beat them all back. We decided we needed a little extra help."

"You decided. I still haven't agreed," Angus countered.

"Right. You are the one driving, remember?" Fritz scowled at his brother. "Regardless, we're not going too far out of the way and should still arrive with plenty of time to prepare for tonight."

Unsure how much he believed and surprised at the simmering rift between brothers, Daniel was distracted by the ridiculously large Confederate flag flying on a pole in the middle of a field in the middle of nowhere. He'd seen it before, and it never made sense. How many thousands of travelers saw that obsolete relic and were insulted over the years? How people wanted statues torn down, but no one mentioned the giant flag just off the major interstate. "Prepare for what?" he asked.

Relief washed over Fritz's face. As much sport as it proved, arguing with his brother was tedious. "Goblins are notorious creatures, but they seldom come out in daylight. They used to lurk in caves and underground complexes before humans came along and changed the world. They prefer skulking, even now. It's a safe bet most will be either asleep or disinterested in anything until nightfall. As you can see, the sun is just rising. We have time to get there and do a little recon of the nest before retrieving your friend."

"You mean breaking down the walls and burning the nest out," Angus countered with his usual dour countenance. "We're in for a fight, one way or the other."

"Which is why we're making the detour," Fritz returned. He made to punch his brother but met Daniel's gaze and stopped.

Angus' face darkened. "Doesn't mean I have to like it. He's bad news and you know it, Fritz. We're making a mistake on this one."

"He's also our best chance of coming out of that nest alive. The idea of a full nest worries me. We haven't faced a threat that large in a long time."

"Who is a mistake?" Daniel injected before they devolved into a conversation filled with what ifs and ancient history. "Who are we going to pick up? Some troll under a bridge looking for a fight? I can make a call and have a team meet us if we need it."

In truth, he doubted any of his team from New York would answer his calls, nor would D.E.S.A. agree to them freelancing for unsanctioned mayhem.

"Thanks to my forward-thinking brother here, we are going to get our father," Angus grumbled.

Daniel felt his stomach clench. Now there were going to be three of them. If Angus and Fritz were any indication, their father was going to be more than he was willing to handle. *Wally, you freaking owe me big for this one.*

The suburban rambled on, slipping off the interstate for a country road quickly turning to dirt a mile beyond the solitary gas station they passed. Daniel knew recognized they were just across the border and heading east. Unfamiliar with the area any further than that, he kept his comments private. Tensions already ran high between the dwarves. Daniel suddenly had no problem sitting in the back seat and, for a moment, considered slipping into the third row in case the brothers came to blows.

Discretion being the better part of valor, he pulled out his phone and sent Sara a text letting her know he was all right and the wrinkle the brothers threw into the plans. Adding how she was better off at home, with her taciturn gargoyle protector keeping her safe.

Daniel snorted after he reread what he wrote. He had deployed three different times, and never once could he remember dwelling on what happened at home while he strode into harm's way. Most soldiers protected themselves from thinking of home or their families during deployments. Thoughts of home often resulted in accidents or, worse, deaths. Daniel stayed focused on the mission and only worried about home when he redeployed out of the combat zone. Conversely, he never paused to consider what those at home thought, how his loved were affected with him at war.

It was different now. Now he worried. The first time he recalled doing so was after hearing about Sara's time among the elves. Even then it was too late to do more than think of ways to ensure it never happened again. Daniel hated feeling impotent when it came to caring for his family. Their safety remained his priority, forcing down his unspoken addiction to action. His mind had failed to fathom how or why, but Sara had never been one to embellish a story. Direct to a fault, she reduced his flair for words and crafting elaborate tales to trifles of fancy wasting her time.

The knowledge that then Sara participated in her own mission left an impression, even if he had no time to worry over her until after the fact. The thought of werewolves stalking his home terrified him on a visceral level, robbing the strength from his veins. Locked in the hunt for Xander, Daniel was thankful for the distraction. He wondered how he might have reacted if he had been home when Sara was forced into the night with a gargoyle and a bitter sword.

His thoughts jarred when they pulled off on a single lane, cruising past the mailbox and down the hundred meters to the quaint ranch style home nestled in a grove of sweet gum and oak trees. Rose bushes decorated the front of the house, running the length of the structure and wreathing it in a thousand light red blooms. Crepe Myrtles of various colors dotted the front lawn, creating a pleasant environment without stress or worry.

Daniel spied the pond off to the right, just large enough to take a john boat out and spend the afternoon fishing. The older he got the more he longed for simplicity and quality living. Birds and bees flitted around the property, making this a scene from a painting. Daniel doubted there was anyway a dwarf, especially a Schneider, who could live like this.

Try as he might, he failed to discover any hidden bunkers or trenches as they parked. There were no machine gun emplacements concealed in the trees. No closed-circuit cameras recording their every move, leastwise none visible. He couldn't even see a security sign outside the front door. The idea a dwarf of this caliber lived completely defenseless was just plain ridiculous.

"Your father lives here?" he blurted out.

"Going on thirty years," Fritz replied. "He always did like keeping roses."

Daniel's eyes widened. "Your father? The man who created the two of you."

"Dwarf," Angus corrected and killed the engine.

"Sure, dwarf. He's responsible for you and he lives like this?"

"Yeah, so? We're not all bloodthirsty warriors who spend our days sharpening axes, drinking mead by the flagon, and belching," Fritz told him. "Some of us happen to enjoy the finer side of living."

"I would kill for a good axe right now," Angus said. "Anything is better than walking into this unarmed."

"You know how he is about weapons in the house." Fritz turned to Daniel and winked. "There's an old tobacco barn out back where he keeps everything. Mother would never let him soil her dream home with so much as a boot knife."

"Can't wait to meet her," Daniel replied absently. "You two did let him know we were coming, right?"

They exchanged private looks. Daniel thought he saw Fritz's face redden beneath his beard. "Right?" he asked again after neither answer.

Tugging on the beard, Fritz replied, "Well, you see, Father is an eclectic man. He doesn't like surprises, but he also despises talking on the phone. Which leaves us in a bind if you follow me. Best if you follow our lead. Oh and, Daniel, for the love of all you hold dear, don't answer any of his questions. Father really detests humans."

"Crusty old man detests everything," Angus added.

"Maybe I'll just wait in the truck," Daniel offered. Already the endeavor proved more than he wanted to deal with. At least now he understood where Angus got his charm from.

"Don't be rude," Angus warned with a set jaw. "Come on. No point in delaying. He knows we're here. Be best to leave your weapons here."

Feeling trapped, Daniel unclipped the pistol at his hip, and set it on the car seat.

Fritz clapped him on the back, driving the breath out of him with a cloud of dust from his jacket, and barked a laugh. "Relax, it shouldn't be that bad. Maybe Mother with have a nice breakfast for us. She's always been the nicer of the two."

"We just ate," Daniel muttered.

Fritz cocked his head with a queer look. "Daniel, that was hours ago. We're going to need a fully belly to tackle the goblins and my doctor tells me to stay away from fast food." He lifted his nose and sniffed the early morning air. "Ah, nothing says home like mother's cooking!"

Daniel caught a hint of coffee and fresh baked bread. Frowning, he failed to reconcile basic home cooking with the ferocity of the Schneider clan.

They ambled up the path the front door. Angus went to knock but his hand never touched wood.

The door swung open, revealing the bulkiest dwarf Daniel had ever seen. Thick ropes of beard hung from his chin, braided and decorated with gold rings. Grey, like the carpet of hair covering his head, his eyes took in his oldest son before shifting to Fritz and then falling on Daniel. Before any could act, Father Schneider bellowed in rage and charged.

SEVENTEEN

The air stank. Old and fetid. Countless years of filth and worse were congealing in the hidden corners of a world few knew existed. A moldy flavor lingered, just enough to kiss the tip of the tongue. Lights dim and swinging from the ceiling thanks to a slight breeze blowing in from outside, a slender corridor was revealed. It tunneled down, far underground.

Wally Rutherford, sack removed from his head, took in the impossible sights as his goblin captors led him deeper underground. He stumbled down the moisture slick ramp and almost fell before a goblin jerked him upright. Cursing his hands being tied, Wally journeyed down a small flight of steps and found himself staring at rooms filled with depictions of pirates, torture, and more. His mouth hung open.

A closer inspection showed the mannequins wore Revolutionary War period costumes, from uniforms to tattered rags of the dregs. Several of the rooms showed elaborate recreations of torture, with other figures imprisoned. Wally's mind struggled to understand what he witnessed. He was ushered past a room filled next with raucous pirates drinking and lording over their booty.

"Where am I?" Wally muttered.

A prod, just sharp enough to produce a wince, kept him moving. Wally slipped around an old cannon and was jerked to a halt before a slime slick wall.

One of the goblins turned, his flesh a sickly hue of green-grey. "What? You've never been to Disney?"

Confused, Wally remarked, "Pirates of the Caribbean sure has gone downhill I guess."

Snickering laughter spread through the group.

Wally swallowed his fear. Multiple hands pushed him toward the wall, muttering and chanting in their native tongue. Bile rose in his throat. The acidic flavor urging him to vomit as the foul taste flooded his mouth. Wally threw his hands out, hoping to stop from being crushed into the dirt and brick. He didn't want to die. Not like this. The goblins pushed harder. He felt his muscles tighten to brace for the impact only to have his hands plunge into the wall and through.

Eyes squinted, Wally felt cool on the backs of his hands. He was shoved the rest of the way through the wall before he had time to think. Again, the goblins prevented him from falling. The sound of ripped fabric echoed.

"Clumsy man!"

"Clumsy!"

Frowning, Wally fully opened his eyes and took in the sheer impossibility of what sprawled out before him. A glance back showed the same wall, but his mind whispered it was an illusion.

So this was the nest. Hundreds of squat creatures devoid of human semblance walked, ate, and talked in groups. Fires burned across the cavern. The smell of roasting meat tickled his nose. Heads perked up as they were noticed. Groups of three or more dropped what they were doing and headed toward Wally. At the chattering, others crawled from tents and dried mud caves until the crowd surrounding him stretched deep into the cavern. Bobbing heads and wringing hands mingled with sharp, pinprick fangs and leering eyes glowing unnaturally in the dim light. He would have collapsed if not for the tiny hands propping him up.

Crispus Goldfarb stepped beside Wally and raised his arms to the crowd. His gaze swept across the gathering, impressed with numbers no nest had enjoyed in a thousand years, after the dark years. After the massacre. All those hungry faces eager for a return to grandeur staring up at him. Power ran through his veins like electricity. He had been a child at the time of the last war but old enough to remember the great purges of his people. Those handfuls scattered across the globe, desperate to flee the punishing justice of the elves. So many were lost, left behind. So many.

Into shadows they went. Hiding. Waiting. Years passed and the nests slowly regained a fraction of their fallen glory until now, amid the great human expansion, they were almost ready to reemerge and make their claim for dominance over the clans. All they needed was a catalyst and Crispus finally had the strength to make his move.

Hands still raised, Crispus waited for the voices to still before launching into the speech he had spent the last few years preparing. "Friends, family, goblins! I have returned with the one who will pave our roads to return to the surface!" He stabbed a finger at the human he had kidnapped. "This man will deliver our glory to the world the way we have longed for! No longer will we be susceptible to the injustices of the great queen of the dark elves. Today we begin the reclamation! Today, we take our rightful place among the elf clans and in this entire world!"

Cheers erupted. A thousand voices crying in jubilee, fists pumping and tears flowing. Crispus fed off their enthusiasm, tipping his head back to relish their adulation. Their energy strengthened him, bolstering his resolve with unprecedented vigor. Cries of more rang through the gathering. He gave it to them.

"Many of our ancestors fell to dwarf and elf. Many of us were there to witness the fall. All these long years we have harbored hatred and despair in equal measure. This ends now! Wally Rutherford is our salvation! Soon, the world will know our plight and our voices will be heard from one side of the planet to the next! I give you the future!"

The roars were deafening. Satisfied and realizing he was speaking in circles, Crispus turned to look at their captive, noting how his mouth hung in shock. The human's name began to be chanted. While Crispus didn't like how it was said with adoration he winked anyway when he caught Wally's gaze. "This is all for you, Wally Rutherford." He stepped back. "My friends, show our honored guest to his new home."

Wally disappeared into the throngs of cheering goblins.

Wally expected to be cut up and thrown into a cauldron for food, the way movies depicted. Realty far exceeded those expectations. He stood, hands unbound, in the middle of a large tent made to look like a room with a bed, drawing table, and a desk with a pair of antique lamps providing just enough light. A copper platter sat in the middle of the desk, beside a stack of blank paper, filled with fruits and cheese. Soft jazz played quietly from a machine in the corner. A bearskin rug covered the center of the room. Wally felt like he had been transported to a demented writer's retreat. Until Crispus appeared behind him.

"Do you like it? My people put great effort into ensuring your needs are met," he stated. "Ah, you do not have water. I will fix that."

"Water isn't the issue." Wally exhaled, unable to hold his tongue any longer. "What is this place? Why am I here? You do realize people will be looking for me, right?"

Crispus chuckled. "I was told you were a funny man. It is good you do not disappoint."

"Thanks," Wally muttered.

Crispus blinked several times before continuing. "This, Wally Rutherford, is where you will create our story for all the world to enjoy."

"Your story?" Wally asked, stepping aside as a young goblin brought in a pitcher of dubiously clean water. "What story? How?"

"Questions. Questions. Ever do humans suffer from too many questions." Crispus shook his head. "Better to act than think, I say. You are an artist. One of the best. You will translate our story into images for us."

"Images? You mean comics?" Wally's eyes widened as he took in the elaborate set of colored pencils and pens sitting next to the blank paper he had seen earlier. It was everything he needed to draft a comic book. "You kidnapped me so I could make a fucking comic book?" His voice rose, carrying out the chamber and back into the cavern where he caught the sharp intake of several breaths.

Wally paused. It wouldn't do to be cooked and eaten for yelling at their leader.

Crispus maintained his composure, smoothing the front of his Black Sabbath t-shirt before replying. "Yes, your images will restore our glory and show the world they have been wrong about goblins for decades. Think of it, Wallace. Our story. Your pictures. It is a creation you were born to complete!"

"Waldo," he murmured, still in shock.

Crispus jerked his head up. "What's Waldo?"

"My name. Waldo Rutherford the third."

Face twisting like he bit into a lemon, the goblin fussed and waved his hands about. "Nonsense! That is a terrible name. We will call you Wally."

"My father was big on tradition," Wally retorted, defensive. "Let me get this straight. You kidnap me, transport me across state lines, and expect me to do your bidding? For what? Everyone knows goblins aren't real." A jagged fingernail slipped through Wally's beard to prick his chin. He gulped.

"We are very much real, Wally. And you will do our bidding. We went to great lengths to find you specifically. You are the one mentioned to us."

"By whom?"

A cruel glare settled over the Nest Father's face. "Oh, that is not your concern for now. He is a friend of yours." Crispus grew disappointed after his comment sparked no reaction. "Now, will you help, or do I send you to the chefs?"

"It doesn't look like I have much of choice, does it?" Wally replied. "Will you release me when I finish?"

Crispus clapped, the sharp report ringing in Wally's ears. "Good. Good. See! I told them you were the one! Very good. We will accomplish great deeds, Wally!"

"What about my family? What happens when they figure out I've gone missing?"

Crispus was already stomping away. For small people they walked heavily.

"My family—"

"No need to worry, Wally," Crispus interrupted, stopping at the room's door. "No one will notice you missing for another three days. It is Sword and Sorcery Con this weekend after all! Get your rest and nourishment. We begin in the morning."

Wally considered following and wringing the smug man's neck, figuring if he took out their leader the others would back down, just like in the books and movies. The quadruple guards slipping into place on either side of the entrance to his new quarters convinced him otherwise. Each armed with curved daggers matching the tufts of wild hair jutting from behind their ears. Unlike the crew responsible for bringing him here, these were wild, almost feral in appearance. That knot returned to his stomach, and he slumped down on the surprisingly comfortable mattress.

Soon sounds of merriment assaulted his ears. Broken songs on instruments in name only, he felt his skin crawl. Wally laid back, placing his hands behind his head and contemplated his predicament. Without knowing where he was, other than the port city Charleston, he had no wallet or cell phone and no one to call for help. Who would believe him? *Kidnapped by goblins. They'd lock me up in a padded cell in no time.*

Wally vowed to make the goblins' lives as difficult as possible without provoking them to injure him. *Or eat me.* Growing up in the country with three brothers toughened him at a young age but not even the typical torments of brothers were enough to fend off a thousand goblins. Frustration grew. Too many variables rattled around in his fogged brain, all leading to one inescapable conclusion. The only way to survive was through doing as Crispus commanded. Even then the goblin might kill him after.

Groaning, he rose and decided to enjoy the food. Perhaps he would think more clearly on a full stomach.

EIGHTEEN

The blank page stared back at him, daring Wally to mar the innate perfection of emptiness. Three crumbled sheets lay on the floor beside the small trash can in mockery of his failures. All morning and not one spark of creativity despite the piles of jumbled notes and key points provided. Wally pressed his clenched fists to his head and growled in frustration. Everything rode on him envisioning and completing the goblin tale. Each successive failure stymied his creativity further and awakened thoughts of never going home. He wanted to cry. To punch the wall. Scream at the top of his lungs.

None of it would do any good. The goblins, for the most part, chose to ignore him since his initial introduction to the nest. Wally caught prying eyes peering around tents, tiny faces filled with hope, as he moved among them for inspiration. He felt nothing. They failed to give him the spark he needed to begin. Frustrations rising, he ambled back to what he deemed his cell and sat down to draw. A small line, then nothing. He dropped the pencil on the desk and went back to bed.

Flopping down, Wally sank into the mattress with relish. Sleep proved elusive. He spent half the night imagining little knives coming for him in the dark. Boogeymen lurked in the shadows. A host of monsters and assassins awaited him should he slip up. His eyes burned.

The one decent factor of his captivity came from the food. He expected gnawed on bones with strips of ragged, uncooked flesh drooping from them. Moldy bread and rotted vegetables. Wally never accounted himself a high-class traveler but the food the goblin women brought far exceeded any hotel expectations and there was plenty of it.

The wet slap of bare feet on the moisture slick floor announced a visitor before Wally caught the stench of body odor. He screwed his eyes shut, praying this was all a bad dream and he would awaken to find himself in his Raleigh hotel preparing for the second day of the con. He knew better.

"Wally, Wally, Wally. You have accomplished nothing since we brought you into our home." Crispus tsked from the edge of the room. "My people went to great lengths to welcome you, ensuring all your needs were met. You have food. Clean water. A bed worthy of kings. Why do you not have anything written yet?"

Groaning under his breath, Wally pushed himself up and stared into the goblin's yellow eyes. "What am I supposed to write about? You've given me nothing. All I know is what I've read or watched, and no show has ever made the goblin the hero. The world sees you as villains, hungry for human flesh and dying by the score and working for some dark lord."

"Those were ... different times." Crispus shifted. A flicker of irritation passed through his eyes. "We are more civilized now. We have learned. We evolved. What you see before you is the promise of a new day, under my magnanimous leadership."

"That sounds great, man, but I don't have any context. There's no backstory. You've given me nothing to change anyone's mind. Not even my own!" Wally replied. He felt his cheeks flush, heat pouring up from the collar of his t-shirt as he tried staying calm. "All I hear is some narcissistic bullshit. You can't expect me to do your dirty work without any creative fuel."

Taken aback, the nest leader ran a grime-stained finger over his bottom lip, caressing back and forth repeatedly. "You need motivation. Very well. I know what will do the trick. Come with me. It goes without saying do not attempt any, how do you say, funny business, yes? My guards will cut you down before you can blink. Come."

Without waiting, the Nest Father stalked through the cavern, waving and greeting those of his nest pausing to acknowledge him. Crispus clearly thrilled at the adoration. Wally found the nest leader enigmatic and egocentric. A combination of toxic qualities waiting to spill over into madness, devouring him in the process if he wasn't careful.

"Where are we going?" he asked as the guards closed in around him.

"You will see. I am going to give you all the motivation you require, Wally Rutherford. Come."

Walking faster, Wally soon found himself impossibly lost and numbed from the sheer size of the cavern. His senses were assailed in a constant bombardment of smells and visuals—ones he guessed no human had witnessed and lived to tell. The cavern eventually tapered down to a slender corridor. Wally had to turn sideways to fit without tearing his clothes on the jagged walls. Not that could suffer from any worse embarrassment than on the trip south.

He felt the flush of heat long before exiting into a smaller chamber that looked to had never seen the light of day. Fear rose in the pit of his stomach. He wanted to vomit. *This is where they kill me.*

One of the guards scurried ahead to light a pair of torches flanking the chamber entrance. The rot of feces and worse tickled Wally's nose. *What is that smell?*

Flickering in the darkness, a figure came into view. *Is that a man?!*

Wally squinted to get a better look. The man stood close to six feet and had long greying hair, thin and brittle, hanging down past his shoulders. Atrophied muscles sagged off his frame. His arms were manacled above his head. Red sores were visible beneath the faded leather. His clothes were tattered, little more than rags. Prison style flip-flops kept his feet from sinking into the muck.

Crispus stood beside the man and gestured to him with a triumphant grin. "See! This is what happens when you fail. He was a most stubborn subject and earned every moment of the torment our torture masters delivered. Do you wish to share his fate?"

Not trusting his tongue, Wally shook his head.

"Good. I didn't think you did," Crispus affirmed. "Though, there is room enough for two if you do not fulfill your holy task. The goblins must be shown in our true light. It is inevitable!"

"Who is he?" Wally's voice was breathless.

Grey hair stirred as the man's head lifted at the sound of his voice.

Crispus paused, casting a cruel gaze upon the human. "A mistake. Will you join him or is the great Wally Rutherford wise enough to his place?"

Unable to pull his eyes from the broken man dangling from the ceiling, Wally shuddered at the thought of suffering a similar fate. *No one knows I am here. I'll die forgotten and alone. Looks like you little monsters win this round.* "Fine, I'll create your story for you. Will you let him go?"

"And give up our favorite decoration? No," Crispus feigned sorrow. "I am afraid he must remain here and atone for his failures. Perhaps one day he will know freedom again. Perhaps not."

Dagger butt prodding him, Wally turned from the prisoner and followed his captors back to his room. The future had never looked bleaker. Any disillusion of being a guest shattered with the new reality of his predecessor suffering in chains. However nicely appointed his "room" was,

Wally viewed it for what it was; a cell holding him without modern rules.

When they entered the main cavern, he raised his head high, acting confidently. Yet sadness crept through the already fragile façade. Questions tormented him, mostly of his wife. *Was she right? What was she thinking after not hearing from me in over a day? I usually call her to tell her about how the sales were.* He'd given anything just to hear her voice right now.

"Do not fail me, Wally," Crispus warned and walked off. Wally collapsed on his bed once more and turned his thoughts to beginning his task.

Goblins, from what he could tell, were miserable creatures best suited to remaining deep in the earth. Filthy and feral, despite the false images Crispus and the others presented, Wally found them unlikeable by every metric. He also knew them to be dangerous. He suffered no illusions about ever being allowed home even if he completed their story, just like their prisoner tucked away. Nightmares seldom ended and he was trapped in one. Unable to discern a single redeemable quality among those goblins he had encountered, Wally worried he might not be able to create a story in which they were the heroes.

Soft coughing coming from the edge of his room caught his attention. Looking up, he found a young goblin woman waiting patiently. Her thin hair scraped more than laid over her shoulders. She had small, deep-set eyes of the slightest shade of crimson. A single tooth, fang, jutted from the right corner of her mouth. She rose no higher than his chest and, despite her simple appearances, bore the same haggard edge so many others carried.

"What now?" Wally asked as his patience washed away. "Hasn't your supreme leader tormented me enough today?"

The goblin cocked her head with a curious look. "I do not understand. I am here to help you with your task."

Another warder for the prison. "Help how?"

"I have studied with the wise women of our nest and am now meant to relay our story to you for your pictures," she replied. "My name is Irma Stain."

Of course you are. Why am I surprised? "Well, Irma, I don't see how you can help me. You can recite your entire history but if I don't feel it in my pencils there won't be a story. You can go tell Crispus thanks but no thanks."

She sidled a step closer, remaining at the far edge of the rug. "I am afraid you do not understand. I have been assigned to you until the task is complete. Should I return now, the Nest Father will remove my head and cast my family down in shame for six generations."

Briefly flirting with the idea of working that same magic among as many goblins as possible, Wally instead saw a pitiful creature filled with fear and hope. Because she was a goblin did not mean she needed to suffer for his lack of creative spark. Could she be turned to help him? It was worth a shot.

Wally prided himself on his compassion. He was the sort of man who got along with everyone regardless of their personal beliefs or how they chose to live their lives. The only people he had a problem with were the ones who had the problem first. Live and let live, he liked to say. That philosophy stood in jeopardy thanks to a handful of impatient goblins.

It was through this moral conviction he discovered the first crack of doubt about the goblin nest being all bad. Irma Stain seemed desperate to avoid punishment for herself and her family. Wally was the only factor deciding her fate. How could he abandon his principles now when others, when she, depended on him?

After she coughed again, he relented. "Well, Irma Stain, it looks like we've got some work to do. I'm Wally."

She beamed with glee. "Wally! It is my pleasure to know you. Thank you. Thank you. Thank you."

He held up a hand. "Don't thank me yet. I haven't done anything and, regardless of what Crispus says, I have no idea where to begin."

"But your desk is fully furnished with comic book materials!" she protested. "The Nest Father went to great lengths to ensure you had it all."

"That maybe but he failed to account for the one thing I need more than anything else," Wally replied.

Inching close enough he caught the first whiff of spice and armpits, she asked, "What is that?"

"A creative spark."

NINETEEN

Daniel felt like he had stepped back in the past to his grandmother's living room in the late 70s. There was a massive floor model television encased in decorative wood, walls were covered with family pictures, and houseplants in various stages of life dominated the room. Oil paintings clearly done by relatives or friends also decorated the wood paneled walls, marring the effects of the plush, dark green carpet. Plastic covered the couch, doing little to block his sight of the hideous pattern beneath. A police scanner squawked every so often with reports. Despite the disturbing flashbacks, Daniel almost felt like he had gone home. He shook those thoughts away as the Schneider's mother brought his cup of steaming coffee, black and probably too bitter for his taste.

He smiled gratefully and took a sip, hoping his wince that followed went unnoticed.

"Tell me, Daniel, how did you meet my boys?" their mother, Nancy, asked as she took a seat beside him. He half expected a motherly hand upon his knee as she waited, giddy with excitement for him to tell his story.

Unsure how deep to go into the truth, Daniel swallowed the acid coffee taste and returned her smile. "Ma'am, I just happened to stumble upon these two a few years back. It really was all by accident. I ran into a jam, and they helped me out. Your boys earned my respect that night."

Her mirth faded, causing him to gulp. *I guess the bullshit meter spiked. Should have known better with this family.*

"Did they now?" she said in a way only a mother could. "My boys haven't earned anyone's respect in a generation. I know a little about that night, you know. We all do. The human author stumbling into our world and playing key role in the events the night the high king was assassinated. Tweedle Dee and Tweedle Dum out there managed to get themselves involved and here we are. Sipping coffee in my living room years later. You don't have to pull punches with me, Daniel Thomas. No one understands those two more than me."

He laughed despite himself. Regardless of the species, there was no fooling a mother's instinct. "As you say. Believe it or not, they really did keep me alive that night. I won't go into details, but we were the main team sent to stop Xander and the princess. We almost succeeded too."

Nancy spat. Dark clouds rolling across her face. "Those pesky dark elves have been nothing but trouble for far too long. I don't know why we tolerate it. I wish those two acted sooner. Perhaps then we wouldn't find ourselves in this predicament."

He paused. "What predicament is that?"

"All of it!" she exclaimed before regaining her composure. "Morgen is losing control. We have already lost so much. The Champion. The Prime Minister. The King. All of them gone, leaving that twisted woman spinning her webs unopposed. We deserve better and its clear she cannot handle it alone."

Daniel had seen enough despots and dictators over his years to recognize the first signs of rebellion fomenting. Dwarves were more than capable fighters. Warriors of renown, should they rise against the throne … He let the thought fade, knowing no good would come from it. Besides, it wasn't his fight. His world had enough problems without getting involved in the inner intrigues of elves and dwarves. *She's practically giving me a new book here.*

"I'm sure she means well," he managed.

"What she needs is a boot in the backside and a slap upside the head to knock sense back into her," Nancy fumed. "Bah, don't mind me. I'm just an old dwarf fussing over what I can't control."

"I understand, believe me."

The anticipated leg pat arrived, and Daniel felt the tension release.

"Daniel, dear, do you think you could do an old dwarf a favor?"

"That all depends," he replied with a chuckle. "What do you need, Nancy?"

Her cheeks colored. "Well, I was sort of hoping you could sign my copy of your last book. I laughed so much! What a pleasure to read."

Trying not to glower over the concept of his epic fantasy novels reduced to comedy among the clans, Daniel presented a tight-lipped smile and said, "Absolutely. Anything for the mother of Fritz and Angus."

Clapping in joy, Nancy scurried away to retrieve her books. Daniel rolled his eyes. Some things never changed.

He glanced at the time and winced. Spending time at the Schneider homestead wasn't as bad as he expected but they were wasting time. He wondered how much longer it would take to recruit the their father and be on their way.

"You dare bring *him* here? That son of a bitch almost ruined our entire way of life!" Max Schneider roared at his sons.

The elder dwarf cut an imposing figure. Bulging muscles strained against the fabric of his clothing. Rings decorated his thick fingers. Bald and covered in scars from long forgotten battles, the dwarf stood every inch a warrior. And he knew it. Neither of his sons wanted to reply, he saw their looks, knowing his temper.

"Well? No one wants to speak now they have a chance? I thought I raised lions, not sheep." Max cracked his knuckles. "I think it's been too long since I last busted your skulls. Living among the humans has made you soft."

"Father, we have come to an understanding with Daniel. He is not the man you believe," Fritz said to placate him. "He knows honor and is a warrior in his own regard."

Max spat. "Warrior! What do humans know of war? They stumble through each conflict, allowing politicians to dictate the course of the fight instead of true soldiers. Always making a mess of things and we are the ones to suffer for it. How many lives were lost that night at zoo? How many friends you convinced to join you did not return to their families?"

"Too many," Angus simmered. "But that was beyond our control. We fought hard, worthy of the annals. Many dark elves fell to our blades, Daniel's included."

"So? I'm just supposed to forgive him from dragging you two knuckleheads into the middle of a war for the throne?" Eyebrow arched, Max waited, inching for a fight. "I knew I should have beat him the moment you set foot on my property!"

It was Angus who broke the silence. "Father, we did what we thought was right at the time and we do so again now. Besides, the queen believes some dark plot is afoot."

"Afoot? What is this, the eleventh century?" Max snapped. "What sort of plan? She rules everything now."

"That's the problem," Fritz cut in. "She wouldn't say it, but we think there are factions within the clans seeking to overthrow the throne once and for all."

Max gaped in shock. "That would cripple us for centuries. Another civil war! We cannot be involved in this. None of us. We barely survived the last one. Another would finish us."

"Father," Fritz attempted to calm him now. "There is more and potentially worse."

Unsure what could be worse than another civil war, Max paced around his workshop briefly before sitting on an old oak bench he carved long ago. Placing both hands on his knees to brace the blow he knew as coming, he beckoned with a hand for his son to continue.

"A goblin nest is active again," Fritz said without delay.

Color left Max's face. He stared first at Fritz and then Angus, searching their faces for any sign of duplicity or prank. "Which one?"

"Ok'tal'med out of—"

"Charleston," Max finished. He slammed an angry fist into his palm. "I told the king we weren't done with them! But he didn't listen. Couldn't stand to have a dwarf offering military strategy. We should have wiped them out long ago. What have they done?"

"They kidnapped a human right off the street," Fritz answered. "I suspect more than one missing person's case has gone active in the last few weeks or months as well. Goblins are never satisfied with a handful of victims when preparing for their war. We are going with Daniel to rescue the human and put an end to the nest."

"The three of you? You'll never survive." Max scoffed.

Angus shrugged. "Queen's orders. Fritz here got the bright idea to ask you for help."

"Right. Which is why you brought the hummie here, to my home." Max sighed. "No doubt your mother is fawning over him as we speak. I don't know what that woman sees in his books, comedy or not. I assume all this will be another part of his sad excursion into our lives? A new story to wow audiences at our shame?"

"He hasn't written about us yet," Fritz offered. "At least not from what I've read. His stories are a little more realistic but still heavy with comedic flair."

"How can you read that filth?"

"It's called knowing your enemy," Fritz answered. "Regardless, I don't care if we become characters or not. We have orders to rescue the human and we need your help."

Max rubbed his jaw. "Well, I can't let you go off and get killed by yourselves. I'd never hear the end of it, and I'll be damned if I let the queen get the better of me again. Things have been peaceful since the last time."

His sons exchanged grins but were wise enough not to comment. They waited hands clasped behind their backs for him to sort through his ragged emotions. Left outside the power struggle in Raleigh by design, Max Schneider wanted nothing to do with the royal family or the clans. He claimed retirement from court intrigue and sought to live a life of value by returning to his woodworking roots. Unlike many dwarves who were born with a hammer in their hands, Max had always been drawn to the grain of quality wood.

His fingers brushed over the polish of the bench. The care and passion involved in coaxing the finished project out of the tree thrilled him even after all these years. It represented peace. An end to the violence forever miring his people. Max longed to lose himself in the grain and forget the problems of the clans. If only for another day. Alas, he knew his fate was tied to the schemes of elves and men. And it seemed his sons.

"When did this man go missing?" he asked at last.

"Two days ago. Nabbed from the Sword and Sorcery Con in Raleigh," Fritz explained.

"Where you two no doubt dressed like dwarves and caused havoc."

"We were trying to, until Damon Pender showed up," Angus grumbled.

"The lich? I thought you killed him," Max mused. *Does nothing stay dead?*

"So did I."

"Damon's being handled by Constantin Andros," Fritz injected.

"Don't forget to tell him about the Tinker while you're blathering away every detail," Angus scolded.

Max sighed. Fritz ever sought to prove himself to him, even if it came at his brother's expense. Just like when they were toddlers.

"Damon Pender and the Tinker? Maybe your mother was right. We never should have let you go into the world," Max shook his head and rose in one fluid motion, causing his sons to step back. "Very well. My path is clear. You two are not going to engage an entire goblin nest alone. Give me a bit to collect my gear."

"You can ride with us," Fritz said with a grin.

Max paused, fixing his son with a withering stare. "In that thing? What's the point of having a bike if I'm not going to use it? Besides, the sun is out, and the day is perfect for a ride." He stormed off, muttering, "Go get your friend away from your mother before she has him writing a book for her."

TWENTY

Daniel wound up being dragged away from Nancy Schneider by both of her sons while her husband dragged the tarp off his Harley and prepared his bike for the short ride down to Charleston. Arms full of snacks and goodies for the road trip, Daniel grinned and laughed to a chorus of jokes the female dwarf tossed out as she followed him to the car.

"Mother, we need to get moving," Angus protested as she wrapped her burly arms around him and squeezed.

"Yes, yes. Always on the go. Never have time for your poor mother," she said into his chest. "Do take care of yourself. Those goblins are pesky creatures. Maybe I should go with you."

"No!" the brothers shouted simultaneously.

Nonplussed, Nancy backed away. "Fine. It was only a suggestion. Your father will be more than enough to deal with this nest."

They exchanged worried looks, nervous at the unspoken implications. Daniel could understand.

Concern shone in her eyes though she refused to speak the words aloud. Too many times had she watched her sons, and husband, march off to war while she stayed behind, fretting and worrying over matters beyond her control? Was this how Daniel's own mother reacted but he hadn't seen it or wanted to?

Chills ran down Daniel's spine. Old sensations awoke, reminding him of those precious days leading up to each deployment. Frantic hours spent trying to convince Sara it was all going to be fine while continuing training at an unsustainable pace. Fragile hours in the middle of the night when they should have been sleeping, instead both lay on opposite sides of the bed staring at the ceiling.

The scene on the Schneider homestead was all too real. He swallowed the lump in his throat, scowling at the foul taste lingering on his tongue. Daniel shoved the snacks into the backseat and turned back to Nancy with his best, forced, smile.

Nancy Schneider was no fool. Her sons were born for battle. Every dwarf was. But knowing and accepting were vastly different. She knew better than to suggest they turn away. Impugning a dwarf's honor proved the greatest sin an elder could deliver, far worse than any rebuke or reprimand. Nancy gave each of her sons a hug, pausing to pat each on the shoulder before turning away so they didn't see the tears filling her eyes. A dark foreboding filled her heart. The thought she might lose all three of the men in her life trembled her shoulders. She would get new gray hair and lines on her face now for sure.

The roar of a motorcycle gunning to life drifted over the property.

Come home to me, you stubborn men. All of you. And if you don't, Morgen will have hell to pay.

Daniel caught Nancy's gaze. "Mrs. Schneider, it was my absolute pleasure meeting you," he said loud enough for the brothers to hear without being too conspicuous. "I don't know what is in store for us, but I promise to take care of your sons like they were my own soldiers."

"Thank you, Daniel. Your words mean more than you know," she said with a sniffle. "You hear him, knuckleheads? Don't cause this man any trouble and do what he says or else."

"Yes, Mother," they mumbled together, lowering their gazes to the dirt and grass.

Smirking, Nancy patted Daniel on the cheek and went back inside.

"You know, Mother Schneider, you'd make one kick ass character in a book," Daniel grinned.

Before any could comment, Max roared his Harley from the back garage and down the lane before hitting the road. The haft of a battle axe jutted from his back; wild hair blew in the breeze. Daniel caught a whiff of cigar smoke. He liked the father's style already.

Clicking in his seatbelt, Daniel stared at the backs of the Schneider's heads when they got into the car.

Angus glanced back at him with a glare. "Not one fucking word," he warned.

"I wasn't even thinking of it," Daniel lied then burst out laughing.

"Let's go," Fritz cut in when Angus growled. "We don't want Father getting there before us. You know what happened the last time."

Grumbling under his breath, Angus threw the truck in gear.

"What happens now?" Daniel asked once he got his laughter under control. Gone were any thoughts of writing new characters. Once more he settled into soldier mode. "We could spend days trying to find the nest."

"We have a good idea where it might be," Fritz answered. "Goblins are social creatures, contrary to popular belief. They will make their nest close to the heart of the city where they can move about without being noticed."

"You do know Charleston is a major tourist town, right?" Daniel balked. "There must be thousands of people there every day. I don't see how goblins could go without being seen like that."

"Daniel, do I need remind you we have existed alongside humans for centuries without detection? You didn't even know your own agent was an elf before watching her die," Fritz replied. "Goblins are masters of disguise. If what I remember of Charleston still stands, not many drunks are going to catch on to the fact they're not alone."

Confused, Daniel asked, "So they're just there to have a good time? That makes no sense."

"Look at us," Angus said. "We were having a blast at your little con before Pender showed up. We know how to have fun."

Daniel cocked his head, struggling to hold back a number of retorts before choosing to ignore that statement. "Doesn't explain why they kidnapped Wally. What do goblins do with prisoners?"

"Eat them," Angus said.

Daniel balked. "What?"

Fritz punched him in the shoulder.

Angus flinched, swerving the truck into the next lane to the wail of an angry horn. The dwarf flipped off the semi barreling down behind them and kept moving.

"We don't know that." Fritz glowered. "Sure, they love the taste of humans but why would they go all the way to Raleigh to kidnap their next dinner? What does Wally do?"

"He's a comic book creator. I think he does IT on the side."

"Why would they want that?" Fritz rubbed his chin. "It doesn't make any sense. He is not a high value target. Are you certain he does nothing else? No government contractor? Ooh, what if he is a secret undercover agent for D.E.S.A?"

The thought of Wally working undercover at comic book conventions wouldn't be that farfetched considering all Daniel understood of the inner workings of both D.E.S.A. and the clans, but he thought himself a good judge of character. He'd certainly seen plenty of people who might fit the bill. But Wally? Nothing about him screamed secret agent.

"There's no way," he said with conviction. "Wally is a solid guy but he's not the one to wear a badge. There must be some valid reason for the goblins to snatch him specifically. Unless they have a habit of doing random acts?"

"Goblins seldom travel far from their nest without great purpose. This Wally must have some secrets or knowledge they need," Fritz said. "But what?"

"Wouldn't that be nice to know," Daniel agreed. Not knowing disturbed him on multiple levels, some he wasn't prepared to accept. Elves killing elves was one matter, goblins stealing humans a complete different one. Instincts warned some dark plot was afoot and, with limited intelligence, he feared they were playing into enemy hands.

Daniel realized he couldn't see Schneider's father any longer in the flow of traffic. "Where'd your father go?"

"Same old dad. Dear old Father charges off in search of fortune and glory without waiting for backup or gathering proper intel." Angus frowned. "How he hasn't gotten himself killed is beyond me. But the queen loves him for his blunt approach to handling matters of state."

"Huh," Dniel replied.

Fritz gave his brother a look before turning back to Daniel. "More often than not we have to pull his bacon from the fire. Recklessness is a dwarven trait, I'm afraid. Don't worry about our father. He'll be all right. What we need is a rally point in Charleston to begin searching for the nest. How well do you know the city?"

Despite it being his favorite city, Daniel had only visited a handful of times over the years. The first was with his ex-wife for an action filled weekend of drinking and sightseeing. The second was for a week with Sara where they toured everything on the main peninsula, from the famed park where pirates were once hung to the haunted prison. The only other time was a brief stopover on his way to Afghanistan on his first deployment.

Part of him wanted to live there, but then summer hit with the heat, humidity, and hurricanes, and common sense took over. Raleigh was as far south as he felt comfortable living. Guilt crept in, slight but enough to throw him off, as he thought of visiting his favorite city without Sara.

"Well enough, I suppose, unless we are heading anywhere but the historic district," Daniel admitted. *Maybe I can bring her back something*? "If we go anywhere else, especially the north side across the bridge I'm no good."

"Sounds like we are about to have an interesting time." Fritz sighed. "Hopefully father doesn't tear the city up too much before we catch up."

The Suburban rolled on. Daniel drummed his fingers on the door.

Viviana Cal hated the south. Too hot. Too humid. Too slow. She preferred the fast-paced environments of big cities where her true talents shined. Stepping off the queen's private jet, she lowered her sunglasses lest the blazing sun burn her eyes and scowled. Attendants hurried to see to her needs, but she waved them away. Her mission to Charleston dominated her mind. Viviana spied the car waiting at the edge of the tarmac and headed that way. The click of her heels on asphalt reassuring.

"Ms. Cal, I am to take you to your lodging," the driver greeted with a tight smile. "If you please."

With a nod, she waited for him to open the door. She climbed into the backseat of the sedan and pulled out her phone when it started to ring. "Yes, your Majesty. I arrived just now. What are your orders?"

Viviana fell silent as Morgen detailed her expectations. Her face remained expressionless. A weapon, a blunt instrument born and bred for the field, she shed her polished persona and slipped into a role she wore as a second skin. Today, she once more became the warrior.

The faintest hint of a smile crossed her lips when Morgen fell silent. "Yes, ma'am. I will see to it personally. I do not believe we will have need of the Old Guard," she replied. "Not yet. I will be in touch as soon as the dwarves make contact."

Slipping her phone back in her purse, Viviana pursed her lips as the car wove through tight streets and throngs of people. She knew events had the potential of slipping out of control fast. Maintaining control over the dwarves as they rampaged their way through the city should prove her greatest challenge—if no other issues arose. Her natural disdain for dwarves notwithstanding, Viviana now had to factor in the unpredictability of a human. Focused on that, she paid little attention when the car pulled into the hotel parking and a young elf opened her door to escort her to her suite.

TWENTY-ONE

The incessant drone of the phone ringing coaxed Thaddeus Blackmere from his slumber. With a groan, he glanced at the clock to discover he'd only been asleep for a few hours. He despised being woken up early and vowed to make whoever calling him pay, especially if it wasn't important. Sleep seldom came easy to him the older he got.

"This is Blackmere," he said through a yawn. His eyes burned and he discovered he needed to go to the bathroom. *It sucks getting old.*

"Thaddeus? This is Sara Thomas. Is this a bad time?"

Blinking to clear the crude from his eyes, he replied, "That all depends. What can I do for you, Sara? Daniel's not in trouble, is he?"

He damned well better not be or I'll have his hide. I knew that man was trouble the moment I met him. I don't know what I see in him.

"That all depends on your definition of trouble," Sara hedged. "He's gone south with those dwarf brothers to try and rescue a kidnapped friend. I don't know what to do." Blackmere felt like cold water had been thrown in his face. He sat up. "Slow down. Gone south? To where? Who was kidnapped?"

She took a deep breath. "Daniel and the Schneider brothers are on their way to Charleston to rescue one of Daniel's friends from a bunch of goblins." She paused before adding, "I think he's in over his head this time."

"Why didn't he notify us?" Blackmere asked. Existing treaties and overwatch committees ensured all active goblin nests remained localized to prevent precisely this. For them to have kidnapped a human … He expected another phone call in short order. This wasn't good.

"He claims Morgen didn't want to get the government involved. I don't trust her fully, not when my family's lives are at stake."

"The queen knows?" Blackmere blurted out. "How big is this operation, Sara? Did he say anything else?" *He saw his entire career flushing down the drain. Once again because of fucking North Carolina. I really hate that state.*

She proceeded to tell him all she knew, he noted how cautious she was and how careful she chose her words. remained cautious. She wasn't telling him everything, but he didn't have the time to pry. "When did he leave?"

"Last night. I'm worried, Thaddeus. This is the first time he's gone off on his own without your agency pushing the buttons."

The meaning was clear: Daniel was in over his head. *Shit. This could be bad.*

"All right. Let me make a few calls," he hedged. "You said Charleston?"

"That's what he told me." She said flatly. That was a conversation for another time. Sara knew better than to start an argument while her husband was heading into danger. Nothing was stopping her from unleashing the moment she found out he was safe.

How did I not know of this sooner? Why wasn't anyone notified? As the chief office liaison for the east coast, Blackmere knew it was a matter of time before he was called to his supervisor's carpet for this mess up. He was supposed to track every nuance of the elf clans in both states. Yet here they were. Goblins illegally crossing state lines and a pair of rogue dwarves, with a human, rampaging their way south.

"I'll take care of this, Sara. I promise. You just stay there and if he makes contact again relay the message to me,"

Blackmere instructed. "Let's hope this isn't as bad as your adventure."

"You don't need to worry about that," she promised. "Thank you, Thaddeus."

Don't thank me yet. I still have to figure out what's going on and get authorization to act. "You're welcome. I'll be in touch."

He set the phone down and groaned. Some days it didn't pay to work for the federal government—his was one of those days. Unable to delay any longer, Blackmere headed to the bathroom before making that dreaded phone call to the deputy director.

"Where are they now?"

Aislinn stared back at her with a blank look.

Her assistant had no answer to provide. Morgen knew this but was trying to keep her anger at bay after being given the report the dwarves either disabled the tracking device in their vehicle or left it behind.

"Your Majesty?" The clipboard was clutched tightly in her hands and pressed against her breasts, at her further silence Aislinn trembled, just enough for Morgen to notice.

Morgen pursed her lips, reconsidering her words. Aislinn was her loyal attendant and had yet to fail her. Certainly, this was not her fault. Dwarves. Always fouling matters at the wrong time. Instead of lashing out, Morgen paused to sip the steaming coffee before her, relishing the hot sensation as it burned down her throat. The aroma of freshly perked coffee proved almost hypnotic. She was going to need more to deal with this mess.

"I am unable to track them," Aislinn clarified with as level a voice as possible. "I have teams scouring the area, but they have been unsuccessful thus far, your majesty."

"Typical. I expected nothing less from our rebellious Schneider brothers. I don't know how my husband ever put up with them. At least their wretched father isn't involved," she muttered. *Viviana can't help me until they reach the city. Damnation.* "Has Constantin reported back on the lich?"

"He has." Aislinn's demeanor perked. "He reports the den has been cleansed and Damon Pender is in custody. The lich is being transported to the Grinder as we speak."

At least something has gone right. I grow so tired of failure. What I wouldn't give to have a firm power core in place among the clans, yet everywhere I turn my efforts are stymied by those sensing blood in the water. She had not felt this impotent in centuries.

"Inform Constantin I don't want that creature to see the light of day again," she ordered. "And contact Viviana. She has developed a rogue personality since her assignment to retrieve my daughter. An asset like that needs to be kept under heel before she spirals out of control." Another gulp of coffee helped to steady here. "Aislinn, what else do you have?"

Finishing making notes, Aislinn scanned her clipboard. "The mayor plans on having a parade at the end of the month. Some sort of agreement with the con founders."

"Wonderful. Not only must we endure four days of humans trespassing on our traditions but now we will be forced to shepherd a parade full of willful idiots," Morgen fumed. "Best have our security forces brought in now and look into opportunities to ingratiate us further with the local human authorities. A little good will goes far. I have no doubts too many of our kind will slip into the parade and cause havoc if they believe they can get away with it. Has any word come from Europe on the new prime minister yet?"

"Nothing I have heard, your majesty."

Morgen took another sip of coffee to stop a frown far too familiar these days from forming. No prime minister meant the power vacuum remained. The royal families across the pond were constantly positioning themselves to advantage, seeking personal glory and standing over unity. She needed a counterbalance to the throne if there was any hope of preventing another civil war among the clans. Without balance, all hope was lost. There was one elf she might try to sway to her side, but he had proven unpredictable for most of his life.

"Wheels upon wheels," she said aloud. "Aislinn, clear my schedule for the rest of the day and close the door on your way out. I have an important call to make. Report back the moment you hear from the Schneiders. I have a feeling they are about to do something rash, even for them."

"Yes, your majesty." Aislinn bowed and left. Despite their gruff demeanor and penchant for ignoring the laws, she had grown rather fond of the dwarves over the years. Not that she'd ever admit to the queen.

Morgen waited for the younger elf to depart before finishing her coffee.

An hour passed as she worked through what she wanted to say and how best to approach it, but the dark elf she intended to call had proven ever unpredictable. There was no guarantee he would agree to her proposal, but it was a chance she had to take. Back to the corner, Morgen found herself preparing for the political fight of her life.

She sighed and reached for the phone.

Charleston, South Carolina was a premier tourist destination on the eastern seaboard. Filled with rich history as well as moments the country seemed desperate to forget at times, the city had been a prominent figure in the shaping of the country. From being a central hub during the height of the western hemisphere slave trade to holding the dubious honor of having the first shots of the Civil War fired, the city plodded along. The old slave market was now an endless row of shops and stores filled with unsuspecting tourists. Church steeples dominated the city. Cruise ships docked a little north, close to the aquarium where visitors could see dolphins splashing in the open water.

Across the peninsula sat the mighty USS Yorktown in all her fading glory. The aircraft carrier dominated the surroundings, easily overshadowing the Coast Guard cutter and World War II submarine docked beside her. Pelicans and gulls swarmed the skies like enemy fighters in the hot summer sun. Plantations and resorts peppered the area for miles north and south, but it was the old city that remained the thriving heart of Charleston. Palm tree lined roads led down past historic homes anyone could tour for a price, and through the Battery, a defensive seawall turned destination park where pirates once hung from mighty oak branches.

Charleston was the sort of city that didn't shy from a checkered past and, for the most part, people came and went in steady lines. A nearby Air Force base ensured a steady influx of military personnel. For some, life continued at an old South pace. Others ensured progress arrived, forcing the city to grow and adapt to the changing world.

Daniel knew all this history and usually appreciated it. Yet, his sole focus rested in finding Wally and, if necessary, beating the goblins down enough they did not make the mistake of kidnapping anyone again.

They plunged deeper into the historic district. The city proper extended to both sides of the small peninsula and for miles back in the direction they had just come from. He did not know how many people lived here, maybe a hundred thousand, and would not have cared if not for the danger posed by the goblin nest. One of his biggest concerns, and one he still wasn't sure if the Schneider brothers shared, was preventing civilian casualties.

The debacle at the hotel in New York where his team of D.E.S.A. thugs refused to listen and almost exposed the operation to countless passersby hung heavy on his neck. Especially knowing the Schneiders, and the father he guessed, were prone to brash behavior. Keeping them calm and collected might prove impossible now that their father was in play. He hadn't counted on the old dwarf's participation despite their debacle with the Tinker last night. A wild card was the last thing he needed. Wally's life sat in the balance.

"We're going to need a place to hole up and use as a base of operations," he commented when they stopped at the next red light.

Fritz bobbed his head, the angry lyrics of *Let the Bodies Hit the Floor* cranking from the radio. "We have another matter to take care of first. We need intel and there's a lady here who can give it to us."

Angus' eyes bulged. "Wait, you don't mean…"

Fritz beamed as his brother's surprise. "You know it and I don't want to hear it. We need her help."

"Dad is going to be pissed."

TWENTY-TWO

"Perfect. This day keeps going from bad to worse."
The light changed. The truck turned right.
Angus continued, a fresh tirade. "You know she's nuts, right? She almost got us killed the last time."
"How was she supposed to know a British patrol was happening by?" Fritz protested. "It wasn't her fault!"
"My shoulder still hurts where that lobster-back shot me, Fritz," Angus growled.
"Quit whining. It builds character."
"One more surprise and I'll build your character through your nose. I'm about tired of being ambushed," Angus warned.
His voice carried a hard edge making Daniel tense. He listened to their banter and, despite the similarities he shared with his own estranged brother, Daniel felt the first pangs of concern they could come to blows. Between the inclusion of Max Schneider and now this mystery woman, the mission bordered on total collapse. If that happened, Daniel feared the worst for Wally and anyone else the goblins might have abducted.
"Who are we supposed to see?" he almost shouted above their bickering.
The brothers ignored him. Fists clenched; muscles stretched and bulged. He felt the stress pouring off them, filling the cabin with raw aggression. Already pushed to the edge and growing more concerned the longer their mission stretched, Daniel was torn between wanting a stiff drink and abandoning the dwarves for saner, more dependable company. *Maybe I should have called Blackmere after all.*

Their bickering rose—Daniel was unable to take it any longer. "Hey! That's enough! We have a job to do, in case you have forgotten!"

Stunned silence filled the cabin. Daniel saw Angus clenching the steering wheel that much tighter as his brother licked his lower lip and peered at him from the mirror. The color in their faces returned when they reached the next streetlight. Daniel held his tongue. It was a rare thing to get the better of one of the dwarves.

"We are going to see the one person in this town capable of helping us find the goblin nest before the sun sets, Daniel," Fritz said after some thought. "She is an acquired taste and easily crosses the definition of insane, but she is the best chance we have to finding your friend and stopping our father from unleashing a new war on Charleston."

"Wait, your father wouldn't do that, would he?"

Images of the elder dwarf rampaging through one of the east coast's most prevalent tourist destinations filled his head. Not that it was much of a stretch to believe Max would. He'd already seen the full effects of the man's sons as they tore across half a state. Violence ran in their blood. He was the only one capable of mitigating that intensity. Maybe.

"You've met the man. What do you think?" Angus asked and took a left, turning the truck around and heading back in the direction they had just come.

Daniel wanted to scream. Through gritted teeth he asked, "Where are we going? Shouldn't we be trying to find your father first?"

"He'll keep, for the time being," Fritz replied. "We need to get to Constance before the boats stop running."

"Boats?" Daniel asked. "She's not in the city?"

"Not exactly," Fritz hedged.

They said nothing more as the Suburban rolled into the parking garage between the aquarium and the Fort Sumter museum. It clicked for Daniel then. Whoever Constance was, she was either on the old Civil War fort or one of the nearby islands. He watched Angus cover their bags filled with weapons and ammunition under a black tarp before locking the doors and donning a pair of sunglasses.

"You still look like a dwarf," he said.

"Says you. No one here knows that," Angus fumed.

They strolled down to the museum entrance to purchase their ferry tickets. Daniel's mind stayed focused on the unpredictability of their father when Fritz told them to wait before he got in line. Max's hint at haste threatened to unravel the entire operation while Daniel and his sons were on a sightseeing tour. A glance at the clock showed it was just past noon. They had nine hours before the sun set, and the goblin nest stirred.

"Next ferry leaves in thirty minutes," Fritz announced as he returned with tickets in hand. "Would you look at this place? Hard to think it was all war and chaos not that long ago."

"The war was a hundred and fifty years ago," Daniel countered, pausing to read through some of the historical displays.

"A drop in the bucket for us," Angus replied. "Fritz and me were picking off Confederate scouts during the siege."

"I didn't know you fought for the Union." Once, he would have been fascinated by that detail. Now it just made sense.

"Who says we did? We were just stretching our legs at the time, waiting to see which way the wind was going to blow," Fritz countered. "We didn't officially sign up with either army until a few years later. Hell, Angus and I were at Gettysburg when Pickett made that dumbass charge across a mile wide field. I almost felt sorry for those boys."

Angus snorted. "If they were dumb enough to make the assault, they deserved to get shot. That was a fun day."

Daniel blinked, not at the fact the Schneiders fought for the Union at the battle of Gettysburg in 1863 but from their making sport of the carnage. Over fifty thousand casualties were had by both armies in a short three-day period, making it the bloodiest battle of the Civil War, and the dwarves reveled in it. He wondered how many other dwarves and elves joined the ranks to slake their thirst for bloodshed during that time.

Shared bonds of military service aside, he failed to enjoy much of his time in uniform. War, from his experience was ninety percent boredom mixed with ten percent sheer terror. Nothing in life compared to the sounds, sights, and smells of combat and the horrors humanity was capable of inflicting on itself. Humans were a violent species with a thirst for blood and had been since Cain killed his brother Abel. Some patterns seemed incapable of breaking.

"You should have seen it, Daniel." Fritz's eyes glassed over as old memories resurfaced. "Thousands of men marching up that slope and right into our guns. I've been around for a long time, been in plenty of wars, but I have never witnessed an act like that. Say what you will about those Virginia boys, but they had steel balls."

"Yes, they did," Angus echoed.

"We should get aboard the ferry," Daniel suggested after an uncomfortable silence settled between them.

Dark possibilities crept into his head. Visions of similar bloodshed approaching with the night as they declared war on the goblins to save Wally.

"Might as well," Fritz agreed with a smile. "It takes about a half hour to reach the fort. Finding Constance might be a problem, depending on how many tourists there are."

In single file, they marched onto the waiting ferry and took seats close to the bow, away from other passengers and, more importantly, out of earshot.

A flight of pelicans swept a few feet above the churning water, reminding Daniel of the final scene from Star Wars. He laughed quietly, thinking how much easier it would be to assault a Death Star than invade a nest of human hating goblins.

"Is anyone going to tell me who this Constance is?" he asked, staring after the birds.

At a grunt, Daniel glanced to see Angus with an uneasy glare, refusing to make eye contact with Fritz.

Clearing his throat, Fritz explained, "She is a sore subject among many of the clans. Constance deLange was the royal librarian, historian if you will, before the split. It is rumored she heavily influenced both the king and queen in their decisions and was thus a major proponent of the war."

"That's no rumor. She twisted their minds until neither could stand the other and set us all on a course for endless war," Angus growled. The words flew out with an escort of spittle. "We should have killed her when we had the chance."

"Did you lose anyone close because of her actions?" Daniel asked, fearing the dwarf's tone might induce unwarranted attention from the others taking their seats.

"Too many to count, Daniel," Fritz revealed. "Alvin deployed a company to bring her in. The hunt stretched across the North American continent before we finally cornered her outside of what is now Montreal. Her guardians were among the best, subverted high elves and wholly loyal to her. They … did not want to surrender her.

Many dwarves were slain that day, including our brother. Angus has never forgiven her for that."

He cleared his throat, adding, "Nor will I."

Daniel's heart tugged. Losing a loved one was never easy and it explained a measure of the inherent animosity the brothers clung to. Their father too. The thought of endless war and being forced to endure with others who either wronged you or fought against you repeatedly staggered him. Yet for Fritz to insist they seek this woman out, the apparent instigator behind the great elf schism, and ask for her help spoke volumes to his character. Daniel wondered if he could do the same.

"If she is the person responsible for it all, why is she not rotting in the Grinder?" Daniel asked.

"Who told you about the Grinder?" Fritz asked before waving the question off. "She was, for a time, but Morgen decided she had suffered enough after Alvin's assassination. Constance was set free with the charge of earning her way back into the crown's good graces. She now spends her days seeking to atone for her crimes by chronicling those of us who fell during the long war. It's not much, or enough for that matter, but she is trying. Which is more than can be said for a great many other villains."

"She is fortunate to have the queen's protection," Angus muttered.

He left the rest hanging, but the message was clear. Daniel found himself agreeing with the dwarf. "Does anyone know why she did it? People must have a reason."

Fritz shrugged. "Who remembers? Some say she was a lover scorned. The woman meant to be queen before Morgen wormed her way into Alvin's heart. Others believe Constance succumbed to her ambition, allowing her thoughts to twist until naught remained but the desire for unlimited power. For myself, I cannot say. It is enough she seeks to become a better elf, even if it will never bring our brother back."

Considering himself a forgiving man, Daniel was unsure if he could do what Fritz seemed to embrace. He had no idea how he might react if one close to him sparked a war resulting in the death of countless loved ones. The sickening knowledge might drive him to lengths he was not prepared to explore. *Would I do any less if harm befell Sara or the kids?*

The ferry pushing from the dock stole his attention. Daniel grabbed the rail to keep from losing balance as they pulled out into Charleston Harbor and began the slow voyage to Fort Sumter. A pod of dolphins broke the waves along the bow, escorting them out. Daniel might have found the moment enjoyable if not for the feeling of impending doom. He closed his eyes, attempting to enjoy the wind caressing his face.

TWENTY-THREE

Fort Sumter was built upon a small man-made island at the mouth of Charleston Harbor in 1829. Originally emplaced to defend the harbor from another naval incursion and with the memories of the second British invasion still fresh in the government's mind, Fort Sumter boasted walls fifty feet high and five feet thick. Over one hundred and thirty cannons gave the fort teeth, more than enough to prevent enemy ships from pushing through the bottleneck the island created.

By 1861 it was garrisoned with almost seven hundred Union soldiers and became the location of the first shots fired to start the American Civil War. The legacy of the fort remained firm in minds for decades after, before being decommissioned and turned into a historic monument. Today, the combination of Fort Sumter and Fort Moultrie built on the north shore attracted three quarters of a million visitors annually and was one of the main historic attractions Charleston offered.

Daniel had been here once, long ago. The only memory he had was of a young boy running around before getting sick and depositing his lunch in the water then seeing the original American flag which flew overhead during the Confederate siege preserved and encased in glass for all to see. As they approached, and like most battlefields he toured as an adult, Daniel attempted to envision himself there in the moment. Surrounded by mayhem and glory and the screams of officers and wounded mingling into one drowning chorus of insanity. How or why anyone willingly strode into danger remained a mystery, even for himself.

They set foot on dry land, much to the thanks of the passengers who suffered a thrilling half-hour ride bouncing over unexpected high waves and chop. Daniel let the dwarves take the lead, knowing better than to attempt to exert any sort of authority. First standing in the crowd awaiting was the park ranger gathering those he was meant to begin the tour for.

After a brief hushed conversation, the dwarves announced they were certain they knew where to find Constance. Without knowing what she looked like, it's not like elves walked around with their pointy ears showing, Daniel deferred to them again. Besides, he knew enough to know anyone around him might be an elf or dwarf, or worse.

"Ladies and gentlemen, welcome to Fort Sumter, South Carolina. It was here at 4:30 in the morning of April 12th, 1861, Confederate soldiers under the command of Brigadier General P.G.T. Beauregard opened fire on the Union garrison and began what became known as the American Civil War. The siege lasted only thirty-four hours, but its effects continue to reverberate through history today. If you will follow me, please."

With nods from the group around them, they started to follow the elder man in brown shirt and horrid green pants as the tour began.

Daniel stepped forward only to be held back by a backhand across the chest by Angus. His glare was met with a silent shake of the head by the dwarf. They allowed the tour to enter the fort, Daniel catching snippets of historical facts about the construction and purpose before they slipped around in the opposite direction.

Daniel did his best to remain focused. As an educated historian, his instincts screamed to explore and learn. The tour guide hadn't seemed that bad either. But Daniel stayed true to their mission. *Wally. Think of Wally.* They wormed through empty casemates once holding cannons before stumbling on a trio of people working to restore an era eight-inch cannon. To Daniel, they appeared like normal government employees doing their job. Angus stiffened immediately, however. They had found Constance deLange.

Fritz stepped between her and his brother. "Constance," he called. "We have need of your assistance."

She stopped what she was doing, pausing to set the small brush down before she straightened. Her weathered face took them in, eyes narrowing with recognition. Constance pursed her lips, flicking her gaze to the pair of elves flanking her. They stepped aside without a word but never took their eyes off the newcomers, who now stood in defensive postures. Daniel longed for a weapon.

"Fritz and Angus Schneider," Constance announced. "Has Morgen decided to revoke my charter? I can think of no other reason for your presence, unless you have come to avenge your brother."

The crackle of Angus' knuckles was sharp following her words; Daniel shifted his stance, eyeing the elves.

"We come of our own accord, Constance," Fritz soothed. "The queen does not know we are here nor have we any wish to harm you."

Daniel caught the hitch to Fritz's words. He empathized with the emotions consuming the dwarves.

Constance peered over Fritz's shoulder to Angus, the simmering mountain of hostility that moved protectively closer. "Angus does not seem to share your sentiments. While I have no qualms against giving you your pound of flesh, I fear my Old Guard protectors will not allow violence of any form."

Old Guard? Daniel's day just worsened. His lone experience with the defenders of the throne remained prevalent in his mind. He had never seen their like in the field. Unlike the commando team deployed to the

Fainting Goat, the pair guarding Constance appeared tamed.

"Angus has no love for you, Constance. Neither do I, but we are not here for ourselves. We… we need your help," Fritz admitted.

"What help can a disgraced old elf provide you?" she asked and looked his way. "Who is the human?"

Daniel started. "I am Da—"

"He's helping us with an important mission," Fritz cut in.

"Mission? I wasn't aware of any sanctioned operations in Charleston. Why have you come and why have you come to me?" she demanded. Daniel saw a flair of what she had likely been like before the war, reminding of the natural arrogance high elves exuded. Something he really wasn't fond of, neither were the dwarves by their stiffening.

"The Ok'tal'med nest is active, and we have intelligence suggesting they have kidnapped at least one human," Fritz revealed, looking harried. "We need your help discovering the entrance to the nest so we can retrieve the human and take necessary actions after. This order comes from the queen herself."

"Morgen never did have patience for goblins," Constance commented as she studied each of their faces, pausing to look into their souls …Or so it felt to Daniel.

He swallowed, unsure what to say, if anything. He learned long ago the best way to learn was by staying silent. Fritz already cut-off his introduction, prompting hasty introspection. Either the dwarf did not think it important enough to introduce Daniel or Constance had a problem with him or his writings or both and might shut down without telling them what they needed to know.

She suddenly pointed a gnarled finger at him. "Before this is finished, I will know who you are."

Daniel stood his ground, lifting his chin slightly in defiance.

Constance purred, a sound Daniel found creepy, the pink tip of her tongue slipping out like a snake tasting air, before returning her attention to Fritz. "Promise me Angus will not interfere and I will tell you what you need to know."

"Lady, you're lucky I haven't ripped your head off already," Angus rumbled. The dwarf stood tense, a coil waiting to spring.

Fritz's groan had Daniel holding back a laugh. "Maybe you and Daniel should go ahead and take a tour of this place. I'm sure it has changed since we were last here."

Seeing Fritz's look of pleading, Daniel grabbed Angus by the forearm and pulled him away. The two Old Guards shifted stances so imperceptible he almost missed it. The last thing he needed was a brawl with so many tourists around. Surprisingly, the dwarf didn't shake him off and followed a respectable distance away.

"Let's go look at cannons. Those should cheer you up," Daniel said as they walked away.

Fritz's sigh of relief echoed through the casement. Sweat beaded his brow. *Okay, focus. Angus is okay. We are fine.* He returned his attention to Constance, warring with his own emotions. "There. Now we can talk."

The high elf made a show of flattening out the wrinkles in her ankle-length skirts before gesturing to the bench against the far wall. Fritz followed her lead, pausing to allow her to sit first. The smell of saltwater hit hard, tickling his nostrils just uncomfortable enough to make it itch.

"Goblins have ever been a thorn in our side," Constance said, dropping her voice to a whisper. "Alvin and Morgen once attempted to subvert them to play by their rules at the beginning of the war. Their efforts resulted in greater violence and the near extinction of all nests in the Americas. A shame. No species deserves extinction."

"Did you play a role in that as well?" Fritz couldn't help himself and had to ask.

She paused, startled. He watched as she buried her frown beneath the mask she had worn as long as he had known her. "The past is the past, young dwarf. I have many regrets to atone for before I can sleep eternal. Now, you say the local nest is active once more?"

Letting the insults fall from his tongue, Fritz said instead, "They have. We have reason to believe they went as far north as Raleigh to kidnap a friend of the human with us."

"Humans aren't important, Fritz Schneider. They never have been." She waved him off.

"The queen feels differently," he replied, a dangerous edge lacing his words. Constance was the sort who seldom took much beyond her self-interests seriously unless pushed. "That man's family has been involved with our kind for years now and is connected to D.E.S.A. The kidnapped man is his friend, making this a high priority. If the goblins are emboldened enough to cross state lines and violate all existing treaties, they must be preparing to launch another campaign. We cannot allow that to happen."

"And you come to me for what precisely?" she pressed. "I am an old woman. Do you think I want to be here? In this relic? This is my penance for crimes against elfkind. I will have no part in harming another creature in this lifetime, dwarf. Go back to your queen and tell her I do as instruct and to leave me out of her future schemes."

She made to rise before Fritz slammed a fist into the aged brick wall. Pebbles and mortar broke free, raining down in a trailing dust cloud. The Old Guard stirred, advancing on the dwarf, hands dropping to their concealed handguns. Constance held them at bay with a stern glare before she prompted Fritz with, "Well?"

"This isn't a game, deLange! You know what happened the last time. I'll be damned if I let that happen again. You may not want to be part of this, but you know the city inside and out. You know where the nest is. Help my brother and I and we will get out of your hair and never see you again. Don't forget, Constance, I don't like you any more than he does," Fritz explained. He grabbed her arm, stunning them both.

She leveled her gaze, studying him for a few moments. In a controlled voice she said, "Take your hand off me, dwarf. You would not want to make a mistake you will regret. Not now."

"Just tell me where the entrance to the nest is."

Smoothing her clothing again after he left her go, Constance offered a false smile. "Very well. I shall tell you, though I suspect you are concealing secrets capable of sending us all to ruin. Tell me, young Fritz, what are you hiding?"

"The nest first." Exposing his father's presence might well tip the balance against them, for Constance bore no love for Max. Their hatred ran back a thousand years, long before the schism and the time when elves and dwarves engaged in hostilities. The longer he kept his father a secret the better the chance of success.

"No."

Her refusal didn't surprise him. He opened his hands, presenting empty palms to the elf. "You expect me to believe you have no idea who that human is?"

"I should have known you held cards close," she tsked. "Perhaps you can bring him to my apartments after this mission is finished? I would very much like to speak with him. Alone."

Fritz failed to conceal his surprise with how easy that proved. "Yeah, maybe. We still have to neutralize the goblin problem before it becomes one."

"Ah, yes," Constance said with a smile. "The nest. Very well. Pay attention. I will only say this once."

TWENTY-FOUR

Irma Stain frowned upon skipping into Wally's chamber. She expected to find an empty platter, full bedpan, and sheets of comic genius waiting for color and dialogue. Instead, she discovered spoiled food and stacks of crumpled paper mingled with broken pencils. Wally should have been at his desk, furiously translating all she told him the day prior. He was lying on his stomach, face buried in dirty blankets, weeping.

Irma grew angry and kicked his shin. "Wally Rutherford! You do me great shame! The Nest Father will punish me for your sins," she exclaimed before getting her voice under control. She ignored his yelp when she kicked him again. "You must complete the story, Wally. You must or I will be punished."

Pulling himself up, Wally reached down to rub his leg. "Like you just punished me? Maybe you deserve it, Irma Stain. I'm not a piece of meat to be treated like this."

She sniffed and crossed her arms.

Wally was angry. If not for the four guards hovering outside his chamber, he would have retaliated and thrown the young goblin off, punishment be damned. Filthy and kept in a constant state of panic, Wally could not remember the last time he endured such inhumanity. Growing up with an army dad numbed him to many of life's hardships, hardening him for when times turned rough. But his dad's hard life lessons hadn't prepared him for this.

Glaring at the goblin, he noticed her quivering. Real fear tremored through Irma, but it wasn't from Wally. He began to think there was an even darker side to Crispus Goldfarb than he first imagined. Wally decided to change tactics. If the man was willing to harm his own people, there was no telling how far he might go to wring all he wanted from a human prisoner. *There is my predecessor too to consider…*

"Look, Irma, I think we got off on the wrong foot," he attempted to soothe her. He even tried to smile. "You and me, we're not so different. You care about your family. I care about mine. In fact, it's all I can think about lately. I really want to go home again, Irma."

She stopped shaking, daring to look up with tear-filled eyes. He didn't like seeing her tears, it made her more human to him. "Wally Rutherford, you are a brave man, but you must not be so naïve. The Nest Father will not let you see the cursed light of the sun until you complete our story!"

"I understand that," he replied without believing her. He fully expected to never see the sun again, but he had to try. "But I need that creative spark. It doesn't help knowing one of my people here."

"He came first," she answered after looking around conspiratorially and lowering her voice. "He did not finish the story either. That is his punishment. I … I do not want to see you suffer similar."

"You and me both, Irma Stain," he admitted. "Do you know who he is?"

She paused, glancing over her shoulder to see how closely the guards were listening before continuing. "I do not remember his name. It was only spoken once, when the Nest Father introduced us to the man who would bring our story to the world. Jerry or Jordy, I believe."

Wally froze. A sickly feeling spread through him as he recalled the haggard man in chains. The hair. The build. The clothes. Realization dawned and it robbed him of what little strength he had remaining. *It can't be.*

"Jimmy Harper," he muttered aloud.

"What did you say?" Irma leaned closer.

"His name is Jimmy Harper," Wally repeated, mind in a haze.

She broke into a feral grin, cracked and broken teeth poking from wet lips. "That's it! You know him!"

"Yeah, I know him. We were supposed to be best friends," Wally's shoulders slumped. He hadn't seen Jimmy in a few years. Now he knew why. "I guess not. Irma, do you know how Cri…er, the Nest Father got my name?"

She bobbed her head. "I am not supposed to know this, but I overheard your friend tell the Nest Father about you. He had such praise for you, Wally. You should be proud to have friends like that!"

Friends like that. The son of a bitch sold me out. A million comic creators in the country, so many you can't swing a dead cat without hitting one, and he fucking picked me! Anger flooded his veins. He wanted to lash out. Smash things to get the hurt from his heart. Most of all, he wanted to confront the man once proclaiming to be his friend and demand answers. Once business partners, Wally had trouble reconciling how or why Jimmy sold him.

Sensing danger, Irma stepped back to the threshold and clasped her hands before her, her face twisting in worry. The warts and pustules under her skin rolled as she knit her fingers together. It hurt a little but helped her focus. Far younger than one in her position deserved to be, Irma had been chosen to help the creators find their genius and tell the goblin's story. Should Wally not discover his creative spark, she feared the worst. The Nest Father would punish her. Others had been sent to the nest cookpots for lesser offenses. While she had no qualms against serving the greater community, Irma believed she had much life left before her.

"Do please calm down, Wally," she whimpered. "I thought this news would be welcome. Is he not your friend?"

"Not after this." The hard edge in his voice unlocked the tears she was holding back.

He watched her cry, her loud sobs filling the room, not caring if the guards heard and sent word to Crispus. Irma Stain, though young, was a goblin and, in his eyes, now either a dupe or part of the problem. The sooner they were destroyed the better. Yet he still needed to play nice, just to stay alive.

Wally hung his head and wiped a palm over his face. "Stop crying, Irma. I'm sorry. I shouldn't have yelled at you," he told her. He half believed the sincerity he heard in his words. She was but a pawn in a greater game, same as him. Instead of treating her like the enemy he could still try and turn her to his side. "Look, I'm sure we can find a way to work through this. Let's forget you ever mentioned Jerry and get back to business."

She sniffled. "You said it was Jimmy."

Wally presented his most charming smile. "See, I already forgot."

Inside, he seethed with thoughts of revenge.

The faintest hint of a smile broke through the grime on her face. For a moment, Wally almost forgot she was his warden. Though no matter how Crispus attempted to shift the narrative, his fate remained tied to creating a comic unlike any he had ever attempted. It wasn't something he could easily, if ever, forget. It didn't help that the storyline hadn't been told and he had no outlet to pull inspiration from. And while plenty of books focused on the villain to hero transition, most, from what he knew, were not true. Nor did they attempt to present a lie.

Goblins as heroes… Who would believe it?

Wally slipped back to trying to find the value in the goblins. His motto of 'be cool with me and I'm cool with you' had so far worked in his favor, until now. Considering himself a good judge of character, Wally found Irma an interesting confusion. A goblin presenting human traits. He refused to believe anyone was inherently evil. Perhaps turning Irma Stain to his side might allow him to win his freedom.

Or perhaps not. She was young and eager to prove herself to her nest, making her dangerous to Wally. One wrong move, a misspoken word, and both of their lives were forfeit. Wally had no disillusions about sharing Jimmy Harper's fate. The thought of his former friend, *former friend,* rotting away in a forgotten cell deep under the earth inspired conflicting emotions. He hated the man for selling him out to the goblins while still wanting to help Jimmy escape. The pain of it mocked his psyche.

Giving himself a shake, Wally focused on the goblin standing before him. "Irma, how about we start with your story. I need a jumping point to being the comic."

"Oh yes, that would be nice." She bobbed her head with a big smile.

He blanched at the sight of strings of chewed meat caught between her jagged teeth. *Girl, you need a dentist.* "Cool. Where do we begin?"

The crisp report of her clapping almost hurt his ears. Irma stormed further into the chamber, helping herself to a seat on the chair beside his desk. "It begins at the beginning! The very first goblin stepped from the earth and into the sunlight, long before the time of the elves. We were a proud people with nests across the world."

"How long ago was that?" Wally asked as he returned to his drawing table and selected a sharp pencil.

"Many thousands of years now," Irma said. "I am told there were real dinosaurs walking around! Can you imagine, Wally? Dinosaurs! It is so sad I will never get to see a live one."

Eyes bulging, despite his inability to accept what she said, Wally gaped, "You were alive during the dinosaur age?"

Irma shook her head. The wet swish of hair scrapping the back of her shirt turning his stomach. "Oh no. I am only a few hundred years old. My great grandfather told me of it. It was an exciting time."

"Exciting? Irma, what about when the asteroid hit? All the dinosaurs were wiped out. How did goblins survive?" he asked, disbelieving the conversation. "The whole planet died."

"Silly, Wally. The planet did not die. How else would we all be here now?" she challenged. "Those that could fled underground. They adapted and thrived, until the elf kingdom rose and established dominance. Wicked, cruel elves! Oh Wally, they are an evil people. They would kill us all if we let them."

"I thought the elves were the good guys. That's how the movies show them," Wally countered.

Any joy on her face died, replaced by raw animosity. "Wally, you should know better than to tell lies. Elves have always been bloodthirsty and evil. They attack without mercy, forcing us to remain underground while they rule the kingdom once belonging to the goblins. We are the true origins of life, Wally Rutherford. We and we alone hold the claim on the world's throne."

"And you want me to show that story," Wally concluded. Eyebrows pulled together in thought, he began tapping the pencil on the table.

"Yes," she said with a straight face.

The smell of roasting meat drifted through. His mouth watered before his mind remembered what goblins ate. *I hope it isn't Jimmy.* He cleared his throat. "I mean, it can be done but you gotta realize I can only draw the pictures. I can't change public opinion.".

Irma cocked her head, looking down at his torso. "You are hungry?"

Wally winced, having hoped to avoid the conversation even as his stomach rumbled. He had eaten the meat they offered previously, but, in his defense, it was before understanding goblins had no compunction against being cannibals. He then ignored the meat brought to him. "I'd love a salad. You know, leafy greens and all that."

Making a point of screwing her face in disgust, Irma laughed. "You are funny, Wally. Salad. Nasty green things. Do you not eat meat?"

Oh, I do, but I know what you cook. You must have lost your mind if you think I'm tasting another bite of one of your friends. Or a human. "I take it you don't eat vegetables down here?"

Muttering under her breath, Irma excused herself to find him a suitable meal.

Wally stared after her, wondering what he had gotten himself into. He stared at the empty page, contemplating all Irma had told him. Mouth twisted in thought, Wally knew there was only so much dissembling he could do about food before Crispus came down on him. He needed to have something to show for all the effort.

The first spark of an idea struck, and he settled down behind the drawing board. Dinosaurs. Goblins. The thought of goblins rising from the remains of the giant lizards brought a chuckle before the reality of his situation slammed home again. Conflicting thoughts dominated the back of his mind, whispering his fate should he fail to appease the goblin hordes. Faces haunted him. Irma Stain. Crispus Goldfarb. Jimmy Harper. Friends and enemies locked in a battle for him—or piece of him.

Wally set the tip of his pencil to the paper and began to draw. Dinosaurs and monsters flowed from his fingers. Soon enough he realized there was no way to tell the goblin story in one volume. Images poured onto the paper, driven by a single sustaining thought of his wife. *I will make it home to you, baby. I swear it*.

Humming softly, Crispus wormed through the nest to check on his latest acquisition. He had high hopes in Wally. The human's work would soften humanity to his plight right before he launched his assault upon the elf clans. If the blasted man ever started the project. Crispus decided further motivation was required. To his surprise, Wally was hard at work creating images. Crispus decided to leave before the human spotted him, there being no point in breaking Wally's concentration. He perked up after noticing Irma marching back to Wally's room with a determined look. *Is that a salad in her hands?* Strange times had come to the nest, and he failed to understand any of it.

TWENTY-FIVE

The ride back to Charleston proper began in silence. Neither of the brothers spoke to each other, leaving Daniel in the cold and unwilling to start a conversation of his own. The cracking of knuckles from each of them threatened to drive Daniel mad, but it was better than the brothers coming to blows on the boat in front of numerous civilians. Throwing both overboard might improve their attitudes... Daniel scratched the corner of his mouth, imagining the dwarves splashing in the water as the boat pulled away. Of course getting that far was no easy feat.

"What's so funny?"

Jarred from his thoughts, Daniel sheepishly answered Angus, "Nothing much. Just enjoying the saltwater smells and freedoms of being on the open water. You never know what you might find lurking out there."

As if on cue, a pod of dolphins popped up along the starboard side, bouncing from the water in unparalleled joy. He envied them.

Glowering, Angus followed his gaze. "Uh, huh."

"Don't take your grumpiness out on him," Fritz said in a rough tone. "You knew we had to see her. It was the only way."

"Oh sure," Angus replied without looking at him. "First father and now that bitch. Who else do you plan on dragging into our little adventure? Any other old enemies we have left alone for too long? Can't wait to sink my axe in all of them, *brother*."

Daniel cleared his throat to get their attention before their banter devolved into a brawl. "Gentlemen, this is not the place. Wait until we are alone, and then you can pummel the hell out of each other for all I care. We need to find the nest and get Wally." At their unimpressed looks he added, "Before your father destroys half the city."

The dwarves glared at him then each other.

Daniel swallowed a groan. *I don't need this. They're like two little kids who pitch a fit when they don't get what they want. Hundreds of years old but I'm the mature one. I guess living forever doesn't mean you grow up. I have half a mind to give Wally a thumping for getting himself, and me, into this mess.*

Turning away from them, Daniel took a sweep of the surroundings. Rows of empty seats separated them from the rest of the passengers. A fact Daniel remained thankful for. The dwarves looked like a pair of angry bikers in jeans and t-shirts. Bulging muscles and decorated beards did little to lend them a friendly air, making him the odd man out. Even with the space and how the dwarves looked, it did little to assuage Daniel's growing fears they were being watched. He had seen the same man staring at them since first boarding the boat to Fort Sumter. Tall, tanned, and with piercing eyes, the man popped up whenever Daniel looked around, always shifting his gaze a fraction of a second too late for coincidence. Daniel felt the need for a weapon, anything to defend himself should this observer prove deadly.

The dwarves appeared oblivious of the attention. Their current spat of animosity directed at each other, for a change, most have robbed them of their spatial awareness. Daniel expected better. He slipped his gaze over the dwarves and dolphins, only to catch the man staring at them from midship. True to form, he turned away upon noticing Daniel staring back.

Hair stood on end down Daniel's neck. "Don't look, but we are being watched," he said, doing his best to not move his lips.

The dwarves paused in the verbal warfare and let him explain the situation. Daniel described the man down to his shoes.

"Is he one of yours?" Daniel asked.

"What do you mean by that?" Angus snapped.

Daniel held up his hands. "I meant an elf, that's all."

Fritz and Angus alternated glances, appearing vaguely interested in the crowd the way most tourists did. Both revealed they had seen him spying on them several times, but it had not seemed notable to them to worry or even let Daniel know.

"You might be jumping to conclusions," Fritz said, his focus once more on the ocean. "It's not like we blend in well."

"He's right," Angus added, supporting his brother as if their disagreement never happened. "Hell, we could easily be heading to prison as taking a scenic tour." He chuckled. "Well, maybe not you."

"Why can't I go to prison?" Daniel blurted out before realizing it made him look stupid. Both brothers laughed. "Never mind. The point is, he's been watching us since we boarded. I'm sure of it."

"That leaves one move," Angus said before glaring at their watcher.

As if sensing his cover blown, the man jerked just enough to confirm Daniel's suspicions and made for the stairwell to the lower deck.

"Got you," Angus growled.

"We have two moves," Fritz started. "Either confront him now where he can't get away and we don't need to worry about violence breaking out. Or we wait until the boat docks and risk losing him in the dispersing crowd. Neither sounds appealing to me."

Exhaling, Daniel felt the sweat beading on his forehead and arms. One thing about South Carolina in the summer you could count on was the debilitating combination of heat and humidity. "Let me go find him. If you two come at him there's a chance that guy will jump overboard or cause a scene. If I go it's just one man."

"I don't know, Daniel. He might be dangerous," Fritz murmured before breaking into a laugh when Daniel grunted. "I'm just playing. Go ahead, but don't do anything dwarvish."

"Dwarvish?"

"He means stupid," Angus clarified. "We'll block the exits. You make contact."

Unsure if the plan was sound or not, Daniel calmed his breathing and rose to his feet. Enough surprises had already been thrown at them, each threatening to derail the mission. *Let this not be a surprise, or at least a bad one.* His time in service taught him the importance of adaptability though. So he needed to be prepared for a bad surprise. "Right. Let's do this," he said, more for himself than to let the Schneider's know he was moving.

Daniel found the man where he expected, attempting to blend in with the rest of the passengers near the aft end of the boat. Undeterred, he strode through the small crowd, bypassing a family with babbling children pointing at the dolphin escort. A few curious glances followed him, but nothing else. Humanity seemed content with letting matters play out without interfering unless it directly affected them. Using this to his advantage, Daniel closed on the man just as he left his seat and made a move for the bathroom.

The man bit back a yelp as Daniel grabbed him by the arm and dragged him to rail. "Why are you so intent on my friends and I?"

Glancing around for any sign of escape, the man answered, "I don't know what you're talking about. I'm just here for the tour, man."

Daniel squeezed, feeling the bone grate beneath his grip. "Bullshit. Try again. One more wrong answer and I turn you over to my friends. They aren't as forgiving as me."

"Fine, just take your hand off me. This is a new shirt," the man replied with the slightest hint of pain.

Daniel released him, remaining close enough to act should the situation deteriorate. He watched, bemused as the man made a show of smoothing out his shirt with a false look of indignity, before fixing Daniel with a strained look.

"Who are you?" Daniel pressed. "Who do you work for? D.E.S.A?"

"My name is Hayf Mansour," the man replied with a resigned sigh, almost as if relieved to be exposed. "I was assigned to watch you by Agent Blackmere."

Blackmere? How did he know? Turmoil erupted in Daniel's thoughts. The queen had been adamant about excluding D.E.S.A. from this affair and, for once, he agreed. No good came from government interference, especially with the shadowy organization charged with overseeing elf affairs. The only person he had talked to had been his wife…

"What does Blackmere know?" Daniel asked.

Hayf stared back, unsure how much to admit as he took in Daniel's measure. "More than he told me, I can assure you. I'm here to monitor and only interfere if you three bumble your way into exposing everything."

"So, you're not an agent," Daniel concluded with some relief.

A quick head shake was Hayf's first response. "Not in the way you are used to. I'm a watcher. That faceless man staring from the shadows. At least I was supposed to be.

I must admit, it took less time than I thought for any of you to mark me. You're the first, you know. No one on any of my previous assignments figured out I was watching or really who I was."

"Great, I feel special now." Daniel rolled his eyes. "How did Blackmere know I was here?"

Hayf shrugged. "I don't know. They don't tell me everything. I'm part of the network, that's all. I get the assignment and make regular reports back to my handler. I don't know Blackmere personally. We've never met or worked together before."

Daniel placed his hands on the railing, running a fingertip over the chipped paint. "What is his interest in me?"

Gaze flitting left and right, Hayf's eyes went wide. A quick glance over his shoulder confirmed to Daniel that the dwarf brothers were lurking at the base of the wide set of stairs. Realizing there was no escape and no chance of summoning help, the D.E.S.A. man told Daniel what he needed to know without compromising his mission.

"From what I gather, Blackmere learned about a human kidnapping that you and the two dwarf brothers were heading to handle yourselves. He knew there was no way to get down here in time himself, so he contacted my handler who activated me to provide surveillance, hopefully ensuring no unnecessary damage is created requiring explanation to the local authorities. My assignment is to monitor your progress without getting involved."

"We're well past that," Daniel said to which Hayf nodded. "Here's the way I see it. You can either report back to Blackmere everything is fine and get D.E.S.A to back off or you can help us."

"Help you? That's against protocol," Hayf sputtered. "I'm an observer *only*. Hell, I'm not even trained for field work."

"Doesn't matter. You're in this right alongside me now. I need to know how to get around town without being seen. We have the location of the hidden entrance to the goblin nest but there has to be a backdoor. I want to know it."

"You really plan on going down there?" Hayf's eyes bulged. "No one has ever come back from the nest, Daniel."

Teeth grinding, Daniel jabbed a finger at him. "Guess it's time to change that. My friends and I are going into the nest and pulling the human out. Alive if all goes according to plan. You get to come along for the ride, Hayf Mansour."

"I don't suppose I have a choice?"

Daniel shook his head.

"Blackmere is going to be pissed," Hayf said.

"That's not my problem."

The tour boat slowly turned, heading for the dock. Hayf and Daniel stared at one another until the deckhands tied off the boat and passengers began getting off. No one paid attention to them, nor to the pair of dwarves guarding the exits.

Hayf's shoulders sagged in defeat as the crew began to cleanup. "Fine. But you're going to regret this. Goblins are nasty little monsters."

"Yeah, so I keep hearing."

TWENTY-SIX

"I say tie him up, slap a gag on him and dump him in the water. We don't need the distraction." Angus folded his arms across his chest. "We're already behind schedule thanks to this little detour and the sun will set in a few hours. Time is up."

Expecting the argument but failing to have any actionable alternatives, Daniel still stood his ground. Winds caressed his face, now oily from excessive sweat, providing the sole relief to the late afternoon sun. The crowds had thinned on the dock, leaving them secluded enough for Daniel to attempt placating the angrier brother.

"We're way past that, Angus," he said. "Hayf here knows more than he should and is expected to report in at regular intervals to our dear agent Blackmere. We need to move past whether we want it or like it and focus on the mission."

"Right, with him sucking bubbles at the bottom of that river."

Damned stubborn fools. And they were worried about me doing something dwarvish! "Look, we need to move. Hayf can get us to the backdoor Constance mentioned without issue and he says your father is already here in the city. We need to pull this together before it's too late."

"Daniel has a valid point, Angus. I don't trust the information Constance gave us. Right now, dear old father is our biggest liability," Fritz added. At his brother's snort, he scuffed his boots and began pacing.

Daniel glared at Hayf when the man stood silent.

"Er, yes. The last I knew, from a fellow watcher you understand, is Max Schneider was at a local restaurant near the Old Market. Not far from the main nest entrance if I am correct," Hayf said with a wince.

Angus stiffened, flexing his muscles to the sound of stitches tearing. "He's already at the nest? Without us?"

"How did he know where it is?" Daniel asked anyone willing to answer. No one did.

Snatching Hayf by the collar, Angus began marching back to the parking area. "We need to move. If he confirmation of the nest entrance he will go in alone."

\

Max Schneider belched loud enough to startle birds resting in the nearby palm trees. Wiping his mouth and beard free from crumbs with the back of a sleeve, he sat back in his chair chuckling to himself. None of the patrons looked his way, not after unveiled threats flaming from his eyes from the other times they had stared at him as he enjoyed his meal. Servers only came close if they saw he was out of beer. Being a dwarf of few words and limited exposure to the outside world, Max took pleasure when he was out and didn't want to be disturbed.

Passersby learned to quicken their step by his table, one situated in the shade just off the main sidewalk that he had selected because of the full view from three directions. He ignored them, thoughts focused on that task at hand. An active goblin nest meant enemy territory and, as far as Max was concerned, he was behind enemy lines. All the weapons and armor were bundled in the back of the truck, leaving him all but defenseless. The idea made him bristle. There was a time when dwarves walked openly with axe and sword. Today they were neutered by societal norms and an overabundance of human laws.

The sickening downward trend forced him into exile. Max seldom left the homestead, especially after the war, choosing a life of solitude with his wife. Together, they raised a variety of animals, tended crops, and did their best to stay off the grid.

That did nothing to prevent the government overwatch. Black helicopters hovering in the distance. Dark SUVs with their lights off partially concealed behind a stand of trees on the opposite side of the main road leading to his property. They thought they went undetected, but Max had every meter of ground plotted and covered with surveillance cameras.

Once considered a foremost tactician among the high elf clans, Max Schneider left nothing to chance. His ferocity in battle was legendary, his axe still sharp, and as the patriarch of the family he created legends wherever he strode. Those battles and campaigns ranged across the face of the world, from the Swiss Alps to Jerusalem and now to Charleston. He took another long pull from his beer and closed his mind to the past. Too many bad memories ruined a man. At least that's what his father preached before the end.

Thoughts of family also threatened to unravel his professionalism. Sure, he had fought alongside his sons in the past, and they were both proven warriors, but this time was different. They did not have the support of grand armies or intelligence networks. Max and the boys were going into the goblin nest blind and with naught but the twisted words of a lich for intel.

More than once he considered they were walking into a trap. But why? He retired not long after the first wars during the schism and remained outside of clan politics for centuries. He held no strategic value for either side, though his sons continued delving into the affairs of kings and men.

Unable to figure out the multiple angles, Max felt like he was caught in a web. Trapped with but one path forward. A path capable of leading them all to ruin. He drowned the last of his beer and slammed the glass down, harder than intended but it didn't crack, and motioned for another. Dwarven capacity for handling alcohol notwithstanding, he needed another round to clear his mind.

The evening crowds were coming out now. Hundreds of people dressed like tourists, you can always tell a local, milling on overworked streets and flooding the rash of restaurants. Max stopped counting the number of horsedrawn carriage rides he had seen in the few hours since his arrival. Those poor animals labored in the oppressive heat, not that any of the humans showed concern. Wives and girlfriends oohed and aahed as they were pulled through the historic district. If Max had his way the drivers would all be flogged with their own reins. Stewing as the server, a friendly enough young girl with flaming red hair reminding him of a forge fire, brought him a fresh frosted mug, Max grumbled a hasty "thank you" and drank deep.

His dour mood lessened, if just, when he saw a familiar Suburban pull past and into the first parking spot available a block down the street. Angus and Fritz hopped out, followed by the infamous Daniel Thomas, a man he wanted nothing more than to knock a tooth or two out of, and a stranger. That made Max sit a little straighter. This was new. He hadn't expected additional forces. From the look of him, the newcomer bore the look of an Arab. Odd, Max did not recall any of the clans claiming the Middle East.

Max kicked the chair across from him out with a boot and gestured to them to join him. His predatory gaze never left the newcomer, not even after the boys explained who this Hayf was and what he brought to the mission. A round of beers were brought, against Daniel's protestations, meant to calm their nerves and enhance the conversation that Max intended to have.

"I thought DESA weren't players in this," he began.

Hayf cleared his throat, disturbed at the ease with which Max identified him, politely declining the beer put in front of him with a wave of his hand. "We aren't. At least not officially. I was not supposed to be part of your operation."

"You're welcome," Daniel said after swallowing a mouthful of his own beer. "Regardless of whether the government is involved or not, Hayf will take us to the backdoor."

"Tonight? Forget about it," Max said with a frown. "Sun's going down. The goblins will be active soon if they aren't already. Best time to strike is at dawn when they are tired or nesting. We go in now and its suicide. As much as I like a good fight, their mother will kill me if they die. I very much like my life, Daniel Thomas."

"We can't afford to delay," Daniel protested, his voice raising enough to draw stares. A calming hand from Fritz settled him back into his chair. "We've given the goblins a long enough head start. What if they kill Wally tonight?"

"Think clearly, man," Max answered and lowered his voice. "If the goblins were looking for meat they wouldn't have left the city. Plenty of homeless lingering on the side streets to pick off. No, they drove all the way to Raleigh, violating every exiting accord and treaty, to snatch one specific person. They need him for something. I'll be damned if I can figure out what."

Daniel blinked, feeling as if he'd been slapped across the face. *Of course!* He chastised himself for not thinking of it sooner. No other explanation made sense. The goblins needed Wally to tell their story!

"They're using him," he said after some thought.

Fritz drained his entire glass in a single swallow and ripped a belch equal to that of his father who had just belched. Daniel was not impressed. "We know they won't kill him without cause, at least not until they get what they wanted from him. I agree with Father. Wally is safe for the time being."

Daniel cocked his head in disbelief. "Safe?"

"As in not dead," Angus supplied.

"I should have stayed home," Daniel muttered. Frustrations mounting, he struggled with what he viewed as abandoning his friend to an additional night of torment and the logical decision to wait until the goblins were vulnerable and they had a plan. Inevitably, his military training kicked in. "Fine. We wait until morning. What's the plan? I know you've tackled goblin nests before."

"Yes," Max agreed, clasping his hands as three trays of raw oysters were delivered.

Daniel frowned. *When did he order those?*

Slurping down the first oyster with a host of disgusting noises, Max went on. "We also had the resources of a full dwarven legion. One thousand of the finest warriors you've ever seen. Even then it was a challenge burning them out. Why, the largest nest I ever saw had well over twenty thousand of the little monsters in it. A tough, but honorable fight."

"How are the five of us supposed to fight twenty thousand?" Daniel dolloped a lump of horseradish on his oyster and squirted it with lemon and let the oyster slide into his mouth.

"That's a good question." Max grinned. The tips of his teeth, stained brown from what Daniel assumed was a lifetime of coffee, tobacco, and who knew what else, poked under his moustache. "Best figured out over a full stomach and a clear head. Eat. Who knows when our next meal will come."

Begrudgingly, Daniel settled into the oysters; Hayf following his lead. Daniel wasn't sure if this was dwarven humor or prebattle traditions. He hoped the oysters were fresh. The last thing he needed was a constant string of trips to the bathroom while attempting to root out the goblins and rescue Wally.

Just when he thought his day could not get any stranger, Hayf dabbed the napkin over his lips and asked the table, "Have any of you ever been to jail?"

Catching the attention of their server, Daniel motioned for another beer. He had a feeling he was going to need it.

TWENTY-SEVEN

Daniel passed his gaze to each dwarf in turn, studying their reactions to Hayf's question. None of them had spoken since. An ominous sign. The brothers had fully absorbed themselves in their meal. A disgusting effort to alleviate the restaurant, and possibly the entire eastern seaboard, of oysters. Butter and cocktail sauce-stained fingers left wide streaks on their napkins. At one point, Daniel felt his stomach turn and he slid his plate away unfinished. Thankfully, the wind carried the aroma of raw seafood back toward the river.

Hayf ate hesitantly, almost as if he feared he was footing the bill because of his status as a government employee. Daniel wouldn't put it past the dwarves if they expected this. The watcher mumbled through bites, offering what tidbits of information D.E.S.A. had on the goblin nest in the hopes of finding the Schneiders' good graces. Their clipped questions usually required detailed answers, which Daniel saw had the man sweating.

Daniel decided Hayf was no threat. The man seemed competent enough, for government spy. The last agent he worked with had been turned by the queen and nearly cost him the mission. Daniel settled his sights on the one person capable of bringing their plans to ruin, or fruition. Max Schneider was an enigma wrapped in a hardened exterior. His gruff demeanor and impossible attitude made him an island, even among his obstinate sons. Burly, rough around the edges, and filled with enough vinegar to pickle a redwood, the dwarf patriarch commanded the area. It took little imagination to envision him dominating a battlefield through sheer will alone. Any weakness he might have remained buried under years of experience, making him more dangerous than even the lich, Damon Pender, in Daniel's estimation. He was the one to watch.

Max wiped his mouth and let out a table vibrating belch. Looking Daniel in the eye, he tossed the shell down and said, "If you have anything to say I suggest you do it now where there are plenty enough witnesses around."

"What are your intentions down in the nest?" Daniel had been prepared for the wave of animosity flowing his way. "I don't give a damn about any vendettas or clan nonsense. I'm here to get my friend out, at the queen's command. Anything else is your issue."

"Is it now, lad?" Eyes the color of obsidian on a cold night on him had him suppressing a shiver. "I don't seem to recall hearing she placed you in command."

"She did," Fritz muttered. "In so many words."

"Did she? Morgen never did have much sense," Max said with a grimace. "You and me, we aren't going to see eye to eye. Not on this. Not on anything. Me and my boys will clear out that nest, give you the diversion you need to sneak your little buddy away—if he hasn't been served as the main course yet, and be done before the sun goes down."

"You're not inspiring any confidence," Daniel told him with as much grit as he could manage. "This isn't an extermination raid. This is a rescue op."

Angus popped a hush puppy in his mouth and, amidst chewing, said, "Just like dragging those boys out of the Chinese P.O.W. camp up on the Yalu River in 51. We can do this, Pop."

"Is there anything—"

The stare down between Daniel and Max drove the server away before she finished.

"You think so, do you, Angus?" Max asked through clenched teeth. His wilting glare remained locked on Daniel. "With this storyteller? He ain't the one, lads."

"He's a veteran," Fritz added. "And he was alongside us from Raleigh all the way to the zoo during the night Alvin died. He's fine in my book."

"That so? Where'd you serve?"

Daniel made a deliberate show of drinking water before answering. He might have to readjust his opinion of Angus once this was done. "I did some time in Bosnia back in the 90s. After that I was in a firebase on the Afghan-Pakistan border hunting Bin Laden and went to Iraq with the 101st Airborne for the invasion. I did my time."

"Good fights," Max admitted. "All right. For now, this is a rescue op. But I'm in command. I'm the only one who has been down in those tunnels and knows how the goblin think. You follow my lead and we all come home again in one piece, including your little friend. Take it or leave it."

"Fine by me, as long as we follow the queen's guidelines," Daniel replied. He tensed when Max tensed. This was the make or break moment he dreaded. A push too far in either direction and it all fell apart. Fickle as dwarves were, he feared the Schneider patriarch might collect his sons and head back for home, leaving Daniel in the lurch and signing a certain death warrant for Wally. He didn't breathe again until Max extended a hand. Daniel shook his, fighting to keep the pain from his eyes as bones cracked from the pressure.

"What about him?" Daniel gestured to Hayf.

"I'm here to observe and report. Nothing else." He wanted no part in their quest. "The agency won't get involved unless I request support."

"Deal. Dawn it is. Looks like we get to go to prison after all," Max said with a nod and resumed his meal.

Unsure at the meaning for the end of that comment, it was then Daniel noticed that passersby avoided them. There too were a pair of police officers lingering beneath a palm, they met his gaze.

When Angus belched, Daniel focused back on the table. How any of them were going to avoid being sick in the morning was beyond him. Daniel figured the dwarves had already put away over a hundred oysters. The question of payment came to mind when the waitress ventured back to give them their check. Sara would kill him if he offered, prices being what they were. Thankfully, Max slapped an Amex on the table. *Problem solved.*

"Now, where do we get some shut eye around?" Max asked.

From the corner of his eye Daniel saw that the officers were sauntering off.

Hayf stirred after a kick in the ankle from Daniel. "Leave that to me. I can book a set of rooms at one of the nicer hotels about a block up the street. On D.E.S.A's dime of course."

"Good man. We should keep him around just in case," Max said. "This is going to be fun. You'll see. Best we turn in now and rest up. Tomorrow is going to be a long day."

He motioned for their reluctant server to close out the tab, leaving Hayf to organize their sleeping arrangements.

Standing outside their hotel, overlooking the calming waves of the Ashley River lapping against the marina, Daniel tried to think of happier times. Rows of boats stretched back toward the Battery. Sea birds nestled in for the night. Music and lights bumped as the local bar dished out as much merriment as tourists could handle. Another time, he would have enjoyed this visit. His heart longed to return to Sara and their family. As much as he loved this city, being here without her felt wrong. They had been part of each other's lives for a long time now. It was Sara who helped him pick up the pieces of a broken marriage and find renewed purpose in life. Together, they were unstoppable. Or so he thought before she reached out to Blackmere. *How many ripples is this going to create?*

The soft kiss of water mingled with the few beers he had at dinner, rendering him sentimental when he least needed it. They were heading into a combat operation tomorrow and he needed a clear head to find Wally and maintain both the known variables the dwarves presented as well as the unknowns of the goblin nest. If the creatures were willing to violate so many treaties with their emboldened move, he knew they wouldn't be playing by the rules. The thought of the goblins being manipulated crossed his mind but without any reason to suspect otherwise, he let it pass.

Charleston was sitting on a powder keg waiting to explode and no one aside from them had a clue. Dependability left him in desperate situations too many times in the past. Renowned for his ability to conduct himself under pressure, Daniel prayed for clarity. Which shouldn't be a problem considering how many church steeples dominated the old town district. He slipped out of his shoes and socks to dip his feet in the cooling water and pulled out his phone to make a call.

They had a lot to discuss.

Pacing from wall to wall in room, Hayf Mansour found himself in an unusual predicament. He might easily lose his job for bungling the assignment. Assets weren't ever supposed to make contact or allow themselves to be made by their targets. Yet here he stood, a victim of his own making. A litany of repercussions detailed in full decorated a healthy chunk of the D.E.S.A. manual. His future was on the line and, depending on the mood of his handler, his ability to continue with the assignment. Hayf calmed his nerves with a quick prayer and picked up the phone. Time for his standard check in.

Midnight edged closer and neither brother could sleep. They lay in their beds flipping through old comedy reruns and horrible movies compliments of hotel programming. Clothing was draped across chair backs, ready to slip into at a moment's notice. Fritz and Angus were seasoned professionals, even if time had passed since their last combat mission.

"Do you think we can do it?" Fritz asked during a commercial break. "We haven't tackled goblins in a long time and if what Morgen suspects is true? We may be biting off more than we can chew."

"Let someone else worry about that," Angus dismissed. "We know what to do, just like dear old Father said. Besides, that man is going to take the brunt of the mission, just like he always has."

"He raised us."

"Mother raised us. He was barely there," Angus countered. "We may be his blood kin, but we're not alike. Don't forget that. He's dangerous and just as likely to go off on one of his berserker fits as maintain a level head." Berserker rage was infamous among the dwarf families but one of those matters few spoke of. Doing so invited temptation. Fritz spat, warding off any foul spirits invoked by his brother's flippant remark. He knew full well the effects of their father's rage. "We will be there to ensure he doesn't," he said. Another worry came to mind that he voiced, "Angus, I don't see how we can find one human among thousands of goblins and get him out alive."

Angus hit the pause button on the tv, the characters animatedly gesturing in the background, and tossed the remote down on his comforter. "What are you saying? That we're going to die down there?" He glared.

"I'm saying none of this feels right," Fritz countered.

Angus paused, running his fingers through his beard in thought. "Maybe, but it's too late to turn back now. The only thing we can do is watch each other's backs and do our best to bring everyone home alive. That's it."

"I hope that will be enough," Fritz lamented. "Mother will be furious otherwise."

Through the wall he could hear his father snoring.

TWENTY-EIGHT

Morgen pushed her plate away and offered a complimentary smile to the man seated across from her. The dining room was filled with many of the city's most influential citizens; businessmen and politicians mostly with tech overlords and sports figures immersed in the local colleges as well. Morgen wined and dined with the elites nightly, conducting power meetings in the back rooms she claimed as her own to maintain her social standing and accrue favors.

Tonight, one of North Carolina's state congressmen was her guest. A shrewd man known for unpopular opinions and managing a tight purse during each election cycle. Salt and pepper hair and a charming smile carried him far on the election trail, ensuring he remained a government staple for the past three decades. Morgen found him a limited man with tempered expectations and a quiet degree of corruptibility. Certainly not one striving to attain higher office after he gotten his current position. She appreciated his aspirational honesty though, having sunk her claws into him years ago. Men like that became useful, to a degree.

"Another wonderful meal, Morgen," he said with a satisfied gleam in his eye. "You certainly know how to host."

"Congressman, as much as I would love to claim credit for this marvelous meal you know it was the chef." She made her voice golden, seductive, as if it was a song upon the air. "It has been too long since our last meal."

"Indeed it has," he replied, his southern accent thick with a drawl. The twinkle in his eye clashed with his natural arrogance. "I suppose now it's time to get down to business though. Never did like mixing fine meals with work talk."

"We do as we must, Colin," Morgen replied. "I was hoping to learn a little more about the state of the construction proposal on Saunders Street. My investors are anxious to break ground."

"Thank the city for that. All the usual red tape," Colin admitted. He glanced around the dining room to ensure no one was eavesdropping before continuing. "Between you and me, I don't see what the delay was, but the governor tries to do what he wants, regardless of who controls the purse."

"And my special concessions?" Morgen pressed. She brightened as the server brought their desserts. Fresh key lime pie for her with a cup of coffee and a slice of red velvet cake for him. "Will they be emplaced?"

"As agreed, Morgen. You have my word."

An inevitable conclusion, Morgen seldom found sport in manipulating human affairs. This current project meant little to the clans. If anything, it increased revenue to the broken throne. D.E.S.A. may regulate modern affairs but it held little claim to monetary compensation or business dealings so long as they complied with the letter of the law. She pretended to offer her backing for his reelection bid while receiving a boon for her people with no one being wiser.

They finished their meal with mild banter, avoiding important topics of business and local politics with deft talents only those in power developed. Morgen took her last sip of coffee, pausing to dap her lips before noticing Aislinn's slender form striding toward her.

"Colin, if you will excuse me, I'm afraid there are other affairs I must attend," Morgen said. "Please, don't be a stranger. It has been far too long, and I do so enjoy our conversations."

He rose, holding his tie down with his right hand as she walked away.

"I expected you sooner," Morgen chided her assistant after they were clear of the congested parts of the club. "The congressman is a social bore."

"My apologies, your Majesty," Aislinn unbothered. Morgen admitted that her assistant had learned long ago how to ignore the rants and focus on her tasks with a level head. It was why Morgen kept her around.

Settling behind her desk, the queen gestured for her to continue.

"The dwarves have entered Charleston and are hunting for the nest."

"But?" Morgen pressed, sensing the hesitation with a degree of concern.

Aislinn cleared her throat. "They have their father with them and have been in contact with local DESA personnel."

Anger flared. Should D.E.S.A. decide the operation violated sanctions the clans would pay heavily. She already clung to a perilous hold, all it took to push her past the brink and bring the throne crashing down.

"Were my orders not clear? Perhaps those damned Schneiders are hard of hearing," she fumed. "Get me Daniel Thomas on the phone, Aislinn. As if Angus and Fritz weren't bad enough now we have to worry about their trigger-happy father ruining things. Oh, and send in Constantin. I have a feeling this is about to spiral out of control."

"Yes, ma'am."

Aislinn ducked out, leaving her stewing. Unless change came soon, the elf clans would fall to their own incompetence—to her incompetence.

Morgen swiveled her chair around to stare across downtown Raleigh, but she didn't see the lights. She reached for the phone. It was time to call Viviana.

"They're going to do what?" Blackmere crushed his cigarette out in the cheap plastic ashtray, smoke billowing from his nostrils. "Who authorized that?"

"I don't think you know these dwarves, sir," Hayf replied through the speaker phone. Receiving a call from his boss's superior unraveled his thoughts in ways he hadn't considered until now. *Why is he calling me direct? This isn't good.* "They are going into the goblin nest at dawn. Nothing I said swayed them."

Confused and impressed by how fast his asset was made, Blackmere struggled with straightening his thoughts enough to adjust tactics before it was too late. Acts of public violence were officially illegal, making the dwarf actions under Charleston a violation punishable by life in the Grinder. While part of him imagined the pair on one of his clandestine teams, no amount of paperwork or backpedaling could cover this unfolding debacle.

He envisioned the worst, knowing his career was on the line thanks to an innocuous call from Sara Thomas. Frustrated and once again held hostage to matters beyond his control that revolved around the ex-soldier turned author, Blackmere didn't know what it was about the man. His life, and career, had not been the same since that first day Daniel discovered the truth.

"Listen to me, Mansour. They cannot afford to be witnessed or noticed until the matter is concluded. Am I clear in this?" Blackmere said.

A pause and huff of surprise. "You don't want me to keep trying to dissuade them?"

Blackmere snorted. "Have you met a dwarf? Once they latch onto something they don't let go until it's over. Keep them from taking this into the human realm as much as you can. Oh, and Hayf, if matters get too far out of control do not hesitate to evacuate the situation. We are a shadow organization for a reason. If this gets out to the local media heads will roll. Yours most of all."

"Yes, sir. I understand," Hayf said fast enough Blackmere knew he did. "I am leading them to the Old City Jail at dawn. From there we will take a hidden tunnel into the goblin nest. They are most insistent on rescuing this human, but I sense the dwarves have something far more sinister in mind."

"We do not involve ourselves in their affairs unless there is the potential of exposing the clans," Blackmere reminded. "Report back in the morning and do not, I repeat, do not enter that nest with them. This isn't our fight."

"Even with humans involved?" Hayf questioned.

Blackmere paused, staring at the last wisps of smoke tickling from the ashtray. One of the benefits of working from home, though his wife admonished him for smoking each time he lit up regardless of whether it was on the back deck or not. For all her chastising, he doubted it was the cigarettes that were going to be the end of him.

"Thomas knows the deal," he replied after silencing the warring voices in his head. The louder voice cried to rush down there and pull Daniel out. It was the quiet voice whispering for him to roll the dice and see what happened. He hated being trapped between them. "He made his choices, Hayf."

"Yes, sir."

Blackmere hung up, unsure whether he made the right decision. "God damn it, Daniel. What are you dragging us into this time?"

Sara settled into the leather bucket seat and closed the door. The smell of Old Spice filled her nostrils, reminding her of her grandfather's bathroom all those years ago. That familiarity, coupled with her comfort around the bulking figure in the driver's seat calmed her rising nerves.

At the gargoyle's silence, she stared out at her front lawn, admiring the way the soft pink knockout roses looked under the solar lights nestled beneath a stand of crepe myrtles. The bushes accented her white home with dark trim, lending it an almost majestic feel complete with wrought iron railings on the stairs and a custom-made wrought iron double door that was the envy of the neighborhood.

None of that beauty and accomplishment lessened the worry in her heart for the man she loved. Well, maybe the twin Bernese Mountain Dog faces peering out at her anxiously awaiting her return did a little. *Had I fed the dogs dinner yet?* She knew better than to ask them but admitted to being distracted. Sara's mind had been unfocused since Daniel first informed her about Wally's situation. While she did not know the man well, having only met him briefly for drinks one night and dinner another, she admired Daniel's conviction.

That he might be a victim of believing his own invincibility concerning elves rattled her. Daniel was a strong personality despite his desire for a quiet life. Trouble seemed to follow him since he stumbled into the world of the elves and, by association, attached her too. She failed to find the allure of rushing into danger, but then again, she had never been a soldier. Reports suggested that addiction to adrenalin remained long after they left military service.

She saw it resurface with Daniel at the worst moments. Thus far he managed to keep it from their children, separating those worlds with surprising deftness. Knowing this did not help Sara, not with the future of her family riding on tomorrow's actions. She needed someone to talk to and, since none of her friends were privileged enough to know about the elves, that left the resolute gargoyle who had taken it upon himself to be her personal warder.

"Good evening, Sara Thomas," Norman Guilt's rumbling voice filled the car. "I did not expect to see you this evening."

"Norman, thank you for coming on short notice," she replied. "I appreciate it."

"This is about Daniel," he guessed after another pause stretched into awkward silence.

She nodded, biting her lower lip gently.

"You are worried."

Sara wanted to scream, irrationally infuriated with the slow understanding of human nature the gargoyle continued exhibiting. She failed to understand how anyone just did not get it. Far from a natural conversationalist, Norman Guilt remained resolute in his approach to dealing with elves and humans.

"When is the last time you heard from him?" he prompted.

"Earlier tonight. He's in over his head. He won't say so, but I can feel it, Norman. He's in trouble. He won't admit it, but I know better. He's in trouble and there is nothing I can do about it other than sit here, worry, and wait."

The gargoyle nodded. "Ever the plight of those left behind when their other goes to war. You must find your Zen, Sara Thomas. It will set you free and allow you to regain control of your life while he is gone. Besides, goblins are not lycans."

"Great. Thank you for that, Buddha," she quipped, pausing to wipe away the tears building. "I'm sorry for lashing out. This is as stressful as his combat deployments."

He laid a hand, massive and rocklike yet surprisingly soft, on her knee. "All will be fine, Sara. You must trust Daniel. He has experience in these matters."

"He's not the one I'm worried about," she explained. "Do you know the Schneider brothers by chance?"

Sara saw that Norman stiffened, as if such were possible for a gargoyle. "There are few who do not."

"Are they reliable?"

Norman's mouth opened and closed several times before he said, "That depends."

"On what?"

"Whether you want them to find trouble or not."

So much for Zen. Sara resumed staring at her home.

TWENTY-NINE

"This is it?" Max asked through a beer stench yawned that had Daniel coughing.

Ignoring him, the elder dwarf stared up at the dilapidated building, looking unimpressed. A rickety staircase led up to the second floor, complete with broken boards and cobwebs from the jail's current residents. Well past it's prime, the jail looked more like it needed tearing down than remodeling. Empty windows stared down on them like missing teeth, lending a supernatural air to the surroundings. Posted advertisements talked of ghost hunters and paranormal obsessives who flocked to the Old City Jail in the hopes of contacting the numerous spirits rumored to haunt it. They invited viewers to join them on their socials to be in on the action too.

Daniel's lone brush with the paranormal at the Fainting Goat in New York had left him unsettled for weeks after. He wasn't interested in following any ghost investigators for their experiences or scary stories. Staring up at the jail, wreathed in predawn gloom, he understood why people looked over their shoulders in the dark, especially here.

From what he knew, the jail was first built in 1802 and closed in 1939 with the reputation of one of the country's most notorious prisons. Over fourteen thousand inmates died while the building was in operation. It was on this spot America's first female serial killer, Lavinia Fisher uttered her infamous last words— *"If you have a message you want sent to Hell, give it to me; I'll carry it"*—before she was hung. Legend said her ghost continued to haunt the jail today.

Daniel was reminded of those bad places he was warned not to go as a child, only to discover the urge too strong to ignore. He shuddered, envisioning nameless torments lingering in those dark, forgotten corners of a building that had borne witness to endless pain and suffering.

"One of the worst prisons in history," Hayf explained as they lingered on the sidewalk. "The secret tunnels are below."

Max cast a disparaging look at the human. "Worst human prison perhaps. We have done worse to ourselves."

"There's no point in standing around," Daniel interrupted, preventing Hayf from sticking a foot in his mouth. A shivered as a stiff breeze caught him, nestling down between his body armor and neck. "I take it we have to go inside?"

Nodding, Hayf gestured to the ominous staircase on the prison's backside where Daniel saw a local ghost tour facility had a sign pointed in that direction. "We do. It will be easiest to go through this door and then down."

"Why not the front door?" Angus asked.

"Too much security. Police will be on us in no time."

The sky continued brightening. Not quite light, but neither was it still dark. Hayf looked anxious, shifting side to side. They had at least twelve hours before sunset, leaving more than enough time to accomplish their goals. It was the unknown which spurred him to action. Countless variables threatening to undermine his objectives before he began. Leaving his companions debating the merits of breaking into private property directly or indirectly, Daniel headed back to the truck to gear up.

The short stock carbine he selected reminded him of his army time. Daniel snatched a several magazines, stuffing them in ammunition pouches on his vest and cargo pockets. Strapping a knife to his left boot, Daniel reached for a handful of grenades Goran the armorer swore were perfect for assaulting a goblin nest. He didn't know what that meant but ensured he took plenty before the dwarves sank their greedy hands into the small arsenal. A pair of 9mm Glocks completed his armament. Daniel shifted the assault pack, adjusting for the additional weight of the magazines, and waited.

The dwarves soon joined him, eager to dive into their favorite weapons. Daniel watched as Angus snatched the light machinegun before either his brother or father claimed it, tossing drums of belt-fed ammunition into his pack and loading another two hundred round belt. His ever-present battleaxe was strapped upon his back before he stepped aside.

Fritz and Max kitted out similarly, each weighed down with enough ammunition to pacify a small nation. Seemingly unburdened by their loads, the dwarven trio presented a most formidable force. Daniel almost felt sorry for the goblins. Almost.

"What about you, slim?" Max asked Hayf.

The asset waved the dwarf off. "Sorry. I have my orders from Washington. I'm supposed to see you here and wait for your return. Agent Blackmere was insistent."

Max glanced at his sons. "Have humans always been this soft?"

"It's a new generation," Angus replied. He studied Daniel before asking, before "Ready?"

"Let's go."

Step by step, on unsteady legs, the small group crossed the lot and made the climb. A sense of foreboding settled over Daniel the instant Hayf picked the locks and shoved the door open with a metal scream. A small fortress, the jail felt alive. Hair stood on end on the backs of his hands, forcing him to calm his nerves before they got the best of him.

The jail was every bit as intimidating in the half-dark as he imagined. Iron bars, aged boards, and, perhaps most haunting of all, a discarded wheelchair strategically placed for dramatic effect on the landing directly ahead of them created a miasmic atmosphere of mental manipulation. Daniel focused on the mission. He jumped as the door thumped closed behind him. Darkness swallowed them.

"Down the stairs and to the left," Hayf instructed. "We still have a few hours before the tour staff arrives to prepare for tonight. Plenty to get you into the nest."

Noticing he left out *and back*, Daniel gripped his rifle a little tighter.

They wormed through the jail behind the blinding power of Max's headlamp. Brushing aside cobwebs as the mythos of the jail dispelled in the light, Daniel soon found himself standing before an iron banded door that did not appear to have been used in the last fifty years.

"All right, the tunnel is directly behind this door. It will take you to the rear of the goblin nest," Hayf explained.

"How far?" Fritz asked.

"Less than a mile." At their grunts, he added, "Sorry, this is the closest I can get you. The only other entrance we know of is under the Provost Marshal office but that will be heavily guarded, especially if the goblins are preparing to act."

"You're sure the tunnel isn't blocked or guarded? We are taking an awful risk here, Hayf," Daniel asked as the watcher unlocked the door and pushed it open.

A musky draft pushed out in a cloud of dust and debris. The tunnel stank of death. Yet another reminder of the nature of the creatures Daniel faced. He looked over his shoulder at Hayf and glared.

"What? There's nothing I can do about the smell."

"No, I thought I saw something behind you."

At the watcher's stiffening, Daniel ignored him and stared into the shadows, convinced he had seen a face leering back at them. One unkempt and garbed in tattered prison clothes.

Angus scoffed. "Nothing is there."

Daniel tried and failed to swallow the lump constricting his throat. The image broke into a leering grin before dissipating into the ether. *I need to get out of here. This place is screwy.*

"Boo!" Fritz laughed. "Come on, don't go getting all spooked on us now."

At the head of their little column, already swathed in the natural darkness of the tunnel, Max hefted his rifle over his shoulder. "Agent man, are you sure this tunnel rans straight? No branching off or possibility of going the wrong direction?"

"I believe it is a straight shot, like I said. Get into the nest and then back out."

Grunting, Max considered the merits of what he considered a cramped battlespace. No actionable intelligence on potential secondary tunnels or open spaces reduced his ability to prepare. They could hold off the entire nest without much problem if this was the only tunnel. Disgruntled, he opted to believe Hayf. Max calculated the distance with how much time it would take to search the nest. Neither projection offered much inspiration. He preferred a clear field of fire and overwhelming superiority.

"That'll do," he said, noticing everyone was getting antsy. "Any nasties down here we need to know about?"

"Our files don't mention anything," Hayf replied. He gestured to the dust coated ceiling and said, "The jail is supposed to haunted, but we haven't heard anything about the tunnel. You have about eight hours to reach the nest, rescue your friend, and return before the ghost tour outfit shows up to prep for the night."

"Right. No time to waste," Max said. "We move now. Single file. Keep your heads on a swivel. I'm point. Fritz, Daniel, Angus next. Agent man, you bring up the rear."

"My name is Hayf," he bristled. "And I'm not coming."

"Good for you, kid. You are." He grunted. "Let's go. I'm tired of waiting." Max stepped forward and paused. "One last thing. We don't go in guns blazing. Not until we secure the target. We do it right and there's no need for the mayhem."

"But I have orders," Hayf protested.

Max spun on him. "And I'm changing them. Look, relax. You're in good hands. We got this. Walk in the park."

"Doesn't sound like you," Angus commented as he dropped the barrel of his machine gun.

"Yeah, well, you get older, and you get a little wiser. Besides, if I know Morgen she'll be putting together an expedition to wipe the nest out soon enough. Might as well save some strength to join the fight when it matters. Any other pointless comments?"

Exchanging a suspicious look, his sons glumly shook their heads.

"Good. On me. No light from here on out. Nods only." He lowered his night vision goggles over his face and headed into the long dark with a pace suggesting total surety.

Daniel figured dwarves were natural cave dwellers, leaving them almost at home in the dark. However, Fritz and Angus both lowered their night goggles, prompting him to do the same. Whether he was uncomfortable or not, moving in the middle of the column offered a modicum of protection. He didn't feel good about Hayf pulling rearguard though, especially with the man now breathing heavily behind him. The man wasn't a fighter, and they all knew it. Perhaps that's why Max set him where they didn't have to rely on him.

"Daniel, can you talk to him?" Hayf whispered. "I'm not an agent. I'm just an intelligence asset. A watcher, remember? Besides, I have orders too. I am not to get involved."

"You think I want to be here? A moment ago, I swear I saw a man standing behind you," Daniel hissed. The rasp echoing off the dry walls. "We do what we must. Period. Nothing I say is going to change his mind. You're in this right along with the rest of us. Sorry, Hayf."

Flustered, Hayf wanted to bellow in rage. Years spent working for D.E.S.A. and he had never once encountered another species, at least none he knew going into his assignments. It was hard enough believing elves and dwarves and God only knew what else walking among us ... It took years to embrace this knowledge and now he found himself in lockstep with creatures that he had avoided till now. Resigning himself to his plight, he glanced over his shoulder to find one of the first aid bags. He hurried to get it before the dwarves advanced too far without him. The prospect of worming through the goblin tunnels alone chilled him.

"Hayf, let's go," Daniel called ahead of him, already hard to see marching into the dark.

"Hold on, we left a bag," he called back and snatched the bag.

He just turned back to the tunnel when the door slammed shut with a resounding clang. A click told him all he needed to know.

"No," he uttered, dropping the bag, and gripping the door handle.

The door didn't budge, no matter how hard he pulled. Fear rose, compounded by the thought of being watched. His skin crawled. The tiny hairs on his arms rising with the flesh. Hayf fumbled through his pockets for the key, only to break it off in the lock in panic. He was cut off from the others, not that he wanted to join their quest in the first place. Unsure how to proceed, he decided it prudent to retreat and contact Washington. Perhaps Agent Blackmere would have a better idea what to do. Offering a heartfelt prayer, Hayf grabbed the bag and hurried up the stairs, certain he was being watched.

THIRTY

Daniel watched, numb, as the door refused to budge. They had quickly gathered when it slammed shut—and locked. *What the—*

The impact sent tremors through Fritz. No matter how hard the dwarf struck, the door did not budge. Frustrated, Fritz slammed an open palm on the aged wood and rusted steel; Daniel was surprised it didn't even bulk under the force. "It's not moving. We're stuck here."

"Could be magic," Angus offered. "Goblin shamans like to do things like this."

"Fucking DESA," Max snarled. "Department of Extra Species Affairs. Bah! I knew he was going to betray us."

"It wasn't Hayf," Daniel muttered. "He wouldn't sell us out like that."

"Says you."

Bristling, Daniel held back his thoughts on whether Hayf was working with them or against them. The last thing any of them needed was a confrontation in such a confined space. "Doesn't matter, does it? We're here and the nest is that way. Let's get this over with."

"Only it does matter, Daniel," Fritz countered, his voice calm and measured. "That was our exit strategy."

"Plan's changed. Now we know no one is coming on us from behind. We don't have time to sit here and figure things out," Max growled.

Daniel knew he was right. Arguing solved nothing. Someone or something, he still had reservations about the reality of ghosts, shut the door and ensured they could not open it. He had seen Hayf had been too far away, leaning down to grab a solo black pack, leaving the unpleasant possibility of supernatural involvement. Without knowing where they were in relation to where they needed to get to, Daniel felt the walls of doubt creeping in until Max snapped, "Same orders. Daniel at the rear. Let's go."

They started off slow through an access point dating back to the American Revolution. The deeper into the near mile long tunnel they traversed the more the walls took on a primitive appeal. Gone was the smoothness and brickwork near the entrance. The floor changed from cobblestone to dirt, untouched by human boots for generations. From the looks of it, Daniel doubted even the goblins used this tunnel.

The air bore a musky taint. Stale but breathable. That initial smell of death was gone at least. Daniel took shorter breaths to compensate for the smell. It reminded him of crypts he'd seen in old horror movies. *What untold monsters awaited us when we reached our destination?* Puffs of dust kicked up with each step, leaving a trail lingering in the air before resettling. Not a footprint remained leaving Daniel reconsidering his earlier thought that it was unused by the goblins. He thanked their luck the tunnel ran straight. Otherwise, they might never find their way out.

Focus. Wally is close, I hope. He had no experience with goblins and what he thought he knew stemmed from ragged old copies of Dungeons & Dragons books. It took little to imagine a vast cavern filled with fires, refuse, and waste. Throngs of bodies sleeping atop each other in the filth. Mangy creatures of boils and pustules, green skin covered in patches of wiry hair. Having already encountered enough gnomes to form a slight opinion, Daniel wanted nothing to do with goblins.

Any questions he had were silenced by the domineering attitude Max Schneider cast over the group. The brothers followed their father's lead, despite any reservations Angus displayed on their way to collect the old dwarf.

Odd man out, Daniel followed suit. There were enough waves between dwarf and human. Creating more served no purpose.

Daniel hated not knowing what to expect. The fog of war always presented uncontrollable variables, inspiring creative leadership decisions. One's he wasn't making right now. Vagaries of battle aside, Daniel felt their initial plan lacked enough details to properly execute. For their part, the dwarves appeared confident in their actions, both present and future. They also were disinclined to share the totality of their knowledge. He surmised the animosity between goblin and dwarf went back thousands of years. This natural hatred, evidenced by Max's aggressive attitude the closer they got to the nest, suggested one or more of the dwarves was going to go off script, endangering the mission.

Unable to proceed without their help and sanctioned by the queen, Daniel floundered as he kept his rifle pointed down and marched on. He had no way of knowing what to expect, what he would find upon entering the nest. The best way to help Wally was by trusting the dwarves to see them through. A trust he did not feel. *I should've trusted Sara enough to call Blackmere in the first place. Stupid me.*

He tried putting himself in a subordinate role, just as he had been the first time he deployed. That mindset kept him alive. The old adage of 'shut up and do what you're told' allowed him to shake free the worries gripping his squad and platoon leaders and allowed him to assault the mission with the vigor of a trained warrior. Knowing he needed to do so now helped improve his attitude.

If the dwarves were aware of his mental dilemma they did not comment. He presumed each was lost in their own private thoughts, having a little rehashing of the dwarf and goblin conflict. Daniel never expected to get along with any of them, nor find common ground. His past adventure with Angus and Fritz showed him the veracity of dwarves and given their propensity for violence, formed an opinion that would not change no matter what else occurred.

Their father remained easy to read. Max Schneider was the sort who came as advertised. It took nothing more than a brief conversation for Daniel to reach that conclusion. The further away from Max he was the better. Strong personalities seldom mixed and the natural distrust and animosity the dwarf harbored for humans all but ensured mission failure if they truly clashed in a battle of wills. At least with the brothers he knew where he stood and could operate.

The scuff of boots on compacted dirt added to the sound of heavy breathing, knowing it was him giving them away didn't help his focus. Daniel began sweating, though whether from the exertion or natural humidity of being so far underground remained unclear. The clamminess on his skin felt wrong. He struggled to suppress the urge to turn back and bathe, anything to clean the fetid touch on his skin. His stomach roiled. The suddenness of it filling his mouth with saliva. He wanted to vomit.

A hand on his shoulder, gentle and reassuring, broke the spell. He glanced at Fritz and nodded his appreciation. The dwarf's head dipped a fraction, and they kept walking. Able to see clearer, Daniel realized what had caused the sudden illness—magic. His entire body revolted from it. Yet all it took was a light touch to relieve the pressure.

"What was that?" his voice carrying despite whispering.

"An old spell," Fritz replied. "There will be more the closer we get. Be thankful that the spell was breaking down. Otherwise, we all would be on the ground in convulsions."

Great. Just another reason to despise goblins. Daniel adjusted the grip on his rifle. Max and Angus were already plowing ahead, undeterred and steadfast in their desire to close with the enemy. Fearing what might happen if the duo broke loose before finding Wally, Daniel picked up the pace. *Get in. Secure the target. Get out.* He hated reducing any life to *target*, especially since he knew the target personally, but removing emotion from the equation was always the best way to enter a fight.

The rest of the journey proved uneventful. No specters or spells. Max led them straight to the edge of the nest, just as Hayf promised. The ground turned uneven. A foul odor assaulted them, announcing they were arriving at their target. One of the brothers spat a mouthful of bile. Max kept going. By now Daniel knew it was only going to get worse. If the nest had been rebuilt like the dwarves mentioned, thousands of goblins were ahead of them. Perhaps more than the dwarves could handle. More than he could handle.

Daniel slowed his pace, pausing to ensure his magazine was fully loaded and rifle still on safe. The last thing they needed was an accidental discharge. He had seen friendlies killed by such ignorance, making it a cardinal sin in a combat zone. Doing what he knew was right did not mean the dwarves followed his example. He had little doubt one or more of them was ready to engage right now. The uncomfortable weight of the pack dug into his shoulders as he came to a halt. Raw pain, burning through muscles that had not been worked like this in years reminded him of some of the worst parts of being in the army. Then again, he was never smart enough to get into a mechanized unit. Most of his career was spent in the Airborne Corps and his body paid a toll for that bravado. A bad back, bad knees, and more aches than he admitted to Sara dogged his days. It was the knowledge he got to go home to his soft bed and a hot bath to soak those aching muscles that was keeping him going.

They huddled just out of range of the glowing reddish light a few hundred meters ahead. Every instinct screamed to go back, even as the trivial part of his mind replayed the Fellowship's journey through Moria. He almost started humming. A fact he did not find prudent to mention to any of the dwarves. Not if he wanted to keep his head attached.

Max had them circle and take a knee the moment they had enough space to spread out. He clicked his goggles off and raised them, pausing to wipe his eyes as he got acclimated to the quasi-light. They followed suit. His gaze went to each of his sons, silently determining their fitness for what came next. He paused on Daniel.

"Right," he whispered, which wasn't saying much for a dwarf. "This is the edge of the nest. If what the agent man said is true, we are about to catch them from behind. I imagine the human is being kept somewhere in the center, close to the nest leadership. Getting him is going to be difficult. The goblins may be asleep, but they will have guards out. Everyone ready?"

Hayf wanted to shout in frustration at the lack of cell service. This was the third spot he had tried. "Why doesn't anything ever go according to plan? Stupid dwarves. Stupid me for letting myself get made. How in the hell am I supposed to explain this to Blackmere?"

Muttering as he gave up trying to find service, he had already given up on opening the door minutes ago, he re-hefted the bag of weapons and hurried back through the prison. People would be arriving soon, according to the time on his watch. The last he needed was to get caught carrying a bag of illegal weapons on private property.

Assets did not get the same get out of jail free card as agents—*Blackmere had reminded me of this.*

Hayf hurried up the steps, tripping over his feet when seeing how the staged wheelchair now faced in the opposite direction from when they came in and ran out the back door.

A quick look around showed the surrounding neighborhood was clear and, thankfully, the truck was still there. Hayf exhaled a sigh of relief and went to lock the door to avoid any suspicion. At least this time he didn't break the key.

He froze. There, just feet inside the prison from a nearby window, fading in and out of reality with the filtering sun, stood three figures. One raised its arm and pointed at him.

Join us.

Join us.

Join us.

Jerking the door closed, he locked it and fled down the steps. All while feeling like he had left a piece of his soul behind, feeding the creatures of the Old City Jail.

He didn't stop running until he hopped in the truck, thankful for the dwarves leaving a spare key under the hood. Lowering his head to the steering wheel and trying to come up with how to call the debacle in. Worse than that, he had no idea how he was going to link up with Daniel and the others once they, if they, secured the other human.

"I hate my job," Hayf said and pulled out his cell phone.

THIRTY-ONE

Some days the words and illustrations flowed. Others felt like being stranded in the middle of the desert with no sign of water for days. Wally found himself trapped in the uncomfortable in-between. Dozens of half-completed images depicting prehistoric events littered a handful of pages. Some had words, some did not. It was more than he accomplished thus far yet nowhere near what Crispus demanded. The idea of forcing creativity rattled him. Wally worked at his own pace, setting manageable deadlines while producing high quality content.

Lines crowded the dark bags under his eyes; he had seen a glimpse of himself in a tray they brought in. His eyes were burning the longer he stared at the paper before him. His fingers shriveled with cramps. He felt terrible. Irma Stain ensured he had plenty of food, though he passed on the rancid meat and drank only the minimum of the brackish water. He failed to see how goblins survived on any of it. Knowing he had only been a prisoner for a few days, three at the most by his estimation, Wally felt weaker than he had ever been.

Dehydrated and cramping from not moving like he usually did, Wally wanted nothing more than to collapse and sleep, hopefully forgetting any of this happened somewhere along the way. He was just turning towards his bed when Irma and Crispus arrived, one looking hopeful, the other anxious with a hint of anger.

"Hi Wally!" Irma gave a small wave.

Wally tossed his head in silent reply. He remained focused on his work.

Crispus was not as welcoming. "I see images. Some words. Scatterings of ideas, but nothing suggesting we have made progress. Very disappointing, Wally."

"Look, man, I already told you. I—"

"I am afraid it no longer matters what you say. You are to be held accountable. Punishment will be decided by the nest."

"Whoa! Punishment? You can't do that!" Wally sputtered. "I'm trying, man. I'm doing what you wanted. Creativity doesn't work like that. I keep telling you this!"

At a shuffling sound, Wally looked to see as one of the guards peeked into his chamber, narrowed eyes. Wally felt his back against the wall with no way out. The closest goblins were shifting and stirring towards him even as the rest of the nest prepared to bed down.

Irma's worried face slipped between her Nest Father and him. Meeting Wally's gaze, she turned away and gnawed at a broken nail.

Crispus shook his head. "It is too late. The Nest Witch has called a trial."

Eyes bulging, Wally asked, "What witch? Trial? What are the charges?"

"The worst possible charge you can imagine," Crispus said and motioned for the guards. "Bring him."

Goblins soon surrounded Wally, prodding him with sharpened sticks when they thought he moved too slow. He went, sullen and defeated. They wormed through a sea of camping tents, mud huts, and burning fires. Wally's mind blurred into a daze. He failed to spot any landmarks or features showing him the way to freedom; not that he remembered much from when they brought him in. Even if he saw an exit there was no way he could run through the nest. It took little imagination to see him hanging beside Jimmy, forgotten and abused until the next poor soul replaced him.

He wondered how much pain he could endure before giving up another name. Would he? Betraying a friend chilled him. Wally would never be able to live with himself if he gave a friend to the goblins. No one deserved the nightmare of being captive to the goblin nest. Steeling himself for the inevitability of his fate thanks to his perceived failures, Wally shoved aside any negative thoughts and focused on his wife.

Knowing she must be getting worried by now… Thoughts of at least fighting for his life, for her, arose. He knew he was good for a few of the swarthy creatures, maybe more before the others would beat him down. Anything was better than the façade of a trial and punishment.

His hopes plummeted upon seeing the massive stone platform looming ahead. Ringed by torches and a score of goblins in ceremonial leather jerkins, knee high boots, and tan pants. Rusted swords hung from their belts and their faces were painted with black stripes. He couldn't write better characters. Too bad that spark of creativity fled the moment Crispus mentioned his trial.

Crispus had the guards lead him up a small flight of steps around the back of the platform; he was halted in the center. He spotted what must be the Nest Witch, a withered and wrinkled old goblin woman clothed only in yellowed bones and bearing a notched staff topped with a fist sized crystal and wreathed in feathers.

Cheers rose from the goblin assembly as Crispus stepped to face the crowd. Wally stared out at hundreds, perhaps a thousand of his captors and knew this was the end. Determined to hold his head high, he stood with feet shoulder width apart and a forced glare. His father always said to meet each new challenge head on and, should the worst occur, accept it, and move on. Those words of wisdom did little to lighten the dread dragging him down. Crispus raised his hands for silence. "Friends, family! I bring before you the man who was meant to be our savior." He turned, jabbing an accusatory finger at Wally.

"This man! This human and usurper of our surface world! Wally Rutherford promised to deliver our story in pictures and words. He has failed. The Nest Witch will determine his crime. Will you abide by her judgment?"

A fresh round of cheers, tinged with bloodthirsty fervor, rose.

Crispus leaned close to Wally and whispered, "I warned you this would happen if you failed."

Before he could reply, the Nest Witch slammed her staff on the rock. The goblins fell silent. Yellow eyes stared up at her in reverence. She spat a wad of black phlegm in her palm and wiped it on the stone. Kneeling, she sifted a finger through the murky liquid. Stiffening, she rose in a flash and stabbed Wally in the chest with her finger.

"Fuckery!"

Fuckery? You have got to be kidding me. Wally wanted to toss his head back and laugh, but instead just stood there, mute and afraid.

Crispus resumed his position to a chorus of gasps, arms raised. "You heard her. The Nest Witch accuses Wally Rutherford of fuckery. What say you?"

"Fuckery."

"Fuckery."

Hundreds of voices echoed the charge until it roared through the nest in a thunderous repetition. Wally's heart sank. A gnawing feeling gripped the pit of his stomach. Hands snatched him, tearing what remained of his clothes. The goblins chanted his crime, building intensity with each chorus. Fires soon blazed, long flames licking the burnt cavern ceiling from tossed torches. Just as Wally was being dragged away to the goblin dungeons the unexpected happened.

He watched as Irma Stain prostrated herself in front of Crispus. Greasy strands of hair draped across her shoulders to touch the rock. "Nest Father. Nest Witch. I beg for Wally Rutherford's life."

"You what?" Crispus gawked.

"What?" Wally echoed, eyes wide in disbelief.

For her part, the Nest Witch clutched her staff tighter but didn't appear surprised. "Let the girl speak."

Forehead kissing the cold rock, Irma said, "I offer myself in tribute. I beg humbly to serve his punishment."

Gasps and muted conversation swept through those gathered.

"You ask what?" Crispus repeated.

"To serve as tribute," Irma affirmed.

"Irma, don't!" Wally tried changing her mind.

"Get up! Do you have any idea what you are saying?" Crispus snapped.

"Yes, Nest Father. I know," she sobbed. A single tear broke free.

"No." Crispus shook his head. "Absolutely not."

"The girl has failed us, Nest Father. She was tasked with ensuring the human completed his task. He did not, nor did she fulfill her purpose. The girl may stand the punishment."

Eyes widening as realization sank in, Crispus Goldfarb relented to the Nest Witch with a nod. True power meant little compared to the dominance of the shamans. "Very well, Irma Stain will stand for Wally Rutherford. Take her away."

Wally watched in horror as guards released him to go and drag the openly weeping Irma away without so much as a protest. Her soft eyes, now filled with tears, stared back at him. He rounded on Crispus and barked, "What are you doing? She's just a child!"

The goblin moved fast, nestling up close to Wally to sneer. "I know that, fool. She is my daughter. I will feast on your bones for this, Wally Rutherford. You will suffer.

Your family will suffer. I will remove the stain of your blood from this planet forever. Take him away!"

Wally started to protest when pain blossomed across the back of his head.

"You know our laws, Crispus. I did what was required."

The Nest Father stopped pacing, making a show of placing his hands behind his back in a display of dominance. "This is not right, Abigail. She is too young to know what she did."

The Nest Witch, Abigail Zorn, sat on the edge of her bone chair, scrapping a stick through the dirt without meeting his eyes. Older by far and bearing the weight of the entire nest, she wore a perpetual frown, as if time and age conspired against her. The crowds were gone. Back to their daily lives with stories to tell of the daring human and the foolish goblin willing to throw away her life on whim.

"I did what the gods decreed, Crispus," she replied. "Or do you think I should have declared in her favor in front of the entire nest? Even I do not have that power. You know this."

"That changes nothing," he fumed. "One of us should not be punished for that *human's* failings. Send him to the cookfires, not my daughter. Please, Abigail. I cannot bear the pain."

"Alas, there is naught I can do," she insisted. "Unless."

Abigail shifted her weight, cocking her hip with a teasing smirk on her face.

He perked up. "Yes?"

"There is the old way. A law unacted for generations," Abigail drawled out. "You may request trial by combat with the human."

Trial by combat. Goblin history was littered with the detritus of failure from challengers and defenders.

Hundreds of Nest Fathers fell in the days following the rise of the elves. His own grandfather fell prey to his challenger and fed the nest well that night. Crispus blanched at the consequences of losing.

"There must be another way," he said, narrowing his eyes. "One where neither of us suffer."

Abigail stopped moving, lifting her stick to inspect the tip before inserting it in her mouth. "Perhaps, but not one you will like."

"What good is being Nest Father if I do not look after all of my people?" he asked. "Especially my flesh and blood."

"Saving your daughter shows favoritism in a desperate time. You know the law, Crispus. We must hold true to the past if we are to find our place in the future."

"Laws. Rules. Codes. I am tired of being bound by obsoleteness. How long must we endure the torments that placed us down here before we break?" he demanded. Anger flared in his small eyes at her shrug. "Abigail, I seek to change the laws for good. No more will goblinkind be subjected to our failings. Tomorrow belongs to us, but only after we shed the dead skin of the past. Our benefactors expect big gains from my ploy, witch. I need you to help pull this off."

Abigail Zorn sat chewing thoughtfully on her stick. Crispus fumed, knowing he was caught in a trap.

Wally awoke to blinding pain thundering in his head. Running a hand over his head, his fingers came away wet with blood at the nape of his neck. Unable to sit up without likely passing out again, he turned on his side in the hopes of alleviating some of the pain.

The events upon the rock remained fuzzy. He failed to understand why Irma Stain offered to take his sentence and suspected she was going to her doom. *Why me? What on earth could possess her to sacrifice herself for me?* Nothing made sense. Rocking in a desperate attempt at clearing his mind, Wally tried processing what he had just witnessed.

He doubted the goblins were going to let him go and Wally wanted to help. Irma may be one of his captors, but she showed him kindness where the others did not. Sacrificed herself for him. He vowed that if he found a way, he would save not only himself, but her as well. Back in his room, Wally stared down at the table but couldn't focus on his work.

THIRTY-TWO

Chanting rumbled through the cavern. Pounded the earth. Vibrated from the walls. Daniel searched for the source, but his limited vision barely penetrated the goblin nest a few feet in front of him. Concealed behind a screen of boulders, he and the dwarves surveyed the engagement zone. There was no logical order, no pattern to the emplacement of tents and structures. Chaos reigned. Daniel wasn't sure what to expect, but it was not this. Images of Civil War encampments with rows of evenly spaced white tents came to mind. His stomach churned.

"Look," Max gestured to the nearest edge of tents. "Most of them are already bedded down. We can slip through the rear and collapse on a singular position somewhere in the middle."

"Do we stop and kill the goblins on the way?" Angus asked. He idly stroked the barrel of his rifle.

Daniel wanted to shout but ground his teeth instead, muttering, "No."

"No. Takes too long," Max replied, casting Daniel a look. "It will take too long to sweep and clear the nest. We need to strike and move, just like the old days."

"Your queen says otherwise, Angus," Max mused. "I imagine she's sending the full weight of the Old Guard at some point. But you are correct about one thing. It is going to take too long to search the entirety of the nest. We need to split up."

"Are you mad?" Daniel couldn't hold back. "We'll be captured or killed in no time."

A twinkle entered Max's eyes; one Daniel knew all too well. "Not if we do it like dwarves. You say you're a fighter. A warrior. Time to start acting like one. We split into two teams, far enough apart to cover twice as much ground and still within sight of each other. We move fast. Stay on line. Angus is with me. Fritz, take pretty boy and the right flank. Don't slow. Don't stop unless you absolutely have to. That means no unnecessary killing, boys."

"What about all the goblins still moving around?" Daniel asked.

Max's plan, sound as it could be all things considered, was still riddled with holes. Daniel recalled a similar mission in northern Iraqi city of Mosul. His squad was tasked with clearing several floors of an apartment building. Suspected al-Qaida fighters were rumored to be in hiding. True to army form, his unit has no other intel to go off and bad things happened. This reminded Daniel too much of that dreadful night. He hoped today's results proved more favorable.

"Stop worrying. Goblins are mostly drones. They need to hit the rack to recharge. We should be fine. Besides, we have the Tinker's little toy. The man may be crazy, but he always makes good devices," Max replied. "Fritz, go ahead and set the scrambler, now that we know for sure this is the nest. Any other questions or concerns?"

Daniel held a litany of them but knew voicing them would only fall on deaf ears.

Fritz rummaged through his pack before producing the Tinker's device. Mouthing a silent prayer, that Daniel echoed, he pressed the tiny button on the side and winced. Nothing happened. They had no way of knowing whether the device worked or not.

"That's it?" Daniel asked. "Is it working?"

"Only one way to find out," Angus suggested.

Max, for his part, refused to wait any longer. "Right. Move fast and silent. We find this human and bounce out of here."

"We need to find the other tunnel then," Angus added. "That door in the tunnel behind us wasn't budging."

"Ghosts did it," Fritz snickered and stared at Daniel.

Max groaned. "Shit. I forgot about that. All right, looks like we're going to need an escort. New plan. Grab the human and find a 'friend' to guide us out. Let's do this. Time is wasting."

The urge to laugh suddenly swept through Daniel. He slapped a hand over his mouth as the image of his grandfather snatching up his fishing poles hours before dawn and admonishing him by saying 'we're wasting daylight.' The dwarves glared at him in a strange combination of curiosity and annoyance. Wiping his eyes, he waved them off.

Max finished screwing on the silence at the end of his barrel and shook his head before slinking away: and Angus shifted left while Daniel and Fritz banked right. Somewhere in the morass ahead was the man they had come to rescue. He hoped. *Wally, where are you?*

Waiting for Daniel and Fritz to move far enough way they couldn't hear any conversation; Max laid a hand across his son's chest. They were still far enough from the actual nest to risk talking in hushed tones without worry of detection, unless the Nest Father maintained a rear guard, which he doubted since they hadn't been discovered yet. Confusion filled Angus' eyes as he silently questioned his motives.

"Are we going to have a problem?" Max asked.

Angus craned his next to watch his brother disappear before focusing on him. "We don't have time for this. They are getting ahead of us."

"You've been bucking my authority since the three of you showed up at the farm. We're not moving until I have a warm and fuzzy on your headspace. Now answer the question. Are we going to have a problem?"

Angus exhaled heavily. "Not down here, but we will if you don't stop playing games. Like you said earlier, this isn't the time or place. Whatever problems we have between us can be solved once we get back home. The old ways."

Max grunted. "The old ways."

Satisfied, he led his son out from the protection of the rocks and into hell. Everywhere they looked stood massive stained and foul cook cauldrons. Piles of bones littered the ground. The sound of bubbling food was loud, repugnant. Scraps of clothing and jewelry sat off to the side. The dwarves knew goblins preferred food. But when no others were available, they turned on themselves.

The throne outlawed cannibalism centuries ago. The goblins did not care. Secluded underground and obscured from the rest of the world unless they wanted to be seen, the nests ate what they wanted without pause. No doubt these cauldrons were filled with a mystery meat soup simmering until breakfast. Undeterred, the dwarves pushed on.

The scuffle of shoes forced them to take cover behind one of the cauldrons. Max lowered his rifle and dropped his left hand to the combat knife belted on his hip. A trio of goblins, seemingly cooks, dressed in stained aprons and laughing about an event earlier in the day moved by. None paid attention to their surroundings or expected trouble. They kept walking toward their tents. As much as he longed to slip into each with a knife, the dwarf forced himself to remain focused on the mission.

Angus exhaled, loosening his grip on his machine gun. "That was close."

Gesturing with his head to move, Max slipped between the cauldrons, pausing to check the immediate area for additional signs of trouble.

They moved on sure feet; left no sign of their passing. Max took pride in watching his son move through enemy territory. They were more alike than either cared to admit. Each knew all it would take was a single spark before the cavern erupted in flames. Should that happen, the dwarf patriarch knew the old rage would overcome him.

They circled around once around the cooking area then scanned the sea of tents for the others. Angus saw them first, thanks to Daniel's taller frame sticking out. Satisfied they were still moving according to schedule, Max slipped past a line of slit trenches, scrunching his nose at the fetid odor of urine and feces, and into the tent city. Whatever commotion occurred earlier seemed to have died down, leaving the cavern bathed in an eerie silence neither he nor Angus was prepared for. He saw Angus frown, tightening his shoulders.

Another hundred meters on were well-worn paths taking them deeper into the nest, surrounding them with thousands of sleeping goblins. Max slowed his breathing, doing his best to make no sound. He felt the old hatreds building. That urge to strike down his foes with ruthless abandon. How easy it would be to slaughter the goblins in their sleep. Grunting, he shook the thoughts away.

The next roadblock presented itself in unusual fashion. Max caught a glimpse of a small group of armed goblins moving through the tents and froze. Fearing they'd been detected when the group's voices rose louder, he gestured for Angus to crouch. Itching for a fight, Max was just about to crouch when he noticed a goblin of importance in the middle of the group. He assumed it was the Nest Father based on his retinue and attire. Plus, few other goblins warranted such a level of protection. What really made him pause was the slender figure pushed and pulled behind the Nest Father. Ragged hair and torn clothes, the figure stood several feet taller than his captors. A smile crawled across Max's face.

They found their missing human.

Now he had to figure out how to contact the other team and reach the prisoner without rousing the entire nest. Never one to back down from a challenge, Max started heading in the same direction as the prisoner and his entourage. He felt Angus keeping close to his back. It had been a long time since they last worked together, but neither had lost a step. Angus stayed close while protecting the rear. His fingers began twitching—there was knife work needing doing this day and he was the one to handle it. Pausing at the end of a row of tents that should've been in a dumpster, Max slipped the pack from his shoulders and withdrew a cylindrical object the size of a frisbee. It was time to start prepping for their escape and this was the perfect tool.

The raw stench of the nest threatened to overwhelm Daniel. He had smelled filth before. Lived in it for years during the span of his deployments. Right now, he would have traded the world to clear out his nose and breathe fresh air again. Daniel looked around, absorbing his surroundings with a tactical eye. He took comfort in seeing Fritz act similarly.

Fritz ignored him since they separated into teams, the dwarf had since gone into battle mode that made Daniel a little jealous. The softer of the two brothers, Fritz was brutal and efficient when necessary. Cold and calculated as well. Daniel wondered if he had misjudged the possible instigator of a mission gone wrong, the silent ones he knew could be the deadliest. Though he did not admit so in any of their conversations, Daniel could tell Fritz hated goblins with a passion. Daniel wondered if he too believed like his father that goblins were the abhorrent stain among the clans; a cancer refusing to die no matter how many resources or efforts were expended. The eldest dwarf certainly had made his opinions on goblins known. Fritz stayed abreast of Daniel, knowing he was struggling; it annoyed Daniel yet he did appreciate it. They slipped through the cooking area, where they had seen Max and Angus, before entering a wide circular spot filled with used paper plates, cups, and scraps being rummaged through by rats and other vermin. A pair of drunken goblins, passed out and slumped across each other in a heap on the ground, was in the center of the circle. Rats crawled over them, nibbling on exposed bits of rancid flesh and burrowing through hair. *Madness. All this is pure insanity*. Daniel shook his head and followed Fritz.

They were well over a hundred meters into the nest and not a single goblin stirred or crossed their paths. *Perhaps the Tinker's toys worked after all.* Not wanting to think of the Tinker, Daniel kept searching for any signs of Wally. The urge to shout his name grew stronger the longer they were in the nest. Panic threatened. *Had he been the "meat" in those pots?* Deep underground and with no viable escape plan, Daniel was assaulted by that old sense of claustrophobia. He would have given anything to see the sun right now. At least the smell no longer bothered him as much as it had. It wasn't much of a victory, but it was the only one he had.

Lost in thought, he almost ran into Fritz when the dwarf halted midstride. A thick arm pointed; Daniel looked to a massive tent less than fifty meters ahead. Ringed with guards, there was little doubt whoever was inside was a person of importance. *But is it Wally?* Fritz gestured at

Daniel's rifle with his chin and shook his head. Nodding back in understanding, Daniel slid his knife free. They advanced on the tent.

THIRTY-THREE

Through his daze, Wally caught the telltale sounds of a scuffle outside but could not be bothered to investigate. The goblins showed their true colors with his farce of a trial. Aside from Irma Stain's heroic, if not unexpected, sacrifice, the entirety of the nest could burn. He at last understood his predicament and what limited value he brought to the goblin propaganda machine. Wally vowed not to help in any way unless Crispus released the young girl. He still couldn't believe Irma was that monster's daughter and refused to help the goblins and their twisted agenda until she went free.

Another shuffling sound followed by a pierced cry, strangled and muted. Wally, back in his confinement, propped up, squinting through the gloom. A cloud of ash drifted into his room. He caught a whiff of charcoal and burnt flesh. *What in the hell?* Two figures rushed into his room with rifles raised. His hopes sparked. For the first time, the possibility of rescue arose. Wally sat all the way up. *Why does one of the men look familiar? Who do I know that—*

"Are you injured?" the burlier of the two asked. His tone reminded Wally of crushing stones. The hardness in his gaze made him shy away. "Answer me. Are you hurt? Can you walk?"

"Who … who are you people?" he asked.

The taller man cocked his head, half turning to cover the entrance. "I know it's been a while, but you can't tell me you don't remember me, Wally."

Blinking, Wally muttered, "Daniel? Why are you dressed like that? What's going on?"

"You wouldn't believe me if I told you. We're getting you out of here," Daniel replied.

"Daniel, the Tinker's device may be working but we cannot place the entirety of our trust in it. We will be discovered," Daniel's partner muttered, his words urgent.

"Who is this guy?" Wally asked. He couldn't help but be naturally suspicious after all that had happened. He wasn't sure he could handle a rescue that instead turned into another kidnapping.

"This is Fritz. We also have a second team searching for you. Call us your rescue squad," Daniel replied.

"I don't understand. How did you find me? Why do you even know I'm here? What is going on? This doesn't make any sense."

"Wally, we need—"

Fritz bristled, interrupting with, "Daniel, are we going to stand here and talk all day, or can we go?"

"Wally, trust me. We can get you out, but I need you to stop asking questions and focus," Daniel said, looking at him and ignored his team member. "Can you do that?"

Looking around the tent, Wally's gaze lingered on the storyboard drafting table. Anger welled. *Goblin history.* He resisted the urge to spit. The world would know their story. That was for sure. Wally intended on blasting the goblins for the murderous villains they were. Vowing to make them pay for their crimes, he steeled himself for the escape. "Yeah, I can do that, but there's something you need to know before we split." He quickly explained Jimmy's position as well as Irma's, refusing to leave either of them behind despite their actions.

"You're telling me there are other humans?" Fritz demanded.

Humans? Buddy, what do you think you are? "At least one."

"We can't leave him," Daniel insisted when Fritz shot him a confrontational look. "Would you leave one of your people?"

His people?

Wally opened his mouth to speak when Fritz shook his head. "Fine, but we need to get word to Angus and Father or we're as good as dead once the goblins wake up." Reaching down, he snatched a spear from the ground and shoved it toward Wally. "Do you know how to use this?"

"What scenario would I ever need to know how to use that?" Wally protested. "Look at me, man. I make comic books, not hunt for my food."

Fritz grunted. "Then I hope you're a fast learner. Just don't stab me in the back."

"Don't tempt me with a good time," Wally muttered under his breath as Fritz exited the tent. Daniel eyed him, waiting. "Daniel, what's his deal? Can we trust him?"

"Fritz? He's a dwarf. They're all like that. Come on, try not to make any sound, and stay two paces behind me. I don't suppose you know the way out?"

He is a what? Nope. Not dealing with that right now. Wally cleared his throat. "Not really. I was blindfolded for most of it." Daniel turned to leave when Wally blurted, "Daniel, wait, what in the hell is going on? How is any of this real?"

Daniel turned back and placed a hand on Wally's shoulder. "Slow down. Take a deep breath and just go with it. Understand there are hidden places in the world we were never meant to know about. This is one of them. I promise I'll explain as much as I can once we are free and clear, but until then I need you to trust me."

Wally thrust the spear forward. "And use this? Look man, I'm not a killer. I never hurt anyone in my life."

"I'm not asking you to. Me and Fritz can handle it. Just keep your head on a swivel and let us know if we miss anyone. Cool?"

"Cool," Wally repeated with an easy confidence he didn't feel.

"Do you two need a condom?" Fritz hissed from outside.

"Yeah, yeah. We're coming," Daniel hissed back.

The chuckle did not go unnoticed as Daniel and Wally slipped out of the tent.

"Not funny," Daniel whispered as he took up a kneeling position next to Fritz.

"A little funny," Fritz countered. "Come on, I spotted Angus heading that way."

Wally decided he wasn't even going to bother asking who Angus was.

They set out once more through the morass of the goblin nest. Wally stared at the four ash piles around the outside of what he viewed as his cell with a quizzical look then hurried to catch up. He thought about going back for his work, even as his mind reconciled with what those ash piles might be but decided against it. Let the goblins suffer with the few images he gave them.

Angus relished the thrill of the hunt. He longed to slay his most hated foe, regardless of what Morgen or Daniel said. Some matters went beyond protocol. Mortal enemies, dwarves and goblins littered history with their dead. Where his brother tried finding ways for peaceful resolution, Angus saw opportunity. The goblin stain must never be allowed to rise again, and they were in a prime position to ensure it did not. He struggled against the urge to rush through the nest, machinegun blazing.

Seeing the Nest Father changed his mind, if just. Nests collapsed with their leadership decapitated. While this was the golden opportunity to cleanse Charleston of vermin and restore the peace between species, he figured hitting the Nest Father would be a great first step. Angus set aside his personal animosity and followed a pace behind his father as the dwarf stalked the Nest Father. The older dwarf moved with uncanny surety through the maze of tents. At another turn, and fearful of losing sight of their quarry, they broke into a tactical jog.

A goblin lurched from his tent, colliding with Angus. They tumbled to the ground in a twisted heap of limbs and gear. Angus snaked an arm around the goblin's throat and squeezed. The goblin gave a strangled cry before his eyes rolled to the back of his head. A sharp snap and he dissolved in a puff of ash in Angus' arms. Disgusted, he got back on his feet and brushed the remains from his clothes. His father shot him an accusatory look before resuming their pace. Angus shrugged, his teeth showing through his facial hair. Take that, old man.

Angus saw that the Nest Father was close. His guards were focused on their leader, while guarding the human in their center. Halfway through the nest he spotted a disturbing complication. There, a pace behind the Nest Father, strode a young female goblin in chains. *A prisoner?* Royal mandate of no unnecessary violence aside, there was a possible mystery worth exploring. If nothing else, it might provide the excuse he needed to cry havoc. *Or it is nothing and they are of no issue to me and would only be trouble.*

His father suddenly dropped to his knee and motioned him closer.

"Why are we stopping? He's right there," Angus whispered, tracking the goblin's march.

Max pointed at the young goblin. "See that? She's a prisoner."

He had seen and it didn't matter to him. "Yeah. So? She's a goblin, Pop." Angus shook his head. "You're confusing the mission. We can kill the leader, grab the human, and clear out before the nest wakes up."

"There's more to that female," Max insisted. "We should try to nab her too."

"We're not here for hostages. You could be starting a war."

The elder dwarf growled deep in his throat, making a clicking sound Angus and Fritz had associated with their father's boiling anger since childhood.

Max gripped his rifle a little tighter. "Look, you're forgetting one thing. Nests are ruled by the father and the witch. Killing or capturing the father is easy enough but won't stop the rest of the nest from coming after us. That female might be key in stopping the witch."

"I knew I shouldn't have stopped at home," Angus muttered. He refused to admit his father was right in his logic. "Fine. Lead the way and let's get this over with. We're running out of time."

Beaming, Max gave a toothy grin. "See, I knew you'd see it my way."

Knowing better than to risk an argument in the middle of enemy territory, Angus relented and slipped in behind his father for the final push to the Nest Father. There were no natural ambush points or secluded places along the trek capable of concealing their actions and, if necessary, hide until Daniel and Fritz linked up with them.

Moving as fast as possible without announcing their presence to the hordes of sleeping goblins surrounding them, they closed the distance. Soon, they crouched behind the final row of tents.

Max scanned the area for potential problem areas before focusing on the large almost circus-like tent dominating the nest. Several guards lurked outside, but their focus was dulled by years of complacency. He gestured to the brace of throwing knives attached to Angus' body armor. His son slowly withdrew four and handed him two.

Throwing up three fingers in a deliberate, slow countdown, they rose together and flung their blades in unison. The second round of knives was airborne before the first pair struck. Four clouds of black ash erupted where the guards had been. Max and Angus raced forward, unable to delay the assault without endangering the mission.

They flanked the entrance, pausing to click off their rifle safeties before giving each other a clipped nod. Max exhaled a slow breath and plunged inside. They counted on there being at least four guards. Using superior fire discipline and thankful for the suppressors affixed to their barrels, they picked off their startled targets in a matter of moments. Only the Nest Father, the human, and the young goblin remained in the main chamber, stunned into silence.

"Watch them," Max ordered. "Any of them try anything and you plug them. I'll secure the rest of the tent."

Angus was glaring at the prisoners when Max returned. "Clear.".

"Friendlies coming in."

They spun on the entrance, weapon raised.

Fritz entered first, followed closely by an unknown human and Daniel bringing up the rear.

Huddling in the massive tent filled with old, broken furniture, carpets and once luxurious pillows used as beds and chairs, they paused to consolidate their resources, take a drink of water, and plan what to do next. Max took in their surroundings before focusing on the prisoners.

"Dwarves in my sanctum!" the Nest Father suddenly exclaimed and earned an elbow to his ribs.

Max loomed over him. "Quiet or I'll show you what we dwarves think of your filth."

Rebuked into silence, the Nest Father folded his legs beneath him and clutched his sore side.

"I thought there was just one human?" Max asked the others.

"That's what we thought," Fritz replied, checking the door for any signs of approaching enemy. He then held out the knives he and Angus had thrown. Max nodded in approval as Angus sheathed them.

As if stirring from a sleep, the long-haired man raised his head and stared at them for the first time. His eyes widened on the other human. "Wally, hey man, I—"

"You son of a bitch!" the human lunged, hands extended and reaching for his throat.

Angus tackled him to the ground just in time, clenching down until the human settled down enough to let loose. Breathing a sigh of relief, Fritz handed over the knives. Max was about to issue the next set of instructions when a shrill voice called in.

"Everything all right in there, boss?"

THIRTY-FOUR

Crispus Goldfarb, hands clasped before him in a humble gesture, stared at the dwarves and humans with shrouded eyes. Wheels turning, he saw no easy way out of this situation, not without bringing the entirety of the nest into it. Doing so meant the lives of countless of his kin, ruining his plans and goblinkind, perhaps forever. Panic set in. Crispus thought himself practical, if ambitious, and the thought of bringing ruin to his beloved nest out of sheer ignorance soured the edges of his soul. Mounting guilt kept him from looking at his daughter.

"Answer him," one of the dwarves grunted. "Nothing funny or you die first."

Crispus cleared his throat, glaring at his captor. "Fine. Just fine. The prisoners must be prepared for their big moment. You may go about your business."

"Good goblin," the same dwarf said after listening to the sounds of old sneakers shuffling away. Rounding on a human Crispus didn't recognize, he asked, "Who is this?"

"Wally, the man we came here to get," Daniel answered Angus who's his rifle was pointed at Wally. He in turn pointed at Wally's friend Jimmy. "How did you find him?"

"Luck," Angus replied. "Pop and I stumbled on this filth bringing him back and figured it was your friend. It was also worth a shot to cut off the head and be done with this whole thing."

"Give me a knife and I'll cut his head off," Wally snarled, surprising Daniel at his ferocity. He was still restrained, by Fritz now, but had ceased struggling to break free. The spear they had given him dropped a few feet away.

Daniel eyed the Nest Father who sputtered, "Wally! I have ever only treated you with respect. Why would you wish to decapitate me?"

"Not you, Crispus. Not yet. Him! My *friend* who sold me out."

Heads turned to Jimmy Harper who, in his defense, lowered his head in defeat. "Wally, I'm sorry. I … I didn't have a choice. They threatened to kill my wife."

"I'll do more than that," Wally snapped. Anger twisted his features, lending him a devious look. Daniel barely recognized him. "I wouldn't be here if it wasn't for you!" Sensing control slipping, Daniel stepped between them. They could beat each other all they wanted once they were free and clear of the nest. Until then, he needed both to cool their nerves if any of them were going to survive. At his interference, Wally shifted away. Now that was solved, they were still trapped in the Nest Father's quarters.

"How do we get out of here?" Daniel asked aloud.

It was the Nest Father who gave a long, slow headshake before he replied, "You don't. Not with my entire family surrounding you. I am afraid this endeavor is most foolhardy, if not brave. The dwarves should have given you better guidance."

"Wrong answer," Max snapped and drew back to strike the goblin again. "You're going to show us the way out that is nice and quiet, or I will personally slaughter half of your precious family before they take me down. Do I make myself clear, goblin?"

The Nest Father stiffened. "My name is Crispus."

"Good for you. Keep talking and it will be ashes. What's the deal with this one?" He gestured to the cowering female goblin who had yet to speak.

Crispus moved in front of her in a protective way. Daniel saw the goblin's right hand tremble. "She is nothing to you. Just an unfortunate circumstance I must deal with."

"She's your daughter," Daniel guessed, noting a resemblance.

His suspicions were confirmed when the goblin lowered his head. Instead of feeling elation at having a way out dropped into their laps, Daniel focused on the manacles, rusted and covered in filth bounding her. He couldn't imagine doing so to one of his children, no matter how much they infuriated him. "Why is she in chains?"

Crispus adjusted his navy-blue track suit top, making a show of brushing crud from the shoulders. "She foolishly offered herself as tribute in Wally Rutherford's place. She is to be punished. She is to be…" his voice trailed off to a whisper. "Sacrificed."

"You sick fuck," Daniel raged. "You're going to murder your own flesh and blood?"

"Goblins never had a sense of decency," Fritz interjected before he went over the edge. "They are one of the most violent of our races."

The urge to burn the nest down threatened to consume him. Daniel paced through the tent, desperately seeking clarity. Despite his military service and wartime record, he despised violence. Yet he found the thought of killing a child revolting. No matter the crimes of her ancestors, there was no plausible way this goblin child was guilty of anything but naivete.

Then a thought had him pausing mid-step. Daniel cocked his head. "Hold on. Why is she here instead of in a cell if she is scheduled to be killed?"

Crispus cleared his throat. "Despite what you may believe of us, we are not monsters. I had every intention of helping Irma escape, though it would pain me to have her gone. She was to be the nest successor."

"Father!" the girl said in shock.

He nodded. "It is true. You were ever meant to lead us into the next generation. But I could not see you die for no reason, especially not for a filthy human. Now, we are all doomed."

"Doomed?" Wally asked.

"Doomed. The Nest Witch will discover my plan, if she has not already, and will use her full fury to hunt us down and make us suffer before we die. If the witch doesn't get us first, there are powerful people out there. The dwarves will die, painfully. You humans will be eaten."

Angus flinched as his father slapped his upper arm. "What was that for?"

"See? I told you," Max said. "Where is the witch?"

"Who can say?" Crispus replied. "I tend to avoid her unless there is no choice. She is a vile creature, even for our kind."

The whole world has gone mad and I'm party to it. Daniel's eyes caught on the golden statue of a two-legged goat with arms dancing beneath a waterfall. He appeared to be playing a flute with water pouring from it. *Right. Mad.* "We need to exfil now. The Tinker's device is still working but who knows for how much longer. Crispus, will you guide us to the exit?"

"For Irma only. I care not whether the rest of you fill our cauldrons."

Daniel had a starting point. He rounded on the Nest Father, forcing him back a step. "Good. You're going to lead us to the exit, and we take your daughter with us. The only way she lives is through us. You get us free and clear, and we ensure her safety. That's the only deal on the table. Take it or leave it."

"What happens to me? That doesn't sound like much of a deal." Crispus stood straighter even as his voice wavered. "I would very much like to live."

"Yesterday you said you couldn't wait to rise again," Wally muttered. He seemed deflated. "We could have avoided it all."

"Choices were made, Waldo Rutherford. Hard choices. Ones I do not envy any parent," Crispus told him.

Waldo? Ignoring that, Daniel recognized it as an apology, a poor one. "I don't care if you live or die," Daniel stated. "One way or the other, your little insurrection is at an end. Get us out of here and we might be able to convince the queen not to send in the Old Guard and turn this nest of yours to slag."

Crispus slumped onto the large zebra striped pillow and planted his face between his palms. Decades worth of dreams were going up in smoke and he was powerless to prevent it. With no clear successor aside from his daughter, Crispus stood on the precipice of vanquishment and, should he find himself in exile, cast to the wolves. He knew elven treachery far too well to expect to be allowed to live long. The remainder of his days would be spent looking over his shoulder for that knife in the back. Still, what choice did he have? Trapped and damned in one fell swoop. "I can lead you to the exit on one condition."

"No." The eldest dwarf's tone resonated with finality.

Crispus ignored him. "The queen must grant me immunity and put both of us in her protection program and leave the nest untouched."

He still had a chance; all be it slim and fading.

"I can present it to her, nothing more," Daniel hurriedly said following the nest leader's words. He could tell Max was about to be unraveled. "Time is running out, Crispus. What's your decision?"

"There is no decision," he lamented. "Let us go but try not to slaughter too many of my people. They do not deserve your retribution. Not this night."

"Not up to me, pal." Daniel wanted to give his assurance, but the three dwarves made that all but impossible as he saw them exchanging looks. "Best I can do is try."

Wiping his grime-stained face of tears, Crispus nodded. "That will have to do. Come, the exit is this way."

He rose in the same instant Angus fell in beside him. No one was taking any unnecessary chances this close to escape. Daniel could almost taste home. He also knew this was the most dangerous part of the mission. Any mistake now might result in catastrophe.

Daniel's beleaguered group formed ranks, keeping Wally and the girl, Irma, in their center and the Nest Father at the point position. If noticed, Daniel hoped that seeing their leader shielding the others might give the goblins pause. Fritz did a sweep through the tent, ensuring they left nothing behind, and pointed to the exit.

They started moving at a deliberate pace. Weapons trained in every direction, they crept across the open area and found themselves creeping through the outer ring of tents. Snoring echoed like a symphony gone mad the deeper into the tent field they went.

Clutching his hand, Irma looked up at Wally and whispered, "I am glad you are here, Wally. Thank you for rescuing me."

Wait, what? Don't get the impression I'm heroic, you might be disappointed. I don't plan on ever seeing another goblin again once we leave this dump. He offered her a tight smile. "No sweat, Irma. Us little people have to stick together."

Her sweaty palm clenched his tighter, producing a sickening feeling radiating throughout his body. Willing to do anything to escape his plight, Wally ignored the disgusting feeling and walked to the point of breaking into a jog before one of the dwarves slowed him down to keep pace. *Dwarves.* Never in his life did he imagine any of this was real …*Goblins and dwarves. Walking among us without anyone being the wiser! What else wasn't Daniel telling me?* If two legendary fantasy races existed surely there would be others. He suddenly wanted to know more. That creative desire bloomed, always at the wrong time. Wally cursed his luck.

The group continued, picking up the pace as they wove through a field of crushing stalactites and stalagmites turning the cavern into the maw of some imaginary beast.

Daniel shuddered at the brush of a stalagmite against his arm. Each step confined the battlespace, limiting fields of fire and reaction time while presenting a host of opportunities for the goblin horde to descend. Frowning at the thought of being ambushed so close to freedom, he looked behind each rock formation that much more.

The group skidded to a halt not long after. Daniel went on edge. They'd gone several hundred meters from the Nest Father's appointed tents, with likely several more to go before hauling back up to the surface and fresh air. He saw it was Crispus who had frozen in place, his already sickly flesh turning pallid.

"What's the hold up? Why aren't we moving?" Daniel hissed.

Angus shifted the weight of his machine gun, clicking off the safety in doing so. "We might have a problem. Remember that witch he mentioned?"

"Oh shit."

Fritz bobbed his head at Daniel's curse. "That pretty much sums it up. I knew this was too easy."

Daniel spotted her waiting atop a flat boulder. Hair wild and bone rattling, the Nest Witch pointed at them with unmitigated hatred. "Traitor!" Her shrill cries echoed across the cavern ceiling. "Awake! Awake! The Nest Father has betrayed us all! To arms!"

THIRTY-FIVE

Max snapped a shot off before Daniel had the chance to react. Rock and dust chipped away from the rockface beside the witch's face. A second shot followed, this one missing as well. Rolling his eyes as the situation got away from him, Daniel turned in time to witness hundreds of goblins, groggy from sleep and whatever else the Tinker's device did, crawling from their tents. They were armed with swords, spears, and the occasional handgun.

"Move!" Daniel shouted before Angus could open fire with his machine gun. "Get to the exit. Angus and I will cover the rear. Don't stop. Go!"

Wally started to say something, but Fritz snatched him by the upper arm, hard enough to produce a yelp, and dragged him toward the stone where the witch had been. The others followed. All but Max. The old dwarf fired into the growing throngs of angry goblins, rewarded by several puffs of ash. Not wanting to start a war, Daniel struggled to find a way out without murdering the entire nest as Angus began firing too. *Kill the witch. Stop the fight.*

"I'm going to him," Angus announced, shifting his line of fire to cover Daniel's right flank.

"No, that's what they want," Daniel shouted over the bark of rifle fire before he could rush to his father's side.

"Look, see how they are gathering to block the exit. We need to shift right and pull back before we're cutoff."

"But my Pop!"

Daniel had a feeling the elder dwarf could handle his own and, in a macabre sense, wanted to be alone on a vendetta mission. A swarm of goblins broke from the group, rushing their position and forcing them to fall back before he and Angus were overwhelmed. Outnumbered and outgunned, they now had one shot at slipping away and that window was closing rapidly.

"Gotta go," Daniel insisted. "Shoot and scoot."

Angus roared and unleashed a torrent of fire into the rushing goblins. Scores burst apart, their ashes staining the red rock.

Daniel dashed a dozen meters back before turning to take a covering position. "Set!" he shouted and selectively picked off targets.

Angus hurried past, fire and hatred in his eyes. Daniel wasn't sure if it was directed at him or the goblins.

They continued that way until the open area condensed down in a funnel. Daniel lost sight of the others. A spear clanked off the wall near his head. He ducked and snapped off three shots at the perpetrator. With fighting space now confined, he and Angus were within a meter of each other and forced to close.

"We got our backs to the wall," Angus announced after a quick inspection. "No way we can continue side by side. There's a passage leading out up ahead, I think. Doesn't look like the exit though."

"Do we chance it?" Daniel asked, feeling his hope fade.

A wild spray of bullets peppered the stone above them, showering them with chips of razor-sharp rocks.

"We don't have much of a choice. Collapse on me and don't stop."

Placing the bipod on a flat surface for stability, Angus let loose a string of short bursts into the milling goblins. Several writhed on the ground from gunshot wounds. Ash piles littered their path of retreat. He searched for any sign of the others.

Daniel saw their hesitation, they weren't coming closer, and knew it was now or never. Surprised Angus chose to wound rather than kill, he said, "This is our chance, Angus."

Angus nodded.

Daniel took a few shots, following the dwarf's lead by wounding his targets. Daniel tucked his rifle down and slipped behind Angus, wishing he had the foresight to put earplugs in. The ringing in his cars alrcady drovc him mad.

"Go!" Angus roared.

Convinced the goblins were either overly cautious and thinking they faced a larger foe or waiting instructions from the Nest Witch, Daniel sprinted to the back of the cavern and took up a good firing position. A hail of spears and pistol shots followed, ever a step behind. He slammed into the nearest wall, regretting the action after hearing the suction of muck that was then unwilling to release him when he pulled forward. The goblins had not moved.

Angus moved at a slower pace, as if daring the goblins to strike him down from behind. Mouth agape at the spectacle, Daniel could do nothing but watch. The dwarf stalked across the angle of retreat, pausing now and then to turn and fire on any goblin daring enough to stand in the open.

Seeing the smear of slime dripping off Daniel's shoulder before looking at the filth covered wall, Angus knelt beside him and loaded a fresh drum of ammo. "There's a lot more of them than I thought," he said between deep breaths.

As if on cue, the goblins stepped forward en masse, chanting with each step.

Covered in sweat, Daniel watched as the slow creep of goblins marched closer. He didn't have enough ammunition to deter them, nor was there enough time to escape through the supposed tunnel. Then he remembered the device Morgen gave him. Digging into a pocket, Daniel pulled it out and pushed the lone button. Nothing happened. "Angus, we aren't going to make it," he said above the din of the chanting horde. "Not like this."

Clothes stained with the red dust from the boulders and a nasty cut across his left cheek from a lucky spear cast, the dwarf spat. "Much as I hate to agree with you, you're right. That doesn't mean we're out of the fight." He slipped the pack off his shoulders and, glancing to ensure the goblins were still a respectable distance, began handing grenades to Daniel with a wild look in his eyes.

"Start throwing on three and don't stop until you're out," Angus ordered. "It might not stop them, but it will damn sure give them pause." At Daniel's groaned he added, "Hey, cheer up. We might just make it out of here yet! Three!"

"Keep moving," Fritz shouted.

Any surprise at the reluctance Wally exhibited in separating from the one man he knew was quickly drowned out by the hurried step with which the Nest Father and Irma Stain moved. Both goblins were intent on surviving. It was almost enough to give him hope. The only dead weight, from what he gauged, was the haggard and abused Jimmy Harper. Fritz pulled and almost dragged the broken man along.

"Quickly! The exit is just ahead," Crispus announced. His words rang with the promise of salvation.

Fritz glimpsed the narrowing tunnel entrance through the gloom. He hated how he was forced to rely on the goblins against his will.

"What about Daniel? We can't just leave him back there," Wally protested.

Heart aching at the thought of the three men left behind in a delaying action, Fritz buried his sigh. The instinctual urge to go back and fight warred with his charge. There was no honor in leaving comrades behind, yet neither was there any to be found in abandoning his assignment. A plan formed in the recesses of his mind. Deliver the prisoners to freedom, or at least the chance to escape, and return for the others. Not answering, Fritz picked up the pace.

They were almost free when Jimmy stumbled and fell, knocking Fritz down in the process. Tumbling in a heap of tangled limbs and puffed dirt clouds, he pushed Jimmy off and rolled to his hands and knees. He took the back of an arm to wipe his eyes clear from the grime, wincing at the feel of a foreign object scratching his cornea. At his side, Jimmy groaned in pain.

"Wally, look out!" Irma's shrill voice pierced his eardrums, followed by the thunk of steel ricocheting off stone.

Forcing himself free of the fallen human, Fritz surged to his feet, bringing his rifle up in search of targets. What he saw paled him. Dozens of the largest goblins circled around in the group, cutting off their escape route.

Crispus spared a look at Jimmy before telling Fritz, "They are the Sorum'kha. The nest protectors. They are the biggest and strongest of us. Fierce warriors with no give and no surrender. They will kill us all if I do not convince them I am hostage."

"And betray us? I don't think so," Fritz countered. Regardless of what happened next, he vowed to kill the Nest Father first. "We fight our way through them."

The goblin balked. "Impossible! These are the ultimate warriors."

"Clearly you have forgotten what a good dwarf can do," Fritz growled, channeling his brother. "Let's get this over with."

He brought his rifle up and fired a three-round burst.

Blade slicing across the goblin's throat, Max roared a dwarven battle cry and strode into the mass of bodies with ruthless abandon. Every goblin killed was a measure of retribution for their crimes. Each target a victim of his rage and hurt only a father who lost his son could feel. Adrenalin fueling his anger, the dwarf unleashed his full fury upon the Ok'tal'med Nest, the queen's orders be damned.

He soon found himself surrounded. His muscles ached, burning from strain. The mixture of sweat and goblin blood wet his lips, dripped into his eyes. He had never felt more alive. They tore at his clothes, ripped his utility belt away. He didn't care. Any thoughts of his sons were shoved aside. The only thing that mattered was the fight and his sole opportunity for revenge. It marked the first time in centuries he had been let off the leash, even if it stemmed from his own actions.

The goblins backed off when they realized he wouldn't be contained, he saw their looks of conflict; their urge to survive vs. their need to kill him—their most hated foe. Forming a circle, they stomped and howled.

Max sneered at their weak intimidation attempt and beckoned for the next challenger.

A pair of warriors, naked from the waist up and covered with tribal tattoos, entered the circle and flanked the dwarf. Each bore a foot long dagger, serrated, and honed to a razor's edge.

"Who's first?" Max roared. His own blade danced in his hand.

They struck simultaneously. The goblin on his left went high, aiming for a killing blow by severing the jugular. At the same time, the second goblin drove his blade for Max's unprotected knee.

Max lunged into the attack of the first, ducking under the stab to punch his blade into the goblin's chest. The goblin gave a confused look before bursting apart in a cloud of ash. Max's move caused the second goblin to miss. Momentum carried him past the dwarf, where he was rewarded with a bone slicing cut across the back of his neck. He fell with a gurgling scream. The entire fight took less than ten seconds but there would be no reprieve for the dwarf. His host of challengers was endless.

The next pair entered.

Then the next.

Max lost track of time and his victims. Soon the cavern floor lay decorated in the dust of fallen goblins and still his retribution continued. The oaths demanded more. The gods ached for sacrifice. Grief crashed like waves upon him.

Bent but far from broken, he was at last driven to his knees. There, breath ragged and body ready to quit, Max heard the chanting stop. The noise ceased until silence reigned. He stared out at the nest, working through potential options for escape.

Ranks of goblins parted, showing him the one creature he needed to kill if he had any hope of survival. For her part, Agatha Zorn stood indifferent to his plight. In her eyes, he was her path to domination; just as she was his. Blue-green magic danced off her fingertips as she stepped forward. Max pushed himself back to his feet and accepted her challenge.

THIRTY-SIX

"Get down!"

The shrill and unfamiliar voice rang over the battlefield, giving the Sorum'kha pause. Fritz saw heads turning, one muttering if they had been recalled by their Nest Witch. A hail of gunfire streamed from the exit tunnel a moment later. Fritz and the others barely had time to drop to the floor before the nest's heavy warriors burst apart. Stray bullets zinged indiscriminately. Irma clamped her hands over her ears and screamed.

The click of a dry magazine cycling echoed. Those goblins still in the fight turned as one to face the new threat and charged. Fritz picked his head up, surprised to find more than half their number whittled down. Whoever the shooter was had skill, but it wouldn't be enough if the goblins swarmed them. Spitting out a mouthful of grime and sand, Fritz gritted his teeth and rose to a kneeling position.

"Cover your ears," he warned as his finger depressed the trigger.

His fire was met with howls of agony as several goblins fell. Not a moment later the mystery shooter finished reloading and continued the assault. Caught between opposing forces, the goblins never stood a chance. The cyclic rate of fire told Fritz the second shooter had a light machinegun and was burning through ammunition at a substantial rate, risking melting the barrel if they didn't slow down and become more selective with their targets. He needed to take some of the pressure off their would-be rescuer.

Dropping an empty magazine and slapping in a fresh one, Fritz told his wards to stay down and watch for anyone coming up from the rear. He didn't wait for a reply before dashing across the cavern to take up a flanking position. The enemy ranks were thinned enough to raise the possibility of friendly fire and he very much wanted to live through this. Setting up against one of the red clay mounds, Fritz became more selective of his targets.

Focused on head and shoulders where the goblins were least protected, he doled out punishment on levels unseen since the Dwarf-Goblin War of 1687. Fritz caught a glimpse of his savior through the haze. *An elf!* Wry grin spreading, he knew Morgen wouldn't leave them to their devices. Regardless of their standing, elves rarely placed full trust in their dwarven counterparts. He was almost tempted to rattle the elf's nerves by placing a burst close to her head.

When the last of the ashes kissed the dirt, the battle ended. Fritz caught the sound of numerous explosions coming from the cavern and struggled against the urge to rush back to help the others. Instead, he reloaded and prepared for another wave of enemy that had yet to materialize.

"Friendly coming in," the elf shouted.

Fritz waved her on, turning his attention back to the small group of humans and goblins under his protection. His relief upon seeing them alive and unharmed drained much of the adrenalin he had used for battle. Holding his rifle by the carrying handle atop the upper receiver, he stood with hunched shoulders and watched the elf close on him. He didn't recognize her, not that that meant anything. Another round of explosions sang from the nest.

"Jesus, what are your people doing in there?" she asked, though he felt it was more of admonishment. "We're you instructed not to engage unless necessary?"

Fritz bristled. "It became necessary. Who are you?"

"Viviana Cal. The queen sent me to look after your crew." She glanced at the ash piles littering the area, staining the red-grey floor. "Looks like I got here just in time. I thought it was just one human?"

He gestured. "Two. They had the second one for a while by the looks of it. We also have a twist. It seems the Nest Father and his daughter are seeking immunity. If it were up to me, I'd plug them both, but they're your problem now, you working for the queen and all."

A dangerous gleam entered Viviana's eyes before she clicked her tongue on the roof of her mouth. "First thing's first. How many more are still in the nest?"

"Three." *If they're still alive.* "We split up once the Nest Witch began her coup."

"Kill her and the nest will fall complacent," Viviana needlessly pointed out.

Fritz turned back to the cavern, a long look on his face. "That's the idea."

Pain wracked his body. Daniel wondered if he was alive, at least until he attempted to move and found he was pinned down by a blanket of stone and debris. Dust filled the area, reducing his vision further, which was already tear-filled and burning. His hands were empty. His rifle disappeared somewhere in the middle of the second round of grenades. No one warned him dwarven grenades were vastly superior to anything in the US Army's arsenal.

His ears rang louder than before. He wasn't sure if any bones were broken but he knew, if they escaped, he was going to be feeling this for a long time to come. When he opened his mouth a gush of dirt and rock poured out. He did his best to clear his mouth and croaked, "Angus?"

"Ughnn."

Good, the dwarf still lived. It was then he realized no goblins were storming them. Whatever punitive force was either destroyed or had the sense to fall back after the first grenade. Unsure what to make of it, Daniel worked harder to dig free. His experience in the nest showed him the depths goblins were willing to plunge deeper into madness and he could ill afford to leave anything more to chance. Rocks began sliding off his battered legs until he managed to work one boot free.

Fresh pain, sharp and invigorating, shot up his leg to his pelvis. Not trusting his strength to stand, Daniel crawled over to Angus, who had yet to rise. The dwarf bled from a dozen places, most looking like superficial injuries. A flashback to his medical training reminded Daniel the face and head bled more than any other part of the body thanks to the abundance of blood vessels. His one concern came from a nasty gash to the dwarf's scalp that needed attention.

Daniel dug through his utility pouch, producing a field dressing and wrapped the wound while Angus remained immobile. Lacking water or antiseptic, Daniel risked an infection from not cleaning the wound first, but they did not have the time. He had no doubts the goblins would regroup and come again once they figured it was safe.

"Angus?"

Angus' head lolled, blood spilling from his mouth. He opened his eyes, but his gaze was unfocused.

Daniel cursed, knowing there was no chance of heaving the dwarf to his feet and getting them both clear.

"Angus, wake up. Come on, man. I need you here with me. Angus." Daniel tried shifting the dwarf and waves of pain rummaged through his own head for the effort. Part of him wanted to slap the dwarf to elicit a response but head wounds were tricky.

Frustration set in. Daniel tried peering through the haze to no avail but spotted the black metal of Angus' machinegun poking from the rubble nearby. At least they were armed again. Leaving the dwarf for a moment, he scurried over and dragged the weapon clear. Any hopes he held of using it were dashed upon seeing the bent barrel. As best as he could figure, the dwarf fired too fast, and the falling rock ruined the superheated barrel just enough to prevent a round from firing. *Useless.* He cast the weapon aside.

"Wha … what happened?" Angus groaned, jerking and twisting his way to all fours.

Daniel glanced at him. "The goblins are gone. I guess those grenades did the trick. We need to get out of here while we can. Can you walk?"

"Dunno. Hurts bad, but I've had worse. Where's my gun?" he asked.

"Gone. The barrel's shot," Daniel replied, expecting a burst of rage. Instead, he got a sorrowful look that tugged at his heart. He placed a hand on Angus' shoulder. "There are more weapons. Come on, we need to take advantage before the goblins return."

"Not that way," Angus said, noticing the constricted tunnel gaping at them. "Head back for the main entrance. We'll never make it through there."

"The main entrance? Are you mad?"

"Daniel," Angus said and paused, grunting from the effort of rising. "If they goblins aren't here, they have to be somewhere else. We have a clear shot to the front door." He paused to spit. "My head hurts. Just head for the front."

Unsure of the soundness of the plan, Daniel relented.

Broken, beaten, and still in the fight, they hobbled through the cavern and back into the nest.

Magic drove Max to his knees. Sweat and blood bouncing off him. He clenched his jaw so hard he felt a tooth break as he struggled against the pain. Smoke poured from him; he caught the scent and sound of sizzling flesh. It had been too long since he last faced a magical opponent and found himself caught off guard.

Far from the one to back down, he redoubled his efforts and was rewarded by the blue waves of power breaking apart. At another sizzling sound, Max glanced down at the burning fringes of his beard and clamped down on the flames with a dirty palm. He rose, pointing at the witch with his blade in challenge. She seethed with anger.

"You should be dead! I unleashed enough magic on you to kill a hundred of your pathetic species!" Agatha fumed.

"You gotta do better than that, toadie," he taunted. "Come on, show me what you got."

Agatha's slight frame trembled. Her lower jaw quivered in rage. Her eyes lit a bright vermillion as she filled herself with magic for the killing blow.

As one, the ring of goblins began stomping their boots.

Max took in the spectacle with mild appreciation. He judged close to a thousand goblins were here to witness. *Good enough.* Roaring his family's battle cry, Max heaved his blade as hard as he could and charged. Agatha deflected the steel with a quick spell but failed to stop the dwarf from crashing into her and driving them both to the ground. Smaller and without the use of her hands to cast another spell, she squirmed to break free.

Max pressed down with his full body weight and placed his hands on both sides of her head—one quick snap and it was finished. Agatha Zorn burst apart beneath him. He shoved upward with a grunt, making a show of wiping her remains from his hands as he stood. The goblins in attendance fell silent. Their fervor gone. Their lust for dwarven blood fading. He broke into a grin. With the power of the Nest Witch broken, the nest lost all will to fight. Max bellowed in challenge.

Many stood there, wandering aimlessly as others strolled back to their tents in confusion. He had seen it before, and it never failed to amuse him. Pain arose in his jaw when he chuckled, and he spit out the broken tooth. Tired and sore and in need of a stiff drink, Max Schneider gave the witch's ashes a final look before stumbling back through the nest, untouched. His battle was finished. Now he needed to see how many of the others, if any, survived.

Max shoved a dazed goblin out of his way and hurried toward the exit.

THIRTY-SEVEN

They stole past groups of tourists in bright colored shirts, men and women who gasped and pointed as they emerged from the deepest part of the dungeons under the Old Exchange and Provost building. Some whispered speculation that they were part of the tour, representing tortured prisoners and long dead pirates. Others crinkled their noses and turned away.

It took the better part of an hour for the entire group to link up. Tired, battered, and pushed to the edge, they gathered in a small group under the shade of a pair of palm trees. The day was ending, leaving them mired in different stages of thought as each processed what had just happened. Max was the last to arrive, covered in grime and worse. The cigar hanging from his mouth spoke volumes.

For their part, Daniel and the others kept their heads down and filed up through the tourists and into the fading sunlight in silence. Amongst his own fatigue and confusion, he saw the others with looks ranging from solemn to angry to saddened. Needing to brood, and suspecting they did too, he focused solely on slipping through the crowds. He saw that only Viviana held her head high. While he didn't like her superiority over them, he had to admit her deeds accounted heavily for the final reckoning in the debacle since she, not him, had led the group to safety. She led them to a small parking lot close to the water where she left her vehicle. Failing to account for the additional people, they were forced to take two trips. Daniel didn't comment on how it would have been easier if Hayf had stuck around with the other truck.

Hours later, cleaned and in fresh clothes, they gathered once more and headed on foot back to the restaurant

Daniel and the dwarves first ate at. To his surprise, Max showed restraint when ordering. This time it was fish fry for everyone with unlimited sides of green beans, hush puppies and coleslaw.

Daniel poked through his food, uninterested in the taste despite it being a perennial favorite. He didn't know how to process the day's events despite having won and escaped relatively unscathed. By far, this was his roughest interaction with elfkind, making him miss Sara and home that much more. He'd called after getting out of the shower. The relief in her voice filled him with enough energy to keep going and see the job through.

He looked across the table, watching the others with casual interest. It wasn't until Wally coughed with his mouth full that Daniel's thoughts turned to the future. Normally he wouldn't care, but events in the elf world translated to his human one. Should their violence spill out he knew his family stood in the crossfire. He briefly contemplated Crispus' warning that another factor was pulling the strings. At this point, he was too tired to care.

Fritz chuckled, slapping Wally on the back.

"What's so funny?" Daniel asked.

The dwarf pointed at Wally. "His name is Waldo."

Cocking his head, Wally prompted, "Yeah? So what?"

Daniel winced, already seeing what came next. *Oh shit! Why didn't I put that together?*

"We just played the world's largest game of *Where's Waldo*, that's what," Fritz roared and soon a contagious laugh gripped them.

Max snorted hard enough beer flew from his nostrils. He slapped a palm on the table and shouted, "Found him first!"

"Says you!" Angus spit a mouthful of beer out.

Dark mood broken, they dug into their meal with enthusiasm. Daniel noticed Viviana picked at her food with disinterest. She studied them with intent that he found unsettling. She was up to something.

"Where are the others?" Wally asked between bites. "I figured they would still be here to keep them from getting away."

Carefully dabbing her lips, Viviana set the napkin down. "Your counterpart, Mr. Harper, is being transported to one of our medical facilities to ensure he does not suffer from his captivity. He will be debriefed and handled according to standing agreements with your government."

"And Irma?"

The tip of her tongue poked out for a moment only before darting back into her mouth. His eyebrow rose, recognizing her sudden nervousness.

"Irma Stain has been marked for future leadership by her father. She will be kept in safety until the time comes for her to ascend. As will her father. Without a witch the goblins should remain complacent. The queen has issued proclamations to maintain stability and peace."

Daniel tapped the tip of his fork on his plate in thought. "What's to keep the nest from continuing their assault? Seemed like they were ready for all-out war."

She hummed, giving him a speculative look. "A delegation is already dispatching. They will contain the nest and prevent further uprisings." She held up a hand. "Before you ask, elf policy of no unnecessary violence takes precedence. No one will be harmed unless they violate the law. With both the witch and father removed the goblins will be complacent. They are a simple people after all. It is our hope to groom Irma Stain to become an ally to the crown."

"Lady's got all the answers," Max grumbled from his mug of beer.

"I wouldn't have my job if I didn't," Viviana fired back. "That brings me to you, Max Schneider. Your role in this was most unwelcome from the queen's perspective. I have not finalized what I am going to put in my report however."

"Hold on," Daniel interjected as the dwarves tensed. "Everything was fine until the witch roused the whole damned nest against us. We reacted to the situation, nothing more. Don't hold him accountable for trying to survive."

Shifting to face him head on, Viviana fixed him with hard eyes. "He is not alone in this. All of you bear a measure of responsibility for what could best be determined as wholesale slaughter. Murder is murder, regardless of the species."

"It was self-defense, not murder," he defended.

She stiffened. "As you say."

"I seem to recall you *murdering* your share of goblins as well," Fritz threw in. "Just wanted to point that out before one of us says something we might regret in *our* reports."

Angus, arms folded and glaring at her as angry as he'd ever been, remained silent. There were times when talking didn't cut it.

A slight hint of crimson crept up her throat. She looked at each of them, clearly deliberating on how best to proceed. "Very astute, dwarf. Very well. Perhaps a truce is best. My report will be curated to reflect popular sentiment."

"Are they all like this?" Wally whispered, leaning closer to Daniel.

He swallowed a mouthful of beer. "Pretty much. You're lucky the government isn't more involved. But it's coming. Mark my words."

"Enough talk," Max announced. "We need to celebrate. This was a monumental victory we dwarves have not seen for decades!"

His sons slowly raised their glasses in toast and the others followed. Tensions dissolved. Daniel saw the shift in mood among the dwarves. Gone was the seriousness of a soldier, replaced by the casual indifference of a survivor. His thoughts drifted back to his final redeployment and the difficulty he had reintegrating into normal society. Doing so took time, patience, and plenty of trial and error. He had no idea how Wally was going to manage, not without a lot of therapy. Then there were the undoubted endless hours of D.E.S.A. interrogation and browbeating to find out what he knew and what it would take to keep him compliant. Daniel didn't envy him.

The sky started changing colors. Long fingers of red and pink crawled across the horizon. Stomach full and fighting his closing eyes, Daniel excused himself to call home.

"Out partying in my favorite city without me?"

Daniel winced at Sara's tone, cringing as a group of tourists gave him odd looks in passing since she had been loud through the speakers. Deciding he needed a more private venue, he headed across the street and found himself beneath a palm tree, leaning against an old stone wall.

"Our favorite city," he said to sooth her. "Remember that place we ate by the flea market the first time we were here? Across the street from that church they converted to a restaurant?"

A pause. "Keep rubbing it in. How do you feel?"

There it is. How do I even explain any of what just happened without sounding like a suicidal lunatic? "It's a long story and I promise to tell you everything when I get home."

"When will that be?"

"Soon. I think we're heading back in the morning, but remember the queen is involved. Who knows what she is going to want," he said. If Viviana and her protocols were any indication, he was in for a long day tomorrow. He caught Wally giving him a pleading look. "Listen, the others are finishing up with dinner. I'll call you when we get back to the rooms. Love you."

"You better," she replied. "See you soon."

Grinning despite the confrontation yet to come, Daniel tucked his phone away and tossed his head back with a sigh. He closed his eyes. Life was supposed to be less stressful the older you got, not more. Instead, he found himself immersed in more action than at any point during his military service. A twinge in his shoulders reminded him of the extensive list of aches and pains he received in the nest. What he needed was a pour of bourbon and another hot bath to soak in before a good night's sleep.

"Daniel Thomas."

Shit. Hands stuffed in his pockets; Daniel was at an immediate disadvantage. He didn't recognize the man standing before him when he opened his eyes. Tall, slender and with a clean-cut suit, half the man's face was concealed beneath the wide brimmed 50s style hat. Pinstripes accented his jacket, drawing focus away from his face. Daniel spied a faded tattoo on the back of the man's left hand before the man noticed him looking and covered it with his other hand.

"Who are you?" Daniel asked. He saw danger in the man's eyes. The kind only a man of violence bore.

"That is unimportant. All you need to know is I have important information you need if you and your family have any hope of surviving the approaching storm."

"Look, pal. It's been a long day and I'm exhausted. Either speak plainly or send me an email detailing all these problems."

He stepped closer to Daniel, cutting off his path. "This is a matter of grave importance."

He saw the bulge of a handgun poking from the man's ribs. Daniel was unarmed and in no shape for a fight. That didn't mean he wouldn't put up one if it came to that.

Left with one choice, he relented, "Okay, tell me.".

Satisfied, the man nodded and began speaking. By the time he finished, Daniel was left with his mouth hanging open, watching the man stroll away into the fledgling night. He had no idea what just happened.

Wheels were in motion. Ones Thaddeus Blackmere was powerless to stop. He spent the last hour racking his brain in a failed attempt at finding a plausible solution but every avenue his thoughts took ended at a wall. The aging federal agent and former Navy man stared at the documents recently delivered by an unknown courier.

The papers on his desk mortified him. Worse, he didn't know who to talk to about. The agency header atop each page suggested the agency was compromised; as if they had been from someone within. He had never felt so alone. Blackmere snatched the papers to reread them, hoping he misinterpreted them. For everyone's sake.

He hadn't.

There, in plain words, was the end of everything he had dedicated his life to. If this happened, the world of elves and men would forever be changed. If any survived.

He crumbled the papers and tucked them into his shoulder bag. The courier had been specific about burning them until no trace remained when he finished reading. Blackmere was seasoned enough to know a problem when he saw it and decided not to take any chances. He went about the motions of shutting down for the night and had one foot out the door before he remembered the detail giving him the most issue.

The man, refusing to divulge his identity, bore a faded tattoo on the back of his left hand. It was a symbol he had seen before. *But where?*

Blackmere clicked off the lights and headed for home.

Outside he was greeted by a storm approaching with unprecedented fury. As he drove home, meteorologists cited climate change and other theories for the out of season hurricane readying to strike the east coast. He'd burn the papers tomorrow. If the storm didn't hit. Glancing at the sky, he shivered. Something was coming. But what?

EPILOGUE

Low clouds wreathed the skyline, concealing the upper floors of the highest city buildings in an eerie glow of distorted lights. Ominous. Deceptive. An indescribable heaviness sat upon the shoulders of those caught outside. Others shivered beneath their blankets, safe inside, and closed their eyes, praying the dawn came swift.

Morgen walked with heavy steps through the pinnacle of her domain. Never in her existence had she felt so alone. So fragile. Aches spread through her hands from clenching them so much. Her jaw was sore from grinding her teeth, though she denied doing so. Morgen did her best to avoid staring out into the night, fear averting her eyes lest remaining strength flee.

Perhaps a trip to the seers might provide the answers she needed. Superstition held no sway in the modern world. That desire to integrate, forcing her people away from the beliefs she found stymying, placed her, and the entirety of the clans, on a precipice from which none might recover.

Lips pursed, she entered her private chambers and poured three fingers of bourbon over a large cube. Swirling the glass a moment, Morgen took a slow sip. For the first time in years, she had no idea how to move forward, nor which direction to move in. She cast her gaze over her apartments, barely noticing the antique chairs and couch she had collected, sweeping over the mahogany desk gifted to her by her late husband on their thousandth anniversary. Paintings and sculptures from some of the world's great masters decorated the hallway and walls. None of it felt important. Nor did it offer comfort.

She snorted. *What good are these comforts if they do nothing when I need it most?*

Grunting her frustrations, Morgen finished her drink in one long pull and slammed the glass down before stepping away from the window. *How had it all gone wrong? Had it?* She no longer knew. Since Alvin's death, the clans were marching closer to reigniting their war. She knew there was no coming back once the first shots were fired, if they hadn't been already. Circumstances worsened by the year, but the government remained curiously absent. She did not know what to make of that. Conspiracy theories swirled to life. It took little imagination for her to envision D.E.S.A. facilitating the toppling of the throne. Humans were by far the most corruptible of the earth's sentient species. Without knowing who instigated the disturbances, Morgen was at an impasse. Having read Viviana's initial report, Morgen concluded the goblins weren't acting alone. Someone was pulling the strings. But who? She dreaded what must logically come next, but the queen would do anything to ensure her people's continued lives.

She turned her thoughts to the Charleston affair. Viviana's reports were concise as only she could manage, but Morgen felt her hired gun left important matters out. The Nest Father and heir apparent were in custody and enroute to Raleigh now. She longed to interrogate the, hoping to find the answers to her questions. Both rescued humans were fully debriefed and awaiting a legal team to ensure they remained compliant with standing treaties. None of this presented an issue. Who would believe them if they talked? Even the battle hungry Schneiders, including their father— that was another mess entirely, were easily dealt with now that their lust for combat was slaked.

That left Daniel Thomas. He had been a thorn in her side for too long. Each instance he interacted with the elves resulted in historic events. Despise him as she did, Morgen knew he was the key to whatever came next. The infuriating man had been there at each of her people's most trying moments over the last decade. But how to convince him they worked in each other's best interests… No doubt the government already sank it's claws into the man, twisting him to believe they were acting in the world's best interests.

Morgen settled into the blue cushions of her favorite couch, wrapping herself in the cool comforts. While Daniel might prove difficult to work with, Morgen had an established, if shaky, relationship with his wife. Sara was her match in many regards but earned her trust and appreciation for helping her defeat the lycan packs last year. Reaching out to Sara Thomas might be her best bet to keep Daniel close.

The phone ringing made her jump. Heart pounding, Morgen scowled at her childish behavior. *A queen knows better.* Disturbed, she answered, "This had better be good, Aislinn. I told you I did not want to be disturbed." Her voice carried an unusual strain that she hated to show. "What do you want?"

"This is not your Aislinn, Morgen, queen of the dark elves," a man's voice replied.

Raspy and thin, almost sinister in her opinion, she did not recognize it. Morgen sat up, looking at the door. "Who is this?"

"That is unimportant. What is important is you are close to losing your precious throne and burning the clans to the ground. It has already begun."

She grimaced. "I don't know what you are referring to. The clans are in perfect order."

His laugh cut her. "Were that true, I would not be speaking with you. We have watched you for centuries. Recording. Waiting. This is your most desperate hour. Your plans will not succeed. Not without sacrifice. Be careful, queen of elves. The world is much more dangerous place than you remember."

He hung up, leaving her mired in confusion as unanswered questions arose.

She felt true fear for the first time in as long as she remembered. Empty promises and webs of lies collapsed down upon her, threatening to unravel all she strove so much to achieve. *'We have watched you for centuries.' Who has? How had he gotten my number?*

The rumble of thunder rolled in from the west, still miles away.

Morgen resisted the urge to smash her face on a pillow. She was surrounded, the walls closing in. Only time would tell if she survived. But no matter what veiled threats she received; Morgen's plans were already moving to fruition yet her confidence waivered. The elves were being hunted. She may no longer be the puppeteer she once thought herself, but the clans needed her now more than ever.

Soon. It would all come to a head soon. How do I get Daniel to come to me?

END

D.E.S.A. returns this fall in the thrilling series conclusion *Save the Queen*!

Check out these other great series by
Christian Warren Freed

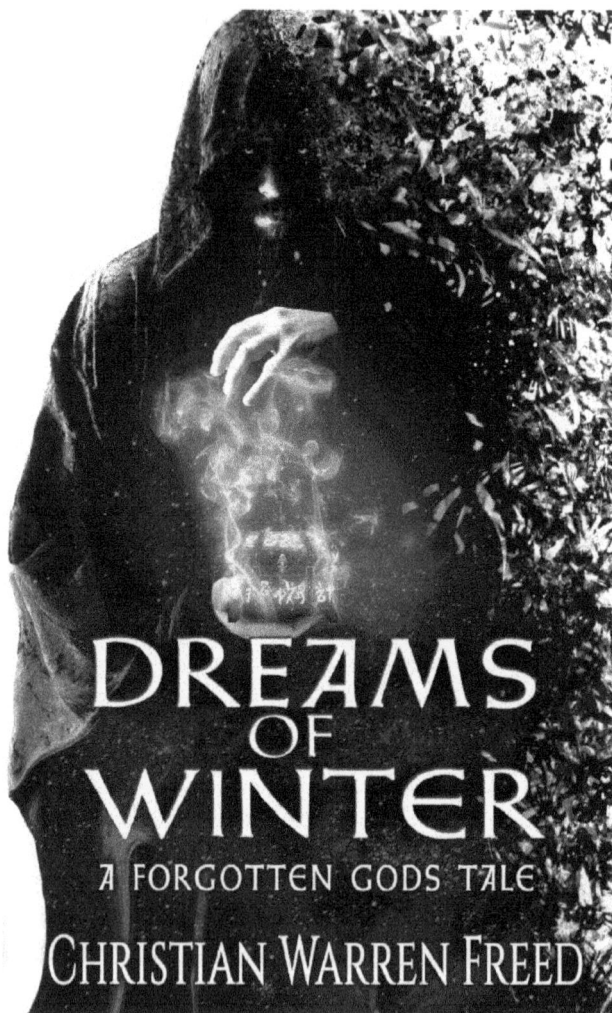

DREAMS
OF
WINTER
A FORGOTTEN GODS TALE

CHRISTIAN WARREN FREED

It is a troubled time, for the old gods are returning and they want the universe back…

Under the rigid guidance of the Conclave, the seven hundred known worlds carve out a new empire with the compassion and wisdom the gods once offered. But a terrible secret, known only to the most powerful, threatens to undo three millennia of progress. The gods are not dead at all. They merely sleep. And they are being hunted.

Senior Inquisitor Tolde Breed is sent to the planet Crimeat to investigate the escape of one of the deadliest beings in the history of the universe: Amongeratix, one of the fabled THREE, sons of the god-king. Tolde arrives on a world where heresy breeds insurrection and war is only a matter of time. Aided by Sister Abigail of the Order of Blood Witches, and a company of Prekhauten Guards, Tolde hurries to find Amongeratix and return him to Conclave custody before he can restart his reign of terror.

What he doesn't know is that the Three are already operating on Crimeat.

Start reading today:
https://www.amazon.com/dp/B0794D68MX

CHRISTIAN WARREN FREED

COWARD'S TRUTH

A NOVEL OF THE HEART ETERNAL

Welcome to Ghendis Ghadanisban. City of god-kings. City in turmoil.

The god-king is dead! Whispers of murder spread through the city known as the Heart Eternal. His death allows an ancient evil Razazel to return and resume its quest to dominate all life. As if that isn't enough, warring factions threaten the jewel of the desert. The only way to prevent this is by a group of reluctant heroes to escort a young boy filled with the dying god's essence to the ancient mountain of Rhorremere so the god-king can be reborn. It is a quest bound to claim lives, for evil never stops.

Far off in the mountains, a squad of stranded space marines sells their services in the hopes of being rescued. Their search brings them in conflict with too many enemies. Forced to join the quest, it is a decision that may prove their ultimate doom.

Fate and destiny clash as agents of good and evil set forth to stake their claim.

Welcome, friends, to the Heart Eternal.

THE
LAZARUS MEN
A LAZARUS MEN AGENDA

C H R I S T I A N
W A R R E N   F R E E D

Welcome to the world of the Lazarus Men.

A thrilling sci-fi noir adventure combining the best mystery of the Maltese Falcon with the adventure of Total Recall and suspense of James Bond.

It is the 23rd century. Humankind has spread across the galaxy. The Earth Alliance rules weakly and is desperate for power. Hidden in the shadows are the Lazarus Men: a secret organization ruled with an iron fist by the enigmatic Mr. Shine. His agents are the worst humanity has to offer and they are everywhere.

Gerald LaPlant's life changes forever the day he accidentally witnesses a murder and discovers an alien artifact in his pocket. Forced to flee, he is chased across the stars by desperate men who want what he has and are willing to stop at nothing to get it. Along the way Gerald meets a host of villains and heroes, each with hidden agendas. If Gerald has any hope of surviving, he must rely on his wits and avoiding the one thing that could get him killed more than the rest: trust.

For he has the key to the galaxy's greatest treasure. Half want him dead. Half need him alive.

It's a race against time to see which wins.

THE CHILDREN OF NEVER

A WAR PRIESTS OF ANDRAK SAGA

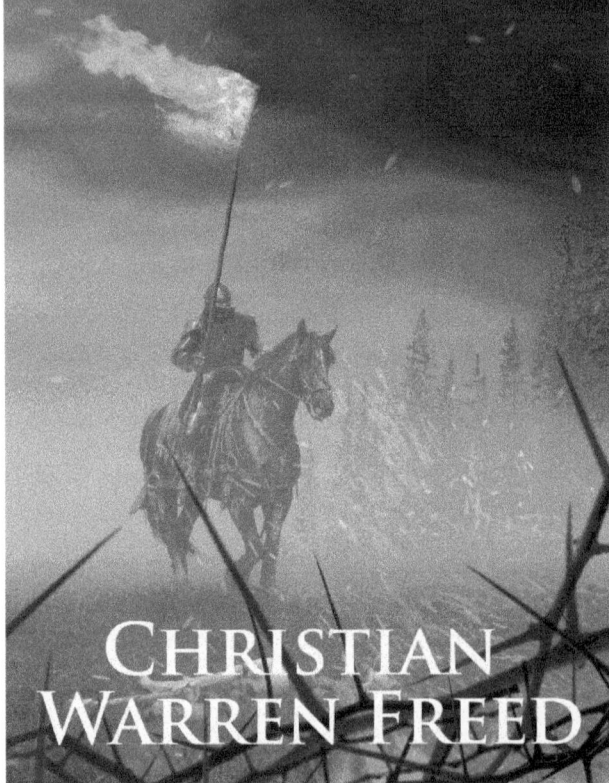

CHRISTIAN
WARREN FREED

The war priests of Andrak have protected the world from the encroaching darkness for generations. Stewards of the Purifying Flame, the priests stand upon their castle walls each year for 100 days. Along with the best fighters, soldiers, and adventurers from across the lands, they repulse the Omegri invasions. But their strength wanes and evil spreads.

Lizette awakens to a nightmare, for her daughter has been stolen during the night. When she goes to the Baron to petition aid, she learns that similar incidents are occurring across the duchy. Her daughter was just the beginning. Baron Einos of Fent is left with no choice but to summon the war priests.

Brother Quinlan is a haunted man. Last survivor of Castle Bendris, he now serves Andrak. Despite his flaws, the Lord General recognizes Quinlan as one of the best he has. Sending him to Fent is his best chance for finding the missing children and restoring order. Quinlan begins a quest that will tax his strength and threaten the foundations of his soul.

The Grey Wanderer stalks the lands, and where he goes, bad things follow. The dead rise and the Omegri launch a plan to stop time and overrun the world. The duchy of Fent is just the beginning.

The follow up to the L Ron Hubbard Writers of the Future award winning short: The Purifying Flame, the Children of Never is an all-new novel set in a world of raw imagination.

Evil never rests and neither can we.
Pick up a sword and join the team!

Warfighter Books

Sign up for our newsletter today and follow us on social media for updates, new releases and more!

Newsletter:
https://www.subscribepage.com/warfighterbooks

Amazon:

BIO

Christian W. Freed was born in Buffalo, N.Y. more years ago than he would like to remember. After spending more than 20 years in the active-duty US Army he has turned his talents to writing. Since retiring, he has gone on to publish more than 20 science fiction and fantasy novels as well as his combat memoirs from his time in Iraq and Afghanistan. His first book, Hammers in the Wind, has been the #1 free book on Kindle 4 times and he holds a fancy certificate from the L Ron Hubbard Writers of the Future Contest.

Passionate about history, he combines his knowledge of the past with modern military tactics to create an engaging, quasi-realistic world for the readers. He graduated from Campbell University with a degree in history and a Masters of Arts degree in Digital Communications from the University of North Carolina at Chapel Hill. He currently lives outside of Raleigh, N.C. and devotes his time to writing, his family, and their two Bernese Mountain Dogs. If you drive by you might just find him on the porch with a cigar in one hand and a pen in the other.

Milton Keynes UK
Ingram Content Group UK Ltd.
UKHW020214040724
444921UK00003B/34

9 781957 326474